Heaven Help Us
By Bryce Main.

Copyrights

Dedication

Every book, published either in electronic or printed form, is a journey. The chances are the author will have benefitted from the help and advice of any number of people, directly or indirectly, somewhere along the line.

Heaven Help Us would not have seen the light of day were it not for the support, encouragement, and copy checking skills of the writer Denise M. Main, the sculptor Shaun Main, the personal trainer and nutritionist Chris Main, and a hundred and one other very talented people who liked what they read before they even saw this published e-book.

A large slice of thanks must also go to Darren Scott of Truth Design, Manchester, UK.

His contribution to the book's front cover was more than just vital. It gave credence to the truism that you never get a second chance to make a first impression.

A note about spelling: Although I may eventually have readers all over the world, I live in the UK, write in the UK and, therefore, spell in the UK. Any anomalies in the spelling of certain words in Heaven Help Us may be due to language and cultural differences. They are not necessarily incorrect spellings of the words themselves, and are definitely not meant to cause offence.

Have a nice day.

Cover concept, design & artwork: Darren Scott of Truth Design.

One

The universe as we know it today wasn't born in a light, happy, smiley place. It came to being in a dark, cold, empty place devoid of colour, humour and matter.

And it wasn't the result of the accidental bumping together and joining of lots of very small things to create lots of very large ones.

It was more like the aftermath of a sound. The kind of humming sound that someone makes, absent-mindedly, as they're thinking. Or the cosmic drumming of fingers, closely followed by the smacking and rubbing together of a pair of all-powerful hands.

It happened in what today's great scientific minds might casually call a really small bit of a nanosecond, or less. And it wasn't anything like a big bang at all.

It was simply God coming to a decision.

"Right," he thought. "Time for another go at this creation lark."

We don't know how many previous attempts there were. How long they lasted, or what went tragically wrong with them.

This time, however, whether by mistake or design, something obviously went substantially right. In the beginning anyway.

Some speculate that the whole thing took as little as a few days, with rests in between for coffee and biscuits. Others are more than happy to go for the Billions of Years theory. The one where time takes time to come about, change is inevitable and microbes don't turn into lumbering great dinosaurs, then accountants and lawyers, without a great deal of trial and error.

Whatever the truth of the matter was, one thing was certain. After all the dust had settled and the coughing had stopped, things looked very different. Very promising.

You know that phrase 'nothing good lasts forever'?

Two

"Ok," said the Devil, "you got me. What is it?"

"Insurance," said God, proudly holding up a fist-sized gem.

The two were sitting on sun loungers on a tropical island beach, complete with palm trees and scorching sunshine. Only it was as far from any beach, or anywhere else, as Heaven was from Hell.

Here and there, the occasional squawking bird dive-bombed the calm sea, fishing for lunch.

God had a cool Helter Skelter Mixer in a frost-rimmed glass with an umbrella in one hand, and a gem the size of his fist in the other.

He took a sip of his drink and tossed the gem at the Devil, who very nearly spilled his Double Miracle Mash (with coconut slice) all over his chest, as he caught the rock.

"Oh well held," said God, smiling and saluting him with a raised glass.

The Devil glared at him, put down his drink on the bamboo side table next to his lounger and looked closely at the sparkling rock, turning it over in his hand.

"Looks pretty much like a bloody great diamond with a bit of a black blob right in the middle of it," he said, dismissively. "This why you yanked me here when I was just settling down for a nice nap?"

God frowned. "I yanked you here, as you so colourfully put it, because that thing you're holding will one day be our salvation."

"Yeah, right," said the Devil, tossing the gem into the air and trapping it with the catcher's mitt that appeared on his right hand. Then, remembering that his companion had an uncanny knack of not only knowing all that was to come, but also arranging it in the first place, he added, "salvation from what?"

God sighed. "It's not a what. It's more like a who."

There was a long pause while the Devil was thinking. Eventually the pause gave in gracefully.

"Mankind, you idiot!" said God, sipping his drink and reaching under his lounger for a small bottle of extra-protective sunscreen. He unscrewed the top, squeezed a blob onto his left palm, then rubbed it all over his face. Not that he needed to. But he had to admit there was a certain primitive enjoyment in spreading the slippery substance over his skin.

The Devil laughed and tossed the gem in the air again, this time a little higher. "What? That lot?"

"Oh you better believe it. Sure...right now they're all balanced very nicely between the God-lovers and the Devil-worshipers. But what happens when the balance gets tipped and they start worshipping you more than me...or worse still, themselves more than either of us?" The possibility made God frown.

A sly gleam crept into the Devil's eyes and his mind went into overdrive at the prospect of a terrifying, but exquisite, opportunity.

"Don't even think about it," said God, throwing him the sunscreen. "Here, put some of this on."

Resting the crystal on his bright red Bermuda shorts, the Devil shook the lotion bottle then proceeded to squeeze a blob onto his hands and from there onto his face.

"What would you say if I told you that one day, all that carefully structured balance might start to disappear? Just drift away like smoke in the wind. What if they started believing they could do without us?"

The Devil stopped rubbing lotion all over his face and turned to God. "You think?" he asked softly.

God nodded. "You missed a bit at the end of your nose," he said. The Devil quickly slapped some protection on the errant patch of naked skin and laid back on his lounger, looking at the sky, momentarily lost in thought. He felt the weight of the crystal balancing on his naval and absent-mindedly shifted it a couple of inches to the left. It sat there. Waiting.

Like a portent of things to come, first one small cloud, then another, then a whole bunch of fluffy invaders arrived on the horizon and threatened to bring gloom into an otherwise uninterrupted blue sky.

God shook his head sadly and a salty bead of sweat dropped off the end of his nose and onto his upper lip, before sliding into his mouth.

He stared pointedly at the clouds, particularly the one nearest. It looked a little feistier, more daring than the others.

The cloud, however, was feeling neither feisty nor particularly daring at all, given the fact that it was falling under the gaze of its creator. In fact the only reason it was there at all was that it was too small to argue with the much larger clouds behind it.

"Go on," the largest had encouraged. "See if you can drift over and find out what's going on down there. It might be something important."

The small cloud had tried, vainly, to explain that covert operations were not really its area of expertise. It was much better at strategic planning and working behind the scenes, it said. It was rubbish at this spying stuff, it said.

"How would you like a swift kick where the sun doesn't shine?"

And so it went, as slowly and inconspicuously as it could. A small, white blob, trying to blend in with the stark blue sky above it. Life as a dimensionally challenged cloud really sucked, it thought.

Down below, God's gaze on the little cloud intensified. "If you think for one second that you can just waltz over here and put the mockers on our day of rest and relaxation, you've got another think coming, you little squirt," he growled.

"Hey, it was you who invited me," blurted the Devil, sitting upright on his lounger, confused and a little angry. He put a slightly oily left hand on the crystal, ready to throw it at God, in self-defence of course, should the need arise.

"Eh? Oh calm down. I wasn't talking to you." God pointed to the little cloud which, by means of a clever series of zig zag movements, had managed to sneak closer, and was now threatening to come between them and the warming rays of the sun.

"You're talking to a cloud?"

"Of course. I talk to everything. Animal, vegetable, or mineral. In fact there isn't one thing or person that I haven't had a good old chat to at some time or another. It's called 'being caring and friendly'. I'm a very caring and friendly God, in case you hadn't noticed. Maybe you could learn a thing or two."

The little cloud, against all its better judgement, began to feel decidedly brave and adventurous. So it thought, "this is what it's like being an operative in the field. Forging ahead and paving the way for the rest of the guys to follow. Going behind enemy lines. Being in imminent danger. I wonder if …"

Just then, God's words of warning came wafting up from down below. It couldn't understand the meaning at first. Then, with a shattering clarity, it knew exactly what God had said. More to the point, what he had said it to.

Suddenly, all its newfound heroism and gung-ho bravery seemed to count for nothing. If it could have shaken in abject fear it would have. Instead, it drifted a little from side to side very quickly which, for a small cloud, was as good a portrayal of terror as it got. It didn't even have enough water in its molecules to pee itself.

"That's it," it thought, "I'm off". And, with a concerted effort, fuelled mostly by fear of imminent non-existence, it charged across the sky, putting as much empty space between its creator and the mass of large, ugly looking clouds behind it.

"Blimey, Tiny's done a runner!" said a solid-looking, puffed-up cumulus at the front of the pack. The whole cloud formation came to a dramatic and very shambolic halt in mid air, apart from a little swaying amongst a few elderly and widespread members of the stratus clan.

"Maybe he knows something we don't!" offered a smaller but quick-thinking cumulus, who was beginning to feel a little edgy.

After a bit of fast-talking and a lot of mumbling, the general consensus was that Tiny was too valuable to be lost to the collective. With him gone, they would have to pick another unfortunate cloud to scout ahead. This normally involved a fair amount of bullying.

"Quick, after him!" yelled someone from the rear. And, with a lot of pushing and shoving, bumping and nudging, the whole sea of cloud wheeled round and began to move off in the direction the little cloud had taken.

"Well, there's something you don't see every day," said the Devil, down below.

"And don't come back!" growled God. At this, the clouds seemed to pick up speed and, like a sea of fluffy white cotton wool, disappeared over the horizon. "Now, where was I?"

"You were at the 'them starting to think they could do without us' bit."

"Aaah, yes. That's why I fixed up a bit of insurance."
"Eh?"

—

Before God could answer, there was a soft scuttling in the undergrowth behind them, and a strange looking feathered creature emerged, heading slowly for the water's edge. It had three legs.

"What the blue blazes is that?" asked the Devil, eyeing the creature as it walked awkwardly over the sand, fluffing its feathers and looking at them suspiciously.

"Watch closely," said God, tugging at his beard and grinning.

Almost on cue, the creature decided to make a dash for the water. The legs were arranged two at the back, one at the front. As the back two dug into the sand, the front one (thicker and stronger than the other two) propelled it forwards and into the air.

The rear two then took the brunt of the landing, and the whole cycle of motion started all over again. It looked ungainly, but the Devil had to admit there was a certain unique style to it. And it wasn't slow.

"Wow," he exclaimed, impressed, as the creature put on a spurt that propelled it into the waves and under them in a flash. It reappeared a moment later with a wriggling slug-like creature stuffed half in and half out of its mouth. The second creature obviously had no desire to end up as dinner, so was doing its best to free itself.

"If you think *that's* impressive," said God, "just watch this."

The three-legged predator, thinking it had successfully nabbed its next meal, made a fatal error in judgement. It failed to notice a small opening appear at what seemed to be the rear of the slug creature, which then proceeded to break wind. The effect was spectacular.

On smelling the evacuated odour, the predator squawked in alarm, waded backwards a step or three out of the waves, and promptly collapsed in a heap on the sand, twitching and moaning.

The slug plopped onto the sand, grabbed its unfortunate and much larger ex-captor and proceeded to haul it, semi-conscious and still moaning, towards the water's edge and into the sea, where both eventually disappeared under the waves.

God turned and smiled at the Devil.

"Oh, I get it," said the Devil, with a penny-dropping look on his face. "This is one of those damned metaphor things of yours. The slug thing's fart was its insurance, right?"

God's smile grew wider. "And that's ours," he said, nodding towards the crystal, which was still in the Devil's left hand. "It's called The Eye of God."

"Very original," drawled the Devil. "What is it?"

"It's a warning device."

The Devil stared at him, unblinking. "Warning about what? And where did you get it?" He was starting to feel the beginnings of bad news.

"Well you know Azriel?"

The Devil's smile froze and his eyes took on a 'thousand yard stare' as he remembered only too clearly the dark angel. "*That maniac?*"

"Nonsense. He's missing a few people skills, that's all. He's really very sweet."

"He's missing a few vital brain cells, that's all!" said the Devil, making circles round his temple with an index finger. "And are you sure he's actually a he, not a she?"

"Just listen," said God in a menacing tone.

"I'm listening, I'm listening!"

"Well Azriel has a cousin called Zaphir, and –"

"Shit! He's another weird one. This tale has a happy ending, right?"

"He might be a bit on the peculiar side," admitted God, "but he's also a bit on the brilliant side. Threw that thing together in a couple of hours. Works like a charm."

"Where's the power source?" The Devil peered closely at the gem.

"Doesn't need one."

"No heavenly mojo involved?"

"Nope."

"Magic?"

"Nope."

"Solar power?"

"NO!"

"Okay, consider me officially interested. What does it do?"

"See that dark spot in the middle of it?"

The Devil brought the gem up close to his eye and concentrated all his attention on the dark spot in the centre.

"Aaaaargh," he yelled, and dropped the gem onto the sand at his feet. "The bloody thing *looked* at me!"

God laughed. "Yes. Quite cute isn't it? Did that to me, too. Zaphir said we could have two trial runs. You've just used up the last one."

"It's an eye!" said the Devil, looking at the crystal, which was staring up at him. "There's an eye, right in the middle. It opened up and looked right at me!" The Devil felt a strange fuzzy sensation, coupled with a powerful urge to evacuate the contents of his stomach.

"That's what it does. It's The Eye of God. What did you expect it to look like – a nose?"

"Of course not, but –" spluttered the Devil looking at the gem sitting in the sand staring up at him.

"Well pick it up, man, it won't bite."

The Devil picked up the gem and held it at arm's length.

"It's still looking at me," he said, feeling queasy.

The Eye of God, almost as if it could hear his words, closed itself slowly.

The queasiness and fuzzy feeling began to disappear, much to the Devil's relief. "So it's gonna save our bacon by staring at folk?" asked the Devil.

God downed the rest of his Helter Skelter Mixer in one large gulp. "Of course not! Zaphir said as long as the balance of belief is maintained, then the eye would be nothing more than a black blob in the middle of the gem.

"Then, when something called Technology comes along and threatens to bugger things up, The Eye of God would open just like it did then. And it would stay open until someone called *The One* came along. Then it would show them the way to get Mankind back on track and us back on top! Well...me. That's the short version anyway."

"Thanks for not telling me the long version," said the Devil, blinking and wondering whether holding The Eye for any length of time would be bad for his health. "What the blue blazes is technology?"

"It's very complicated," said God. "It's got a lot to do with steam engines, computers, and cell phones."

"Cell what? Oh never mind. I get it. These are some of your 'at some time in the future' things, aren't they?

"Correct."

"I think I need another drink," sighed the Devil. The glass on the table at his side refilled itself with another green, foul-smelling Double Miracle Mash, which, like God, he downed in one. He wiped a green drip off his lower lip. "So – where you gonna stash your Eye thing?"

"Well," said God, patting the box at his side on which his drink and cheese sandwiches were resting, "first, I thought I might put it inside my storage Ark. It's only got a few bits and pieces in it. Those stone tablets I told you about last week, and some spare underwear."

"Doesn't sound too secure," said the Devil, looking at the box suspiciously.

"That's just what I thought," said God. " So I think I might stash it on Earth, with The Pope."

"Right! Emm – what's a Pope?"

"The head of the Catholic Church, silly!"

"Okay know-all – what's a Catholic Church?" asked the Devil, confused.

"Aaah, haven't told you about Junior yet, have I? No matter. Take it from me. Some time in the future I'm going to have offspring. Don't ask me how. Haven't figured it out yet. Anyway, a bit later in a place called The Vatican, there will be lots of these Popes and they will have billions of people worshipping my Junior."

"Brilliant. Emm – why would they do that? No, wait. Need-to-know, right?"

God smiled. "And the beautiful thing is, if these Popes say you and I exist, then we do! No questions asked."

"But that's crazy. We *do* exist – don't we?"

"Oh absolutely. Without a shadow of a doubt."

"And all these folk believe that we exist, right?"

"Well, that depends. Lots of them do, and lots of them aren't sure. And a few of them don't really care one way or another."

"Okay. So what happens if all the ones who do believe stop believing?"

"No problem. These Popes and all their friends will do absolutely *anything* to stop that happening. Soon as that little eye pops open, they'll start running around like mad, looking for someone called *The One*, who can help bring all those non-believers back into the fold."

The Devil looked at the blue sky and folded his arms behind his head. "So do we have any leads on this *One*?"

"No. Zaphir has a bit of a memory block about it. We've tried everything. Hypnosis, bribery, pain, the lot. But the fact is the poor boy can't remember who *The One* was, or is, or will be. What he did say, thought, is that *The One* might not even know that they're *The One*."

"Well what about your God thing?"

"What God thing?"

"The 'I'm God and I know everything' thing."

"Oh I do know everything. It's just that, well, I get these teeny weeny blind spots every now and then. Nothing serious. Just a touch inconvenient."

"Right. And not knowing who *The One* is just happens to be one of these teeny weeny blind spots?"

"As I said, inconvenient."

"You don't have any deaf spots to go with them, I suppose?"

"Absolutely not!"

"Headaches?"

"Nope."

"Hearing any voices?"

"Always. They never shut up, but that's normal."

"Loss of sensation at your fingertips?"

"That disappeared a while ago."

There was an awkward silence between them, during which the Devil had the distinct feeling that God was being evasive. What wasn't he telling him? Was this part of a cunning plan? Oh bugger it. He was in his 'up to something' mode. "So, what do we do now?"

"We can't do anything at the moment," said God, "*The One* won't appear until things start going wrong. That much Zaphir could remember. So we'll just have to sit tight until The Eye opens and we start losing our powers."

The Devil swung his legs over the side of the lounger and glared at God. "Losing our powers? You never said anything about losing any powers. That wasn't the deal. Seventy-thirty, you said. Split right down the middle. Top half for you, bottom half for me. Everything in the middle fair game as long as everyone's happy – you said!"

"Yes. And I also said that the powers we have are dependent on the ability of Humanity to believe that we exist in the first place. And the moment they stop believing, *we* start the journey up the proverbial creek without a paddle."

"Hang on, I thought you were the all-powerful creator of the universe? You mean you're not?"

God glared. "Listen. Doing that creation thing is bloody tiring. It takes a lot out of you. If Mankind stops believing in us, I'll go back to my old reduced-level powers. And you, my friend, will disappear up your rear end."

The Devil's eyebrows shot up and he took another large gulp of the green stuff. "Okay. So what do we do if they stop believing?"

"Simple. We help the poor souls start again. And I just happen to have a cunning plan in place and ready to go."

Three

Brothers Carlos and Roberto loved their job. Clerical Monks in the Vatican's Special Investigations Department, they were charged with what they were told was the single most important job in the whole of Christendom and maybe even in the history of the world.

For generations, a few lucky Vatican servants had been the chosen guardians of a gem the size of a large fist. For the past 55 years the task had been theirs and theirs alone.

"Don't take your eyes off it for a second," said the ageing Cardinal David Carlotta, who had sat down with them on that joyous first day in his Vatican apartment all those years ago, and told them of their glorious and highly secret appointment.

"There are no two like you," he said, full of gravity. "The families of Castanada and Lupi have been chosen to be guardians of the single most important item in the whole of the Vatican's history."

The brothers looked at each other, each wondering what could be so important – and why they hadn't heard of it before. He looked at them sternly, then stood. "Come with me."

Walking out through the door behind the old man, Carlos whispered to Roberto, "You see! I knew we were destined to do great things in the service of Our Lord."

After half an hour's walk through endless corridors and down countless flights of stairs, the three arrived at the largest and oldest-looking wooden door Carlos and Roberto had ever seen.

The Cardinal reached out a bony fist and knocked twice on the dark, ancient wood. Nothing happened. He looked at the two young men, frowned and knocked twice again.

"What's all the noise about?" croaked a frail voice from the other side of the door. After a jangling of keys and sliding of bolts, it opened to reveal possibly the oldest, most wrinkled and misshapen monk the two young men had ever come across.

"Good evening, Brother Dominic," said the Cardinal, almost reverentially. "These are the next two."

"Thank God," said the monk, exhaustion written all over his face. "Does that mean we can get a decent night's sleep now?"

"It does," said the Cardinal, patting the old man on the shoulder.

"'Bout time. It's been 74 years and I could do with a bit of a lie-in."

The Cardinal gestured for the two young monks to enter the small, cell-like room, sparsely furnished with two old beds, one armchair and a small dining table with chair. Another uncomfortable-looking chair sat in front of a round table that held a glass box.

In the armchair sat another equally ancient monk, snoring. At the sound of the trio entering the room, the second priest awoke with a start. "Who are you?"

"That's not very hospitable," said Brother Dominic. "Our time's up. These are the lucky two who get to take over."

He walked slowly over to his old companion and helped him to his feet, leaving the newcomers to watch as the pair shuffled slowly and painfully out of the room.

"My sons," said the Cardinal, gesturing to the glass box, "what you see before you is nothing less than the most important item the Vatican possesses. The biggest discovery in the history of mankind."

"What? More important than the holy cross?" blurted Carlos, astonished.

The Cardinal nodded slowly.

The young men looked at each other.

Roberto was the elder of the two and, as such, was in theory the more responsible and sensible. Tall and slender, he had a broad face, intelligent eyes and, some said, intelligent ears, too. "More important than the sacred Ark or the image of our Lord on the blessed Shroud of Turin, or its sinful copies?" he asked, softly.

"Hard to believe, but yes, even more important than those."

Carlos gasped. He was the younger of the two and, in theory, the more easily led and headstrong. He was a slightly undersized member of the brown-robed brethren, with jet black hair and a hook nose that made him look distinctly like a human-vulture hybrid.

"Holy shit of God," he blurted.

"If we had that, it would be even more important than that, too," said the Cardinal.

"The Holy Father himself has deemed this so important and so secret that even though you will be its' guardians from now on, you cannot know what it is."

"It's a crystal," said Carlos, shrugging and wondering what the fuss was all about.

"Very observant," said the Cardinal. "But it's a lot more that just that."

Roberto slapped Carlos on the back of the head. "Slug!" he hissed. "It doesn't matter what it is. If Papa wants us to look after it till the ends of the earth, then that's what we will do!"

"Awww!" the smaller monk hissed, and rubbed his head furiously.

Roberto took the Cardinal's hand and kissed the holy ring on his middle finger. "I apologise for the rudeness and stupidity of my brother."

The Cardinal's face darkened. "This is your task. You will each, in turn, watch the crystal. You will not take your eyes off it. Not for a second. You can eat, sleep and rest in shifts. And you will do this until you are either relieved *or*...until the dark heart of the crystal changes shape."

"Pardon your Eminence, but what shape will it change into?" asked Roberto, trying to imagine what wonders there were locked inside this mysterious gem.

"That I cannot say," said the Cardinal. "But if it ever happens you will immediately press that button over there on the wall."

He pointed to a red button on the wall next to the door. "Is this clear?"

"What about eating and – you know – the other?" enquired Carlos, almost too embarrassed to ask.

"There's a kitchen through that door over there, for snacks and tea and coffee," said the Cardinal, pointing to a door on the far wall. "Your meals will be brought to you every day. And as for 'the other' if you look behind that screen over there, you'll find another door. Open it and you'll find a toilet, washbasin and shower. Any more questions?"

The two silently shook their heads.

The Cardinal looked at them both for long seconds, then did something totally unexpected. He stepped forwards and hugged each one in turn, almost paternally, patting their backs softly.

Then he crossed himself and walked out of the room, closing the door behind him, leaving the two young monks in a silence that clawed at them through their garments.

"Okay, you first," said Carlos.

"Bugger that for a lark. *You* take first watch!"

Carlos looked at his friend, smiled and sat down on the chair in front of the crystal. "Six hours on, six off?" he said.

"Peachy," said Roberto, settling down in the armchair and closing his eyes. He dreamed of things that holy men and women should never dream of – and once again wondered if God could hear his innermost thoughts and look into his dreams.

Mere feet away, Carlos looked at the black heart of the crystal and tried to clear his mind.

Fifty-five years later he screamed.

Roberto leapt up from his sleep, upending the half-finished coffee sitting precariously on the arm of the chair. "*Whooooa!*"

Whatever word he was thinking of didn't even get the chance to finish itself off. He looked over to Carlos, who by now was up off the chair and pacing back and forth, stopping regularly to look at the crystal, muttering, "shit" repeatedly.

Carlos looked at him. "*The damned thing looked at me!*"

Roberto sighed, "I think you've been looking at it for too long my friend."

"No, no." Carlos grabbed Roberto's sleeve and dragged him over to the table. "You look at it and tell me what you see."

Roberto, frowning, sat down and stared into the crystal. "*Holy Mother of God*! Is that an eye?"

Carlos crossed himself and looked upwards. " Thank you God. Thank you for keeping our minds clear for this moment. Thank you for choosing us to be the instruments of your miracle!" He turned to Roberto. "What the hell do we do now?"

"The bell," said Roberto. "Push the bell button!"

"*You* push it, you're taller!" exclaimed the younger monk. "I'm too short for that kind of responsibility."

Roberto grunted, ran to the door and pushed the large red button on the box halfway up the wall.

Nothing happened.

He pounded the button with his fist. "Fine! Sit around for fifty-five years waiting for we-don't-know-what to happen and then when it does happen, *we can't tell anyone!*"

18

Suddenly, they became aware of the sound of running feet. Lots of them. The sound got closer and closer and then stopped outside the door, accompanied by lots of gasping, coughing and wheezing.

Roberto opened the door and was met by a crowd of monks, priests, nuns, cardinals, archbishops and assorted Vatican employees, all in various states of undress. A small, self-important looking, bespectacled priest at the front of the crowd looked at him and demanded: "Well – where's the fire?"

"Fire?" asked a confused Roberto, "what fire?"

"You heard the fire bell, didn't you? This is our gathering point. It has been for the last ten years. Don't tell me somebody set off the bloody fire alarm by mistake?"

There were groans from the crowd behind him and a very tall, half-dressed cleric hissed, "If this is another one of your ruses, Father Scarpetta, and something funny's happened to my poker hand when we get back, may you die of syphilis and go to hell!"

"Fire alarm? What fire alarm? And who are you?" demanded Roberto, glaring at the small priest.

"Father David Munroe, Chief Assistant to the Office of Cardinal Alfredo Bonetti," the priest said, rather pompously.

"Okay, Chief Assistant," said Roberto, grabbing him by his arm and dragging him into the room, "you come with me. The rest of you, stay there!" He slammed the door closed behind them and pulled the protesting priest over to the table with the crystal.

"Right," he said, pointing to the crystal. "We've been guarding this for the past fifty five years and now the damned thing's changed and we were told to ring that bell if it ever did change and now it has and we rung the bell and we don't know what to do now. Okay?"

Munroe reached inside his pocket and took out a handkerchief. He took off his glasses, wiped the lenses, put them back on again and looked closely at the crystal.

He abruptly backed away, knocking over the chair and was only stopped from falling over by Roberto who caught him from behind.

"Oh," he said, a mixture of surprise and panic in his voice.

"Oh exactly!" exclaimed Carlos. "Oh as in 'Oh bugger what happens now?' We don't know what the thing is or what it does. But we think that you should at least call someone very important!"

"Well, I know exactly what it is," said the priest, gulping and beginning to turn a whiter shade of pale. "And if we don't act really, really fast, we're all up the creek!"

Four

It was 11.15pm. Ten minutes after the sound of the fire alarm had drifted up from the floors below, only to be cut off abruptly. Cardinal Alfredo Bonetti, Head of the Vatican's Special Investigations Department was sitting at his desk in his private chambers. His thoughts were far from Vatican business and a whole lot nearer the hot water bottle waiting for him in his bed. He didn't even hear the alarm.

Many years ago, he had been offered a nice new electric blanket to ward off the chills and make his journey into sleep a warmer, more comfortable one.

"Does the Holy Father have an electric blanket?" he had asked the small cleric who came bearing the gift.

"No, Your Eminence," came the reply. "He has a hot water bottle."

"Then that is what I shall have, too," said Bonetti.

"And the cover? The Holy Father has a cover for it."

"Yes, that too," answered Bonetti, impatiently, sending the cleric scurrying out of his chambers to make the arrangements.

So it was that the hot water bottle waiting for the Cardinal in his bed every night since then had a fluffy cover shaped like a teddy bear. Tonight, it would have to wait a little longer.

Whatever thoughts he had in his head at that moment vanished in an instant, thanks to the polite knocking, followed by the loud pounding, on his door.

"He opened the door and stared into the white face of his Chief Assistant, Father David Munroe. "David? What – "

"It's happened," gasped the alarmed priest, almost pushing his way into the room and closing the door quickly behind him.

"Well, as long as it's not the second coming, you can at least sit down, catch your breath and tell me what's going on," said the Cardinal, taking Munroe by the arm and attempting to guide him over to the guest armchair. Munroe was having none of it and stood rooted to the spot, breathing heavily and sweating profusely.

"*The Eye of God* has opened!" he exclaimed in a loud whisper, before making the sign of the cross, grabbing the Cardinal's hand, kneeling and kissing the ring on Bonetti's finger.

Bonetti felt his heart skip more beats than were healthy for a man of his age. "Does anyone else know of this?"

"Only the two guardians, Your Eminence. I kept the crowd out and made the old brothers swear to keep the door closed until you came."

"Crowd? What crowd?"

"When the fire bell rang – " said Monroe.

"There's a *fire*?"

"Oh no, it was a false alarm. But you must come Your Eminence. *The Eye of God* blinked at me!" With that, Munroe dashed to the door, opened it and waited for Bonetti to follow.

"Say nothing of this to anyone, you understand?" said The Cardinal softly, not waiting for an answer as he strode out the door and headed for the room holding the crystal.

Along corridors and down stairs, the priest was his constant shadow. Not uttering a word. Always one step behind. Understanding completely that, unless instructed otherwise, a vow of extreme silence was required of him regarding anything concerning the crystal. From now until probably the end of time.

Eventually they came to an ancient wooden door. The Cardinal knocked on it twice and commanded, "Open up. This is Cardinal Bonetti!"

Almost immediately the door was pulled open and there, wild-eyed and in a state of utter panic, stood Brother Carlos, crossing himself repeatedly. "We did nothing Your Eminence. Holy Mary, Mother of God I swear we kept to our sacred duty. There is an eye in the crystal and it opened and looked at me. I feel queasy." He changed from crossing himself to beating his chest violently with his right fist, gasping "Mea culpa, mea culpa, mea maxima culpa!"

Bonetti stepped into the room forcing his way past Brother Carlos, causing him to stagger back slightly. A following Monroe managed to steady him, before turning and carefully closing and locking the door. The old monk was gasping more mea culpas.

As the Cardinal surveyed the room at a glance, he saw the elderly Brother Roberto standing in front of the glass case containing *The Eye of God,* with his hands over his eyes.

This had the effect of affecting his balance and he was swaying backwards and forwards. He was also muttering.

Bonetti rushed over to him, grabbed him by the shoulders and said, almost tenderly, "Take your hands from your eyes, my son. There is nothing to be afraid of."

"Is it still there, looking at me?" whispered the monk, slowly and carefully uncovering his eyes.

Bonetti looked at the crystal and he had to admit that, even from about three feet away, the blob in the centre had changed in shape to that of an eye. And it was looking directly at him.

What's more, he was feeling a little woozy.

The feeling only lasted a second or two, but when it passed, he felt as though someone or something had been poking around inside his head. And whatever it was had left a message. "I need to speak to the Holy Father immediately," he said, turning to Munroe. The two monks and the priest were looking at him strangely.

"What?" he asked.

"I'm an extremely good linguist," said Munroe. "But you were looking at the crystal and speaking in a language unlike anything I've ever heard."

"And you've been doing it for the past 35 minutes," added Brother Roberto.

"What's happening, Your Excellency?" asked Munroe, mounting concern in his voice.

"I don't know," said Bonetti. "But I know a man who probably does."

"Look!" shouted Brother Carlos, pointing to the crystal. "*The Eye* has closed."

Sure enough, the eye at the heart of the crystal had closed and changed back into the shapeless blob that had existed there since the day the gem had arrived at The Vatican.

"Does this mean our holy duty has ended?" asked a hopeful Brother Roberto, who was looking forward to feeling the warmth of the sun on his face again.

"God needs you to be strong again, my son. Perhaps this is the biggest test of all."

As he spoke, he could swear that the slightly bent back of the monk straightened a little, and his chest attempted to puff out in pride.

"Shit," mumbled Brother Carlos under his breath, but not enough under to avoid detection.

Brother Roberto's slap on the back of the cursing monk's head was swift. "We are the servants of God, and if he needs us to stay here and guard the holy crystal until our eyes wither in our heads, then so be it," he said, crossing himself slowly and nodding at Bonetti.

The smaller monk attempted to cross himself with his right hand and rub the back of his head with his left. He failed miserably at both and eventually stood, eyes downcast, staring at his feet.

Five

After leaving the monks to continue their holy duty, Bonetti and Munroe headed for the Apartamento Pontificio, on the top floor of the Vatican's Apostolic Palace.

Since the 17th century, this has been the official residence of a long line of holy men all known by the titles: Bishop of Rome, Vicar of Christ, Successor of the Prince of the Apostles, Supreme Pontiff of the Universal Church, Primate of Italy, Archbishop and Metropolitan of the Roman Province, Sovereign of the State of the Vatican City and Servant of the Servants of God.

For reasons of convenience and user-friendliness, this collection of titles has been shortened to just two simple but immensely powerful words. The Pope.

Bonetti and Munroe made it to the door to The Pope's private apartments before their forward motion was stopped in its tracks by two Swiss Guards whose joint height and width completely blocked the impressive doorway.

Under normal circumstances and at any other time of day or night, Papal guards would have respectfully stood aside and allowed the Cardinal to enter and conduct whatever business he had with the physical and spiritual head of the Roman Catholic Church.

Once The Pope retired for the night, however, the protection of his slumbering earthly form became the sole responsibility of a band of very determined and, if necessary, religiously violent, individuals. On this evening in particular, the behemoths in question were Papal Escort Captains Emile Dolce and Rodolfo Gabbano.

"Are you going to stand aside or do I have to physically excommunicate the pair of you where you stand?" said Bonetti, testily.

Dolce and Gabbano merely stared at the Cardinal and his companion. The only muscles visibly moving were those behind their eye sockets.

"Stand aside!" commanded Munroe. "The Cardinal needs to see The Holy Father immediately."

Gabbano, the taller of the two, looked down at the little priest and slowly shook his great head from side to side. "The Holy Father has retired for the evening."

"How would you like to retire for the foreseeable future!" hissed Munroe. "This is a matter of the highest importance."

The ghost of a smile passed across the guard's face. "You're very small for such a big man," he said.

"Captain Rodolfo Gabbano. Gabby," said Bonetti, uttering the last word softly, "I remember the day I baptised you. Your father had to hold you because you were too big and heavy for your mother."

Gabbano visibly blushed and altered his standing position ever so slightly. "Your Eminence – " he began.

"It's okay. I know you're only doing your job. But now, you're keeping me from doing mine. The fate of our world is at stake and the only person on God's beautiful earth that can help me save it is behind that door. So, you can stand there and do nothing or move aside and help me. Which will it be?"

Dolce and Gabbano turned their heads slowly and looked at each other, nodded almost imperceptibly, then took one pace sideways, leaving the way clear to the door.

"Thank you boys," said Bonetti, as he stepped forward, grabbed the door handle, turned it to open the large, ornately carved door and walked into the vestibule of the Papal apartments.

Following on behind him, Munroe glared at Gabbano. The glare merely bounced off the guard without making a dent.

Beyond the vestibule lay the 10 rooms that everyone in the Vatican knew of, including the papal bedchamber. Reconstruction and modernisation to the apartments in recent years gave rise to the rumour that there were more, including a highly advanced medical suite, and a specially designed panic room (complete with its own satellite communications link), installed in the event of a terrorist attack. The satellite was, of course, funded and used exclusively by The Vatican. Bonetti was one of the very few who knew the truth of this. It was he, after all, who had approved the new plans and insisted on this final security measure.

The Good Lord sometimes needs a little help when it comes to dealing with the realities of modern-day papal protection, he had argued at the time.

That same argument had resulted in the design and creation of the most unique motorised bubble ever to have transported another Holy Father safely wherever he went. The famed eco-friendly Popemobile. Complete with fluffy dice. The vehicle about which one Pope memorably and sarcastically quipped: "Nothing says 'I have complete faith in you God' quite like a few inches of bullet-proof glass."

The Cardinal walked, calmly but briskly, to the door he knew led to the papal bedchamber. As he prepared to knock, he took a large, slow breath. The fate of the world would turn on the events of the next few minutes.

Before his knuckles reached the wood, the door opened and there, smiling, dressed in his official papal bedchamber attire of striped cotton pyjamas, white toweling dressing gown and red slippers, stood the leader of the world's Catholics, the 87 year old Pope Julius IV. His white hair was wild and spiky, and he was holding a half-eaten chocolate chip cookie in his left hand. His right hand flapped and beckoned them into the room. "Come in Alfredo. You too, David," he said, looking at Munroe.

The small priest felt a surge of pride almost swell his chest to bursting point. *"The Holy Father called me by my Christian name"*, he thought, incredulously. Bonetti bent his head close to the priest's ear and whispered. "Don't think anything of it. He's just trying to make you feel comfortable. He does it with everyone." The surge of pride disappeared quicker than air out of a burst balloon as the three moved further into the bedchamber. The Pope sat in a comfortable-looking armchair and beckoned the other two to sit on the Chesterfield sofa facing him.

"There has been a development with The Eye of God," said Bonetti, preparing to bring his immediate boss up to speed.

"I know, Alfredo," said the Pope, still smiling.

"But – " blurted Munroe and stopped mid-phrase as Bonetti's quickly raised hand demanded silence. He knew better than to question the Cardinal. He had heard the stories, whispered in corridors and behind closed doors, about the ability of the Holy Father to know the unknowable. See the unseeable. Being so close to God was a great privilege. Maybe with it came great powers too!

"So, what's the plan?" asked the Cardinal.

The Pope's voice lowered. "You have heard me speak of The White Room, yes?"

27

Bonetti's heart skipped a beat. "Yes".

"Time for you to visit it, my son. We have guests".

"The White Room?" enquired Munroe, only to see Bonetti's hand rise again.

The Pope, still looking at the Cardinal, enquired in a soft voice: "Tell me, did you look into *The Eye*?"

"It looked into me, more like."

"And what did it see?"

Bonetti felt uneasy. "Possibly more than I'd like it to. But it left me a message, and I think I'm supposed to give it to you."

"So give it."

Bonetti delivered the five words that had been replaying over and over in his brain like a stuck record. "*The One* will save you!" he said.

"That's it? *The One* will save you?" asked Munroe.

"Every last word."

"Pen and paper," said The Pope, holding out his hand in anticipation.

Bonetti frowned, dug deep into the folds of his garment and produced a small black leather-bound notebook along with a black and gold Mont Blanc fountain pen. He handed them to the Pontiff as one would hand over a precious jewel. Carefully and reluctantly. Very few people were privy to the contents of Bonetti's famed little black book. The older man opened the book, scrawled on a blank page, and handed it back. He kept the pen.

The Cardinal waited a heartbeat for the pen's return, then, on realising that his beautiful writing implement would never grace his fingers again, he accepted the loss quickly and moved on. His eyes turned to the scrawl on the paper.

"Time for our friend to come back to us," said The Pope.

"As you wish," answered Bonetti, automatically making the sign of the cross.

"Find him. After your visit to The White Room you'll know why. Now go. It's time for my hot milk."

"But where is The White Room, Holy Father?"

"God will guide your feet," said the old Pontiff, mysteriously.

Bonetti and Munroe stood up, walked to The Pope and each in turn knelt down and kissed the signet Ring of the Fisherman on the little finger of his proffered left hand.

—

28

Before they left the bedchamber, the old man stared hard at Bonetti and this time, the smile had disappeared. "Heaven help us, Alfredo," he said.

Bonetti signed himself, as did Munroe, and the pair departed the bedchamber. In the vestibule outside, the Cardinal tore the page containing the name from his notebook and handed the paper to his Assistant.

The priest looked at the page and saw, scribbled in black, *Father John Wayne Cooper.*

"You can't come with me now David. I need you to find him and bring him to me as quickly as possible," he said.

"This White Room," said Munroe. "Where is it?"

"God knows," said Bonetti. "I only hope that sometime in the next few minutes he has the good grace to tell me."

Munroe watched as Bonetti walked out of the vestibule, on his way to whoever or whatever waited for him. He looked again at the paper and walked along a dimly lit corridor in the opposite direction. A man on a mission.

Six

There was a room in the very deepest part of the Vatican the existence of which had been a closely guarded secret for more than a thousand years. It was simply known as The White Room.

Although that was its name, it wasn't exactly a room in the conventional sense. Of course it had walls and a ceiling and a floor. Somewhere. And there was a vague rumour that there might even be a door, although whether it actually opened and closed was anybody's guess.

Mostly, however, it had whiteness. Lots of it.

Of those who knew about the room, few had ever been in it. Even fewer knew its true purpose – namely, to be the only common ground on Earth where representatives of the three realms of Heaven, Hell and Earth could meet, unseen and uninterrupted, at a moment's notice. With refreshments.

On the night shortly after *The Eye of God* opened in a room elsewhere in the Holy See, The White Room was occupied by a Cardinal of Rome, an Angel of God and a diminutive devilish creature with a personal body odour problem.

The room had three white leather wingback chairs surrounding a small, white, glass-topped table containing 'welcome' drinks and nibbles in the form of tea and biscuits.

In one chair sat Bonetti, dressed in his everyday plain black cassock. The only interesting colour in his personal dress was hidden from the prying and judgmental eyes of others less open minded.

In another, sat Azriel, a six and a half feet tall angel of dubious sexuality but leaning mostly towards the male persuasion. Dressed in a white collarless jacket over a pale blue t-shirt and tight black leather trousers over tooled leather cowboy boots.

In the third chair, filling as much of it as he could, which wasn't a lot, sat Ralph. Personal Assistant to The Devil himself, wearing an impeccable Italian silk three-piece suit. Ralph's chair was noticeably further away from the other two.

"It's okay, you can speak now," said the angel to Bonetti, who was blinking repetitively, in a slight state of shock.

Roughly 30 seconds previously, the Cardinal had been taking large, purposeful steps along a particularly isolated corridor deep in the Vatican. He had no idea where he was or where he was headed. Just that he was going to wherever he was supposed to be. Under other circumstances he might have been just a tiny bit alarmed. However, when *The Eye of God* had given him the message, it had also inserted directions to The White Room deep into his unconscious mind, and he found himself heading unerringly towards it, as if it had been programmed into his own internal satellite navigation system.

Bonetti's blinking slowed and he took a deep breath. Without asking, he knew who they were. More information from *The Eye*.

"No need for introductions, then?" asked Azriel, who noticed a change in Bonetti's body language and the recognition in his eyes.

"No. I apologise. It's just – this is the first time I've ever met an Angel of The Lord and a Personal Assistant to The Devil," said the Cardinal. Then the odour hit him and the effect was mirrored in his face.

Ralph blushed and shrugged apologetically. "Hey, it's an incurable medical condition. So sue me."

"How much do you know?" asked the Angel.

"Not a lot. I guess this is why we're here, right?" answered Bonetti.

"Hey, for somebody who just met us, you're doin' okay. At least you ain't pissed yourself, and that's always a good sign!" said Ralph.

"Right, let's begin," murmured Azriel. The little devil's mouth clamped shut, at least temporarily.

The Angel leaned back in her armchair, crossing his legs. "The crystal you know as *The Eye of God* was created by the Angel Zaphir and designed to be a warning device." He told Bonetti about the creation of the Eye, about its purpose, and about *The One*.

Throughout, Ralph remained silent. Then, as if words had backed up in his mouth and were desperately trying to escape from between his lips, he blurted, "Tell him about the knock-on effect."

Azriel glared at the diminutive creature, then returned his gaze slowly to the Cardinal. "There is a small possibility –"

"Large possibility!" Ralph corrected.

"Fine. There is a *distinct* possibility that if we can't put right whatever's going wrong, we could all die!"

"Pardon?" blurted Bonetti in alarm.

Azriel sighed. "If humans end up worshiping technology more than religion, then we won't exist. And if we don't exist, neither do you!"

It felt as though the blood in the Cardinal's veins had suddenly turned to ice. "You mean GOD won't exist?"

"Of course not. He simply won't be as powerful as he is now, and He'll have to start all over again."

"It's all a matter of arithmetics," explained Ralph. "The more humans there are, the more worshippers there are. And the more worshippers there are, the more powerful we become. And vice versa. Get it?"

"I think so," said Bonetti. "I just don't get the bit about humans not existing."

"That's easy. If you don't believe in us, we don't exist. And if we're not around to believe in you – well, you get my drift?"

The Cardinal drifted into silence while his brain attempted to understand.

"Gotta hand it to the big guy. If you listen really hard, you can hear the cogs whirring round!"

"Then we won't exist, either?" whispered Bonetti slowly, almost to himself.

"Bingo! He's figured out the Mutual Existence Clause! Time for a cuppa, I think."

"Hang on. *What* Mutual Existence Clause?"

Ralph sighed. "The one in the Guide to Creating a Populated Universe, of course! Both parties need to believe in each other, otherwise everything goes pear-shaped and nobody exists anymore, well, except God, of course. Then He has to start all over again with the old blackness and nothing in it. It's quite simple, really."

The look on Bonetti's face didn't resemble simplicity in the slightest. The first glimpse of panic, maybe. "So – what happens now?" he asked slowly.

"Now we have a problem. Well two, really," said the Angel.

Ralph eased himself off his chair, walked in a jaunty fashion over to the coffee table and poured freshly brewed tea into three pure white china cups, without remarking on the irony. "I'll be mother."

Azriel accepted a cup with almost feminine grace. "The first problem is what do we do with *The Eye of God* now that it's moved into glaring mode."

Bonetti, his speech pattern returning to normal, frowned. "We've hardly started and already we have glaring problems?"

"Hey, we're doin' our best here, buddy!" said Ralph, with a touch of annoyance in his voice. "A little love and understanding, if that's not too much to ask."

"Okay, let's go get this *One*. Where is he, by the way?"

"We're working on it."

"Is it even a he?"

"We're working on it."

"So – you don't know what, or where, this *One* is, right?"

"Ain't got a friggin' clue. And then there's the second problem." A chocolate-covered biscuit disappeared from a plate and reappeared somewhere inside Ralph's mouth.

Bonetti tried to imagine anything that could compare to a catastrophic lack of balance between Heaven, Hell and Earth. He didn't get far. "What second problem?"

Azriel's voice softened. "Homer."

"The Greek poet?" asked the Cardinal, confused.

"Oh no. This one would be Homer 3421F, the asteroid that's heading straight for Earth."

"*What?*"

Azriel could see that some sort of crisis overload was taking place inside the Cardinal's mind. He decided to take things slowly. "Which part of everything we said didn't you understand?"

"You mean an asteroid's going to hit the planet?"

"Oh good, we're getting somewhere. Yes, that's the way it looks."

The Cardinal crossed himself again. "How big is it?"

"Put it like this. You know the one that beat the crap out of all those dinosaurs?" asked Ralph.

"*That* big?"

The little devil slowly shook his head from side to side. "Waaaaay bigger amigo."

Bonetti started to cross himself again. Azriel frowned. "Stop doing that so much! First thing in the morning and last thing at night will be more than enough."

The Cardinal lowered his right hand slowly mid-cross.

"I apologise. It's just that, first there's the *Eye of God* opening, and now there's this Homer threatening the planet.

"A person could be forgiven for believing that somebody very powerful is trying to tell us something. Like maybe they don't like us anymore."

The angel smiled. It was disconcerting. "Not necessarily."

"See – in the beginning, everything was about time," said Ralph. "Time to see Homer. Time to realise; 'Shit – it's heading straight for us!' Time to figure out what to do. All that stuff."

"Okay. So, how much time are we talking?"

"Oh, around a hundred years, give or take."

Relief flooded the Cardinal's face. "Thank God. That should be more than enough time to stop it. Shouldn't it?"

Azriel reached for a biscuit. "Not really. That was before."

"Before *what*?"

"Before it decided to speed up."

Bonetti felt as thought he had been handed a lifeline, only to have it roughly pulled out of his grasp. "It can do that?"

Ralph nodded. "This one can."

"Well – how long do we have now?"

"Difficult to say. Could be decades, could be less."

Bonetti looked at Azriel. "So, tell me. At what point did you realise that *The Eye of God* opening and this asteroid heading straight for us were connected?"

"I'd say somewhere in between pretty fast and *wow*!" said Ralph.

"0.00000000000000001 of a second in your time. Much quicker in ours," said Azriel.

"Hey, cheer up! It's not as bad as it sounds. We have a plan."

"To do *what*?"

"Save the world, of course," said Azriel, as if the answer was obvious to anyone with half a brain. "We were thinking that a joint effort might be a good idea."

"Yeah. Like a Superteam! Three heroes. One from Heaven, one from Hell and one from Earth. Magnificent Three – I love it. Whaddya say?" said Ralph, excitement only serving to enhance his distinctive body odour.

Bonetti chose his next words carefully. He was about to say, 'I think you all might be clinically insane!' What he actually said was, "You think *three* is enough to stop an asteroid?"

What makes you think that you can do it now when you couldn't do it before? And how are you going to find *The One* when you're too busy figuring out how to avoid a planetary disaster?"

He finished speaking, took a deep breath and a slow sip of strong green tea in the hope that the pungent odour might spark off even the beginnings of an answer. It didn't.

"That's how The Boss wants it. He thinks it's the best shot we've got," said Azriel, "and I have no intentions of arguing the point with Him. I will be joining the team." He turned to Ralph. "Your turn."

Ralph cleared his throat nervously. "There I was. Ready and willing to die for the cause, as anyone who knows me will testify. But emm – all of a sudden I got important pressing business back at the ranch. An offer I couldn't refuse, you might say. So, at great expense, you got MoMo – pass the bourbons!"

"MoMo?" asked Bonetti, none the wiser and shoving the plate of biscuits as near to Ralph's edge of the table as his sinuses would allow.

"Aaah, best you see him in the flesh," said the angel. "Descriptions don't really do MoMo any justice. Meanwhile, I believe that your team member is being tracked down as we speak."

Bonetti thought again about Father John Wayne Cooper. There was no other priest like him. No other human like him. He was an impossibility that, were it asked, the Catholic Church would deny existed. Angels and demons were easier to accept than Cooper. Easier to believe in.

Yet he did exist. In the flesh. The only shapeshifting priest, alive or otherwise. The only Catholic holy man, or woman, or item of household furniture, who could call Bonetti his friend, The Pope his boss, and The Pope's boss his creator. The only individual for whom a dog collar could either be virgin white and worn with a beautifully tailored black suit – or chunky black leather with shiny metal studs and worn with absolutely nothing else.

"*Time to go back to work Cooper,*" he said silently to himself. "So what now?" he asked Azriel aloud.

"The team will meet here tomorrow to track down *The One*. Hopefully we can get enough information from *The Eye* to stop Homer before things go pear shaped."

"Oh food, that reminds me. About tomorrow. Bring more biscuits," said Ralph.

"A large plate or three of sandwiches would be a good idea, too. And maybe cake. MoMo has what you might call appetite issues," he added.

The meeting over, Bonetti was about to ask Azriel where the door was, when he suddenly felt queasy. He closed his eyes, hoping desperately that he wasn't about to throw up.

When he opened then again, he was back in his apartment, sitting in his armchair.

"Time for bed," said a familiar angelic voice in his head. He got the distinct feeling that resistance was futile.

Seven

At roughly the same time as Bonetti was snoring loudly in the Vatican after his meeting in The White Room, a male Golden Eagle was sleeping peacefully in a nest high up on a cliff, roughly 1,6000 miles away in the Highlands of Scotland. Next to it were the bloody remains of a large mountain hare. There wasn't much left.

Although the raptor's brain was small, this one in particular was experiencing thoughts far beyond its normal physical, psychological and emotional capabilities. In fact it was dreaming about a perfectly grilled, medium-rare rib-eye steak with roasted roots and parsley pesto. All washed down with a small glass of red wine. It was no ordinary Eagle.

Suddenly the dream was interrupted by a soft, unfamiliar voice. "Father?"

The creature ignored the intrusion. The voice became louder and more insistent. "FATHER!"

That did it. In almost one fluid movement, the bird came awake, ruffled its feathers and launched itself into the air, away from the cliff, swooping down through the darkness towards the ground and landing next to a zipped-up one-man tent.

What took place next wasn't the sort of thing that could be explained without offending either religious or scientific minds. The air seemed to move and ripple around the great bird and as it did so, the bird's shape and size altered. In almost the blink of an eye it changed from being an eagle to being a human. A naked man. The man shivered once, crawled into the tent, and emerged minutes later fully dressed in hiking clothing.

"You're needed again," said the voice. "I think it's time to switch that phone thing of yours back on." Without answering, the man reached down and fished around in a small rucksack to retrieve a touch-screen cell phone. He switched the phone on and nearly dropped it when it rang immediately. He raised the phone to his ear. "Yes?" he answered.

A small voice on the other end of the line replied, "Hello. Is that Father John Cooper?"

"Yes."

"Oh thank the Lord I've found you. It's David Munroe here. We need you back at The Vatican immediately. We'll be sending a plane for you. I'll call you again in half an hour with the flight details. Is your phone fully charged?"

"Yes."

"Good. Please keep it switched on. Bye for now."

Father Cooper ended the call and threw the phone back into his rucksack. "Oh bugger!" he cursed.

At precisely 4.30 the following morning, Bonetti was dragged roughly out of a deep sleep by an insistent tapping on his bedroom door.

In other circumstances, he would have cursed softly, turned over, hugged the last vestiges of warmth from his teddy bear hot water bottle, ignored the interruption and gone back to sleep.

But he knew the tap, the identity of the tapper and the reason for the intrusion. Munroe had news. The distance from his slippers, placed neatly at the side of his bed, to the door was approximately 15 feet. Bonetti covered it, slippers on and half awake, in about five seconds flat, pulling on a large red woollen dressing gown as he went. He opened the door to a smiling Munroe, who was holding the page torn from the Cardinal's notebook.

"Got him!" said his Assistant as he walked into the room, a sense of achievement palpable in every spring of his steps. Bonetti was now fully awake.

"Nicely done David. How soon can he get here?"

"Lunchtime. I sent the jet."

Eight

At 11.05 later that morning a private plane landed, away from prying eyes, on a little-used runway at Leonardo da Vinci airport in Rome. Built to hold 10, the mid-sized jet only had one passenger on this trip. A priest in his early 40s.

After a brief wait at the end of the runway, the plane taxied to a private hangar, where a black limousine with Vatican plates was waiting. The priest exited the plane, limping slightly, knelt down and kissed the ground.

"Welcome home," said a voice. This was a different voice to the one that had woken him from his sleep just a few hours previously.

"I remember when home was a small house in a village just north of Glasgow," said Father Cooper, standing up and brushing the runway dust off his knees with the palms of his hands.

"Yeah – and I remember a bunch of villagers burning down that home because they thought The Devil lived inside, instead of a scared kid who could change into anything he wanted to. Animal, vegetable or mineral."

"Hi Gabriel," said the priest.

"Hi Father," said the angel. "We got problems."

"So I guessed."

Fifty-five minutes later, the Swiss Guard waved the car through the gates with a swift and smart salute. Expecting the car to go up the ramp to the St Damascus Courtyard entrance, the priest reached to unbuckle his seatbelt. Instead, the vehicle took a detour and stopped, five minutes later, outside an unremarkable looking doorway.

"So, no red carpet welcome?" asked Cooper in mock disappointment.

"It's probably being cleaned," said the angel.

The driver turned round in his seat. "The Cardinal wants to see you as soon as possible. Through that door you'll see stairs on your right. Someone will be waiting for you on the third floor."

The priest climbed out of the vehicle, closed the door behind him, and stopped to adjust his trousers. He turned to give a nod of thanks and farewell to the driver. The car had gone.

He turned back to see the smiling face of Father David Munroe. "Father – welcome back to Rome. Please follow me. I hope the trip here has given you an appetite. You'll be joining His Eminence for lunch."

"How long did it take you to find me, David?" asked Cooper.

"Oh that. Yes. I had a little help," said the younger priest. Then he turned and walked briskly along corridor that seemed to stretch for miles. The new arrival obediently followed behind.

Fifteen minutes and a maze of corridors later, they arrived at a heavy looking oak panelled door. Munroe knocked twice and entered. The aroma of cooked food immediately escaped from the room and danced wickedly down the corridor, flying up the nasal passages of anyone in its path, exciting millions of taste buds as it went.

Following the priest into the room, Cooper found himself in the private dining room of His Eminence Cardinal Alfredo Bonetti, Head of the Vatican's Special Investigations Department.

"Thank you David, I'll take it from here," said Bonetti, who was carving a thick slice of slightly pink roast beef from a joint large enough to choke a fully-grown lion. The small priest, who until then had assumed that he would be joining the two for lunch, looked crestfallen for a second, before regaining his composure and taking his protesting stomach elsewhere for something less delicious to eat.

"Nice to see you again John," said Bonetti, smiling. He was the only one who called Father Cooper by his Christian name. But only in private. It was a familiarity that had lasted as long as the two had known each other. "Help yourself," he said, indicating the food. He didn't have to say it twice.

When his plate was half empty, the Cardinal put down his knife and fork and looked solemnly at Cooper. "The Holy Father has an assignment for you. Do you accept?"

"Accept what?" asked the priest through a mouthful of meat and roast potato.

"I'm afraid it's one of those assignments that relies on your total acceptance before we can go any further."

Cooper speared a slab of meat with his fork, cut off a bite-sized chunk and held it, poised, in front of his mouth. "You know, I bet that's what they tell all the cows just before they take them into the slaughterhouses."

Bonetti shrugged. "Sorry. Orders from above, so to speak."

"Can't you tell me anything?"

"I can tell you that I can't tell you anything. And I can also tell you that if you don't say 'Yes' before you know the details, we ask Father Roberts."

The picture of a plump priest with eyes that were too small for his head and a nose that never seemed to stop running entered Cooper's head. Allard Roberts had been persuaded by his mother that God had obviously marked him out as special. The fact that there was no evidence to support her opinion was completely lost on the 12 year old boy, who then proceeded to make becoming a priest his one goal in life. It took him another 22 years to come to the attention of Cardinal Bonetti. Not because he was an excellent priest, which he wasn't. Not because he had a superior intellect, which he most certainly didn't. But because he was Bonetti's leverage. The threat of the fat, socially inept priest being brought in to replace anyone on Bonetti's staff was enough to ensure their acceptance of any assignment.

"Isn't he a few beads short of a full rosary?"

"You see our dilemma then, John," said the Cardinal, picking up his fork and prodding a small roasted potato before spearing it, placing it gently in his mouth and chewing slowly, savouring the taste. There was a short silence.

Cooper sighed. He knew he was being played. He always did. "Okay."

Bonetti beamed. "Excellent," he said. "Now, let's get to the details. This is where I tell you that the future of the world's heavenly believers is in your hands. And, come to think of it, the future of all the other believers and non-believers!"

"What, all of their futures?"

Bonetti raised an eyebrow, almost daring Cooper to protest. "Too much to ask?"

"Oh no. It's just – well, I don't suppose, for argument's sake, it could just be part of their futures. Or maybe only some of the believers?"

The Cardinal looked sad and shook his head, almost apologetically. "No John. This time we really are, as they say, up the creek."

The only door in the room opened and a generously proportioned waitress with arms and legs like a Donegal heifer walked in wheeling a serving trolley, quickly cleared the table and left without saying a word.

When the door closed, the Cardinal wiped his mouth with his serviette, looked at each of them in turn, took a deep breath and asked, "Have you heard of *The Eye of God*?"

"Only a rumour. You mean it actually exists?"

"Oh, it exists alright. In the year 1352 a raggedy old man appeared at the gates of the Vatican carrying a crystal almost as big as my fist. He claimed that this crystal was *The Eye of God*, told them what it did and that they should take very good care of it, otherwise there would be trouble."

"And they believed him?"

"They thought he was crazy. But they took it anyway. Then they were going to give him some bread and water and kick him out when something strange happened. Something that made the Church take him very seriously indeed."

"And that was?" asked the priest, looking around the room for any sign of a sweet trolley.

"He disappeared."

"What, you mean he ran away?"

"No," said Bonetti. "I mean he disappeared into thin air. Right in front of their eyes."

"Now there's something you don't see very often."

"Scared them so much so that they locked the crystal up and hid it away in the deepest part of the Vatican. It has been there ever since, guarded day and night."

"You didn't bring me all this way to look at a crystal, did you?"

"No," said Bonetti, settling into his story, "the old man told them that the crystal was a kind of barometer. Supposed to measure the movement of two very particular kinds of power."

"And those kinds would be?"

"Good and evil," answered Bonetti. "Put simply, it tells us how things are doing in Heaven and Hell."

"What – *the* Heaven and Hell? *Our* Heaven and Hell?"

"Well strictly speaking they're not exactly ours."

Cooper sat bolt upright. "Okay, now I'm officially fascinated. No, make that completely hooked. I take it I'm here because things aren't going so well?"

Bonetti's eyes burned with the look of a modern day Crusader. "They're going very badly. The world is turning upside down, John. Good is evil – evil is good. Churches are being sold off and converted into homes. And now the Holy Father has started seeing things."

"Some people would say that's evidence of excellent eyesight." Cooper was about to dig into the last roasted potato on his plate when curiosity got the better of him. "Okay, what things?"

"Dead people," said Bonetti, his voice a whisper. "He's started seeing dead people."

"I know a mortician who sees dead people every day. There's nothing unusual in that."

"There is when the dead people in question are God and the Devil."

"*What?*"

"He sees God and the Devil, dead as dodos," he whispered.

"Okay – that's deeply scary."

The Cardinal sighed, "At first we thought it might just be a nasty case of senile dementia. And to be quite frank we didn't like the idea of the Holy Mother Church being led by somebody who in a few months might not be able to remember his own name. But then something happened yesterday that changed everything."

Cooper began to experience a nasty feeling in the pit of his stomach.

Bonetti took a deep breath. "*The Eye of God* opened and stared at us!"

"The crystal stared at you?"

"Stared and communicated would be more accurate. I think it's time you saw it," he said. "Follow me."

Twenty minutes later the two were standing outside the room where *The Eye* was kept.

Bonetti knocked twice and the door was opened by Brother Roberto. "Have you come to let it look at you again?" he asked, moving aside to let them in the room.

Bonetti didn't answer. He merely patted the old monk on the shoulder as he entered.

"I don't suppose you could ask him to come and take his eye back, could you?" asked Brother Carlos, who was sitting in a chair in front of the glass casket containing *The Eye*. "My piles are killing me!" The comment drew a glare from Roberto.

"Not yet, but if God is willing, you can both go home soon with the Pope's special blessing."

"So," said Cooper, walking over to the crystal. "This is what all the fuss is about?"

He bent down until his face was inches from the crystal, then gasped when the blob changed into an eye, which opened and stared at him.

A strange muzzy feeling came over him and he smiled. "Cool! Now that's something you don't see every day. You know when you said it was *The Eye of God*, did you mean that in the figurative sense – or the literal one! And who the heck is Homer?"

The Eye closed and Cooper realised he was sitting in one of the two armchairs in the room. Bonetti and the two monks were standing over him smiling.

"It spoke to you, didn't it?" asked Roberto.

"You've been staring at it for 20 minutes. I think it likes you," said Carlos.

"I think I'm supposed to know something. Or do something," said Cooper. "Oh wait, it's getting – *wow!* So that's who Homer is." He turned to Bonetti, blinking rapidly. "I think I have to go somewhere."

"This place wouldn't be white, by any chance, would it," asked Bonetti.

"Very," said the priest, with a faraway look in his eyes. "And there are lots of sandwiches!"

"I think you'll find you're expected."

Cooper felt the muzzy feeling again. He closed his eyes as waves of nausea threatened to overcome him. When he opened them again the feelings were gone and he was sitting in a white armchair in a completely white room. Bonetti and the monks were nowhere in sight.

There were two other armchairs and all were arranged around a coffee table piled high with tea, coffee, diet cola, sandwiches, cakes and biscuits. One vacant chair was considerably larger than the rest.

"Well, one thing's for sure. I don't think I'm in Kansas any more," said Cooper softly to the whiteness. He adjusted his position in the chair, sinking into the comfortable leather. As if reading his thoughts, it moved effortlessly into a reclining position, far enough away from the table so as not to upend anything.

The right armrest flipped up, revealing a mini-cooler with ice-cool cans of coke, waiting to be slurped. He reached for one, pulled the ring, took a slurp and waited for something to happen. He didn't have to wait long.

"*So, this is the holy shapeshifter,*" said a disembodied voice. It was deep and slow and vaguely reminded Cooper of a loveable donkey character from his childhood stories.

"*He's one of Gabriel's pets,*" said another voice. This one wasn't so friendly. More abrupt. Maybe even a little impatient.

"Well, are you going to show yourselves, or do I have to catch up on some sleep until you decide to join the party?" asked Cooper.

"*Ooooooh, I like him, he's feisty,*" said the first voice. "*Time to meet and greet, eh?*"

No sooner had the voice finished speaking than two individuals materialised sitting in the other armchairs.

One was an angel. The other very definitely wasn't. Not only was he from the basement, rather than the attic, he was the width and height of an overgrown sumo wrestler, completely hairless and didn't so much as sit in the largest armchair as give it permission to expand to fit his massive frame.

"I gather *The Eye* has been poking around in your head," said Azriel.

"I think maybe it had a pick axe and a shovel," said Cooper, looking at the smaller of the two. "Azriel?"

The angel nodded ever so slightly.

"And you must be MoMo."

The large creature smiled. "I knew you were going to say that."

"Of course you did. You're a direct descendant of the last priestess of the Oracle of Delphi, right?"

"I knew you were going to say that, too!"

"Tell me, is there anything you don't know I'm going to say?"

"Not when I'm running on full Oracle power," said MoMo. "I'm only walking on it at the moment. Something's slowing me down. But I can still guess pretty good."

Azriel pointed at MoMo's head. "See that bump on his forehead? That's his inner eye. The one that can tell what's going to happen, what might happen, and what doesn't have a cat in Hell's chance of happening."

"So what happened?" asked Cooper, itching to touch MoMo's bump and suddenly feeling very defensive towards him.

"Fifty per cent blindness in his inner eye is what happened. Began losing his powers at around the same time as the powers of Heaven and Hell began to go up the spout. Sometimes it sees and sometimes it's as blind as a bat. But even on partial power, it's still the best way we've got to try to figure out what's going to happen next."

"I knew you were going to –"

"Okay MoMo, I know you knew," interrupted Azriel. He turned to Cooper. "Right.

Let's see what you know about *The Eye of God*."

"Okay."

"You know what it does?"

"Bits and pieces."

"Great," said the angel sarcastically.

"You know about *The One* – and Homer?"

"Well nobody's told me directly. But I get the impression everything's in there. Or at least some of it," he said, pointing to his head. "I had a conversation with *The Eye*. Or, more to the point, it had a conversation with me. Forced its way into my subconscious and left sticky notes everywhere. Reading them might be a bit of a problem though. The handwriting's terrible."

The ghost of a smile appeared on Azriel's lips. "Well well. A sense of humour."

"Everybody has a defect," said Cooper.

"Okay. Listen up." The angel filled in the blanks in the priest's knowledge about *The Eye of God*, who created it and why. And also about *The One* and Homer. He was careful to mention only the 'need to know' data. No point destroying the human's brain with the sheer weight of information normally carried in an angel's mind.

While he was listening, Cooper was tucking into what was left of the sandwiches, decimated just minutes before by MoMo. Then it was his turn. "So, *The Eye* not only warns of the shift in the balance of power, it also shows *The One* the only way to reverse the process, equalise the balance between good and evil, stop the worship of technology, give the non-believers their faith back, give God, the Devil, and all the angels their powers back, fill the churches, end world poverty and bring peace on earth?"

"Who said anything about the last two?"

"Can't blame a guy for trying. What about *The One*. Any idea who he is?" asked Cooper.

"Don't know who or where he or she is. Unfortunately the idiot genius of an angel who created *The Eye of God* also told *The One* how to fix it if it broke and how to put the balance of power right if it went wrong. Now he can't remember who or where *The One* is."

"Marvellous. What kind of name is *The One* anyway?"

"The kind you give to *The One* who can fix things, stupid!"

"So let's get this straight," said Cooper. "We know what *The Eye* can do, but we don't know how to find the only bugger on God's green earth, or anywhere else, who can work it?"

"I have an idea," said MoMo.

"You back up to full Oracle power?" asked Azriel.

"Oh no. Just wondering if we could have some more food. I think better on a full stomach!" No sooner had he uttered the thought than the coffee table was replenished with refreshments. He grabbed a ham salad sandwich and reached for the teapot. "Tea anyone?"

The angel picked up a cheese and pickle sandwich and prepared to stuff it into his mouth.

Cooper was surprised. "You eat?"

"Doesn't everyone?"

"Hmm – well, I suppose we start by trying to figure out who and where *The One* is. What was the name of that angel who made *The Eye*?"

"Zaphir," said Azriel. Only it actually sounded more like "Znnnfrr", through the mouthful of sandwich.

"Well, I think we should talk to this Znnnfrr. Maybe a little gentle prodding from MoMo here could help him to remember."

"Oh no. I don't do violence," said MoMo. "I tried it once a long time ago and –" his voice trailed off and there was a look of great sadness in his eyes.

Cooper decided wisely and immediately that any prodding of anyone from MoMo was to be avoided at all costs. Maybe that was the reason he was sent to Hell.

"Who said he was sent there?" asked Azriel's voice. Only this time the voice was in the priest's head. *"A little private word. MoMo went voluntarily. Stop digging."* One look into the angel's eyes persuaded Cooper to put down his inquisitive spade.

"What about you? He's your cousin, after all. Maybe a little family connection could knock a few memory-type brain cells back into place."

There are times in life when you wish you'd said something meaningful and important to someone special, instead of saying nothing and strongly regretting the silence. For Cooper, this was one of the other times. The times when you wished you'd stapled your lips shut.

Azriel stopped chewing and swallowed whatever food was in his mouth. It was obviously an uncomfortable experience. He didn't speak. He simply stared at Cooper, which was, by comparison, an infinitely more uncomfortable experience for the priest.

"They don't get on," whispered MoMo slowly. "In the Great War of the Angels, Zaphir sympathised with the angel Apollyon. The one they called The Destroyer. He wasn't very nice. Zaphir realised his mistake and made up for it by creating *The Eye of God*. But Azriel has never forgiven him."

"You realise I can hear every word you say," said the angel. "In fact if the wind is blowing in the right direction I can probably hear every word you think, too!" He turned to Cooper. "Except for some reason, I can't seem to hear anything going on inside *your* head, collar-wearing shapeshifter! Now why would that be, eh?"

MoMo frowned, picked up a large jam sponge cake and stuffed it whole into his mouth.

Cooper smiled. "You have to be invited in," he said. "Okay, what if I have a quiet word with him?"

"Be my guest," said the angel. "I tried to have a quiet word with him about *The Eye*. It didn't go too well."

"That's because you did violence," said MoMo.

"I was provoked. He did stupidity!"

"He's a genius."

"He's an idiot genius. And now he has the bruises to prove it."

"I still think I should talk to him," said Cooper, bringing the discussion to an end. "So, how do we get to wherever he is?"

"It's okay, I'll see you when you get back," said MoMo. "I know what's coming next."

"Exactly how far does this 'seeing into the future' gift of yours go?"

"Not very far. It's a bit like a short range weather forecast instead of a long range one."

"Aaah – right – got it!"

"We have to go upstairs," said Azriel.

Cooper's heart skipped a beat. "What, Heaven?"

"Not exactly. More like the suburb of a big city. You'll have to close your eyes and hold your breath. You might get a bit of a muzzy feeling. Oh, and you know that thing about asking nicely? Consider me asking."

The last thing Cooper heard after he closed his eyes was MoMo's faraway voice shouting, "Missing you already!" The first thing he heard before he opened them again was the sound of a strange, scared voice yelling painfully, "It doesn't matter how many times you hit me, I still can't remember. I might forget a lot, though!"

Cooper opened his eyes and breathed deeply. He was standing in a clearing in an ancient-looking forest, in front of an equally ancient-looking cottage. Miraculously, he didn't feel like throwing up. Azriel was standing at the door of the cottage, pounding on it with his right fist. "I'm not going to hit you, you imbecile. I want you to talk to someone. A friend of mine."

"Is this an intervention?"

"Eh? No, of course not. Now open the door."

"You don't have any friends. And I still have lots of bruises. You think maybe the two are connected?"

Cooper decided to butt in. "Hello?"

"Who said that?"

"My name's Cooper. Father John Wayne Cooper. I wonder if I could speak to you for a minute or two. Would that be okay?"

"Are you going to hit me?"

Certainly not," said Cooper. "I'm a pacifist. And I have some very good friends who are vegetarians."

"Do you have any very good friends who are females? I feel safer in the company of females. Especially when Azriel is around. He can be very argumentative."

"A female!" whispered Azriel. "We never thought of that."

Cooper thought quickly. "As a matter of fact my colleague is here. Her name is Chastity. You'd like her. By the way, what's your favourite smell?"

"Eh?"

"What's your favourite smell?"

"That's a bit personal, isn't it?"

"I have a very good reason for asking."

"Well – okay. I've always been partial to leather."

"Excellent. So, you fancy having a chat with her?"

There was a pause during which some sort of weighing up the pros and cons was obviously happening inside the cottage. The pros won.

"Okay. She can come in, but you two stay outside. Especially that nutter of a cousin of mine. Agreed?"

"Agreed." Cooper walked towards the cottage and in the space of putting one foot down and lifting the other one up, his physical form changed. From male to female. From handsome to beautiful. From conservative black suited to long, black leather coat over white blouse above tight black trousers with knee-length black leather boots.

Azriel, who had never witnessed such a transformation before and wasn't easily impressed, exhaled slowly, looked Chastity up and own, and grinned. "Very clever," he said. There was something in the grin that was definitely not angelic.

The thought occurred to Chastity that she was going to be inside on her own with Zaphir, so she needed all the help she could get. She returned Azriel's gaze. "Consider yourself invited, then."

The air was suddenly filled with the metallic sound of multiple locks being unlocked on the other side of the door. For a second, Chastity wondered why anyone would think that locks and bolts would be a barrier to any angel. But the thought passed as the door opened and she crossed over the threshold, walking into the maternity ward and birthplace of *The Eye of God*.

The door slammed shut behind her and the locks seemed to have a mind of their own as they made at least that entrance to the cottage secure. As her eyes adjusted to the interior lighting, she could make out vastly more space on the inside of the cottage than there seemed to be on the outside. All of it taken up with desks, drawing boards, machines in every state of unfinishedness, laboratory equipment, and, in the middle, a large Zen garden, complete with raked gravel surrounding large boulder islands.

There was an audible and powerful inhale of breath, followed by a slow, savouring exhale. Zaphir's voice came from behind her. "Oh my. So much leather."

Without turning, Chastity said, "You know, smell is one of the most powerful memory aids there is."

"I can't remember anything about *The Eye*, you know," he said, softly, almost regretfully. "Or *The One*."

Chastity turned and saw an overweight, under-sized man with a shaven head, wearing a monk's saffron-coloured robe and sandles. Over the robe was a work apron that, long ago, had been white but had slowly developed a colour all of its own. He had the same look on his face that Azriel had when he saw her transform outside the cottage.

"Watch yourself. He might be an angel, but he's no angel, if you get my meaning," said Azriel's voice in her head.

"I see you like leather, too," said Zaphir, smiling.

"I thought monks were supposed to abstain from the pleasures of life," said Chastity.

"Monk? Oh I only wear this when I'm in my garden," he said, indicating the robe. "It helps me get into the spirit of things."

"Be careful. I don't think it's the spirit of things he wants to get into," said Azriel.

Chastity smiled inside and walked slowly towards the rotund angel. "Maybe if you had a lie down and we had a nice chat you might remember what you forgot."

Zaphir smiled. "I'm willing if you are."

"Right, that does it. I'm coming in," said Azriel. *"If he lays a finger on you —"*

In his mind, Cooper answered. *"Oh stop it. Chastity's a big girl. She can look after herself. Let's see if we can loosen his tongue, and his memory."*

"Allow me, said Zaphir," and a large double bed appeared to the side of the angel. He sat down on it and patted a space next to him.

"I was thinking something much more intimate. How about a comfy chaise longue for you and a nice leather wingback armchair for me. There's nothing as satisfying as a prod around a beautiful mind, don't you think?"

No sooner were the words out of her mouth than the two items of furniture appeared. Chastity and Zaphir made themselves comfortable and the angel sighed softly as he relaxed in the sofa.

"This is nice," said the angel. "Tell me, do you always wear black leather?"

"I'll tell you if you tell me something first," said Chastity.

"Ask."

"How does the smell of leather make you feel?"

There was a long pause. "The same as the feel of leather. Strong. And secretive. Everyone sees the leather. They don't see me. I'm invisible. That's the way I like it. Your turn now, Bob."

Chastity smiled. "You called me Bob. Why?"

"I never did!" protested Zaphir, opening his eyes and looking a little worried.

"Who's Bob?"

"Don't ask me. I don't know anyone called Bob."

"Is he a secret?"

"I don't know any secrets. Secrets are dangerous. They can be very painful." Zaphir was beginning to panic. "You have to hide them away so nobody can find them."

"*No prizes for guessing who The One is, then,*" said Azriel, with a triumphant tone his voice. "*Now, ask him where he is.*"

"Was that what you did with Bob? Did you hide him away so nobody could find him?" asked Chastity.

Zaphir was breathing heavily. "Can't remember."

"*Quick. Give him a sniff of your coat,*" hissed the voice in her head.

Chastity leaned forward in her chair and shoved her leather covered arm under Zaphir's nose, bumping his jaw on the way. The angel breathed in deeply, moaned and yelled in pain. "Aaaagh! Toothache." He sat up on the sofa and rubbed his right cheek rapidly. "Sorry, I don't like you any more. You'll have to go NOW!"

Chastity protested but the angel insisted. The visit was over. However, they hadn't come away empty handed. They had a name. Bob. Whether he was *The One* was anyone's guess, but it was a start.

As she walked to the door, the locks and bolts undid themselves in what must have been record time, and the wooden slab flew open on protesting hinges. It slammed shut behind her with the kind of speed and venom normally reserved for very unwelcome family members or debt collectors.

Somewhere in between steps two and three heading away from the cottage door, Chastity changed back into Cooper. Although he looked closely, even Azriel, with all his angelic powers, couldn't spot the exact point of transformation. "Very impressive," he said.

Cooper shrugged. "It would have been even more impressive if he'd told me where we could find this Bob."

The angel smiled. "Zaphir can be extremely brilliant and phenomenally dumb both at the same time. He did tell us. He just doesn't know he did."

Nine

"Purgatory? Bob's in Purgatory?"

"Apparently."

Azriel and Cooper had left the suburbs of Heaven and the forest that held Zaphir's cottage and rejoined MoMo in The White Room. The muzzy feeling was just beginning to leave the priest and the three of them were seated around the coffee table which had been replenished with food and drink."

"Well correct me if I'm wrong, but don't you have to be dead to go there? Isn't that a sort of prerequisite?"

"Normally yes, but there can be exceptions."

"Like what?"

"Like if you're there for the day," offered MoMo.

"You mean they have visitors?"

"They do excursions. They're trying to improve their image."

"I didn't know they had one," said Cooper, amazed.

"They have trees. It's a start."

"But how do you know he's even there?"

"Sometimes it's not what a person says that tells you what you want to know. Sometimes it's what they don't say," said Azriel.

"So, because Zaphir *didn't* say Purgatory, you knew that's exactly where he meant?"

MoMo offered an explanation. "No. Azriel knew he meant Purgatory because he said toothache!"

Before Cooper could finish looking confused, MoMo said, "Hey, we could always look in the Registers."

"You got Registers for Purgatory?"

"We got Registers for everywhere. Everyone in, everyone out, everyone staying for the duration. Even everyone everywhere else sitting around waiting to go anywhere else. You want me to check all the Registers?"

"You can do that?"

"Sure. Be back soon." With that, MoMo stood up and seemed to move from a state of being there to one of not being there at all.

In the space of a heartbeat he returned to the being there state. "We got 633,486,399 Bobs, dead or alive, all fully accounted for everywhere – 288,387 are in Purgatory. If our Bob's one of them, we need to go take a look."

"How crowded is it there?"

Azriel answered. "Think of Bob as a single grain of sand. And think of Purgatory as the Sahara Desert."

"So, a quick in and out, search and rescue, smash and grab, then?"

Nobody laughed.

"I got a bad feeling," groaned MoMo.

"Your Oracle powers tell you that?" asked Azriel.

"Nope. Indigestion. I think maybe I ate too much."

"I didn't think that was possible."

The oversized Oracle frowned and looked like he was about to say something. But instead, his sizeable abdomen decided to speak for him. A rush of fetid air escaped from his stomach, moved rapidly up his esophagus and out through his mouth. What followed was the loudest, longest and smelliest burp Cooper had ever heard, felt or smelled.

The priest covered his nose and tried, unsuccessfully, to stop his eyes from watering. Azriel merely sat comfortably in his chair as if nothing had happened. "Is the bad feeling gone now?"

MoMo nodded, smiling more with relief than joy.

"So, road trip?"

"To Purgatory? Us? Now?" blurted Cooper.

"Well, we could wait for a month or two, or maybe a year or two. Oh no, I forgot. There's that small matter of Homer. Maybe if we ask nicely he'll put on the brakes and hang around in space until we're decide what we're going to do next, eh? Your call."

"Fine. Road trip it is. Just remember, I'm human so I can only hold my breath for so long before I start turning purple and fainting."

The last thing he heard after he closed his eyes and before the muzzy feeling came, was MoMo's voice. "Is he really *The One*?"

Ten

"You can open your eyes now," said Azriel, "and that purple colour doesn't suit you, so it would probably be a good idea if you took a breath."

Cooper slowly opened his eyes and looked around, not knowing what to expect. What he didn't expect was what he saw.

He was sitting in a chair in a dental surgery reception area. The room had soothing pale blue walls, a badly framed print of an oil painting of a bowl of fruit – and a dark wood reception desk behind which sat a middle-aged woman in a white coat, typing on a computer keyboard. MoMo and Azriel were standing over him. It was half full of people in pain.

"So *this* is Purgatory?"

"No," said the angel, "*this* is a dentist's reception. Purgatory is through that door over there." He pointed to a white door at the far end of the room with a large golden 'P' stuck on it.

Cooper had a lightbulb moment. "Toothache," he said, remembering the word spoken by Zaphir.

A small, twisted smile attempted to curl up the sides of Azriel's mouth. It nearly succeeded. "Funny how the mind works. My clever cousin's conscious mind couldn't remember where Bob was. But the smell of your leather jacket helped his unconscious one throw out a cryptic clue. Good job this isn't my first visit to the Big P."

Nobody in the room gave the new arrivals a second glance, or even a first one.

"Don't worry. Nobody can see us, or the door. In fact no human can see anyone from Heaven or Hell, unless we want them to. And generally we don't. There's too much explaining to do."

"I get that. But how come we can't go straight there without the detour?"

"Simple," said MoMo. "This isn't a detour. It's their last familiar sight from the old life, before they hit the Big P. And it's where they hand out the welcome packs. Everybody gets one. There's a brochure, a map, and even a toothbrush and toothpaste.

All in a special goody bag. But we won't be staying, so we won't get one." He sounded disappointed.

Azriel walked towards the door with the golden P and knocked three times.

"Stayin' or visitin'?" yelled a rough voice, with a Bronx Jewish dialect, from the other side of the door.

"Three for the guided tour," said Azriel.

"Azzey my boy, is that you?" yelled the voice, even louder. There was the sound of a key turning in a lock and the door flew open.

"You don't write, you don't call, a guy could get the feeling you didn't want to know him no longer!" complained the voice, which now had a face, followed by a body. Standing in the doorway, filling it so completely that it was practically impossible to see anything beyond, was the strangest creature Cooper had ever seen.

It was the living, moving and breathing example of everything that could possibly go wrong if you decided to make a human being from scratch with just the bits and no blueprint or prior knowledge of the end result.

"Guys," Azriel said, smiling "say hello to my very good friend Beebop. Keeper of a million secrets – confidante to the weak, the lonely and the totally insane, and Head Doorman to the Realm of Purgatory."

Beebop smiled with pride at the grand introduction. The fact that his smile wasn't where Cooper expected it to be was neither here nor there. The same could be said of his arms and legs. But remarkably, even though the whole package was soft of jumbled up and mixed around, it made its own kind of sense. And anyway Beebop didn't seem to notice the difference or struggle with any of the anomalies.

He simply extended two overlong arms and pulled Azriel to him in a warped kind of bear hug. The angel had obviously expected this because he showed no surprise. He simply allowed his friend to embrace him for a sufficient amount of time before wrestling himself free and allowing Beebop wipe a tear from one of the eyes on the face in the middle of his chest.

"Beebop," said Azriel, adjusting his garments and wiping something wet and slimy off his shirt front, "meet Father John Wayne Cooper. He's a shapeshifter. And MoMo. He isn't."

"Charmed, I'm sure," said Beebop, bowing slightly.

"No need to go overboard with the introductions," said Cooper.

"Don't knock it. That's the nearest thing to a friendship I ever saw Azriel have with anybody. He must really like you guys."

"I knew you were going to say that," said MoMo enthusiastically.

"He's an Oracle," added Cooper. It sounded like an excuse rather than explanation.

"Nudge nudge, wink wink, say no more," said Beebop, bringing an arm from behind his back and tapping his nose, which happened to be under his mouth.

Cooper was about to say something, when Beebop sort of rolled to one side and for the first time since the door opened, they could see what Purgatory looked like.

Ahead of them lay what should have been a hideous sea of sorry-looking bodies atoning for their earthly sins and waiting for the day when grace fell upon them again and they were plucked from the mire and sent upstairs with a brilliant white gown and a slate wiped clean. Or went screaming into the fires of Hell. Damned forever.

Instead, what they saw was a vast empty plain, a bit like a flat desert with mountains in the background and the odd tree or two in clumps here and there.

"Hang on – you mean this is it? This is Purgatory?" exclaimed Cooper.

"Well," said Beebop, performing the best imitation of a shrug that he could, given that he didn't have shoulders where they should have been, "I must admit there's rather a lot of space and not a lot of bodies."

"Not a lot? *It's empty*! Where are all the screaming masses? Where's all the pain and suffering. All those billions and billions of souls serving out their time, eh?" I expected something a bit more, more – "

"Yes?" asked Beebop, raising his eyebrows which fortune had, somehow managed to place correctly.

"More grand and tortured and cosmic, even!" he said sweeping his hand across the empty horizon.

"Cosmic?" said Beebop, a tone of alarm creeping into his voice. "Nobody said nothing about being cosmic. Don't bollock me, I'm just the friggin' doorkeeper! Nobody said 'Oh Beebop, it's gonna be really COSMIC'.

All they said was 'keep the door locked and don't let anyone out without a pass'!"

"So what happened?"

"Orders from above to clear them all out is what happened."

"Clear them out when?"

"Last week. No wait – maybe it was last year – "

"Where have they gone?"

Beebop yelled, "How the bleedin' gonads should I know? Like I said. I'm the doorkeeper."

Cooper turned to Azriel. "We're stuffed then, basically."

"We were looking for someone called Bob," said MoMo.

Beebop stroked what he thought was his chin in an effort to appear helpful. It wasn't his chin, but it seemed to work. "Come to think of it, there was one skinny bloke who was left when everyone else had gone. Then they must have realised their mistake because after a couple of minutes he disappeared. They probably came back for him."

"Time you went to work MoMo," said Azriel. "What does that bump on your forehead say?"

The large Oracle reached up, gently stroked the bump with the fingers of his right hand, closed his eyes and began humming. After a minute, his eyes sprang open. "He's coming," he said.

Eleven

The darkness was all around him. He couldn't even see his own hands in front of his face. There was no sound and the loincloth he was wearing made him feel not only cold but also vulnerable and naked. It was a very small loincloth.

The voice came from somewhere in front of him. Or maybe it was somewhere behind. "Hello Bob."

He tried to answer but the only thing that came out of his mouth was a breathy silence. It was as if his vocal cords had forgotten how to work. Maybe their ability to make the sounds that made speech was lost. He couldn't remember the last time he had a conversation with anyone. Or anything. How long had it been? Years? Centuries? Aeons?

"Oh come on. You've only been gone five minutes. Well – maybe a day at the most," said the voice.

Bob suddenly rediscovered his voice. "Who said that?"

"Aaaah, now there's a question. Straight and to the point. Remember me Bob?"

"Who's Bob?"

"You are."

"That's funny. I don't feel like a Bob."

"Oh you're a Bob alright. A very special Bob. Long time no see."

"I'm surprised you can see anything in this darkness. I don't suppose you could switch a light on, could you?"

There was a grunt followed low, humourless laughter. "I like the dark. It's very comforting. You can hide things in it. Things like *The Eye of God*. You remember that, Bob?"

"Is there anything to eat here? Maybe some bread with a bit of cheese?"

"Bread? Focus Bob!" There was annoyance in the voice. "*The Eye of God*. I know you know *what* it is. What I need you to do is tell me *where* it is."

Look, I don't know who you are, and I don't know what this *Eye* thing is. But I'm very cold and I'm very hungry, at least I think I am."

A thought crept into Bob's head. "If I'm so special, maybe if you could put the light on and make it a bit warmer in here. Better still – make it a lot warmer! Give me some clothes and something hot and tasty to eat. I might start remembering all sorts of things. Maybe even important things."

There was a sigh. "You don't remember anything do you?"

"Sorry. All I can remember is loads of nothing. Is that any good?"

"No Bob. I'll just have to wait a little longer. Oh well – see you again soon."

"Is there going to be pain now?"

"Not yet."

Twelve

There was a muzzy kind of feeling and Bob realised he was sitting in the sand back in Purgatory. Standing over him were three people, one of them alarmingly large who seemed to be smiling and rubbing his forehead, and a creature that had all the right parts of a people, but in all the wrong places. One of the people with parts in the right places spoke.

"Your name's not Bob, by any chance, is it?" asked Cooper.

Bob decided that, as this was the second time he'd been connected with that name in the past few minutes, there was a fair chance that his name was, indeed, Bob. "Maybe it is and maybe it isn't," he said.

"Do you know?"

Bob frowned and said, "Maybe I do and maybe I don't."

There was a yelp from behind them. "Sweet Mary Hell" said Beebop, "you got him to talk! I tried for years and the only damned thing he said in all that time was, 'Excuse me, am I dead?' In the end I said 'Yes, you are bloody dead, now piss off!' Never spoke to him again after that."

Azriel leaned down, grabbed one of Bob's arms, and pulled him up to something closely resembling a standing position. Given their difference in height, the angel looked down into Bob's eyes and said, "Good news. You're not dead. You're very under-dressed and you're incredibly skinny. But you're definitely not dead."

That seemed to please Bob, who smiled.

"Now. You disappeared from here and then you came back. Where were you before you came back?"

"I remember blackness."

"Did you have your eyes closed?" asked Cooper.

Bob looked at him as if he were looking at an idiot asking a question that didn't even deserve an answer. "I remember somebody talking to me. Asking me about something called *The Eye of God*. I told him I didn't have a clue what he was talking about. I don't think he was very pleased. Then I woke up here."

Azriel and MoMo exchanged the kind of glance normally reserved for bad news.

"Listen very carefully," said the angel, with foreboding and menace in his voice. "Did this somebody tell you his name?"

"No. But he did say I knew him and I hope not because I'm very sure I don't think I want to know him at all."

"Do you remember anything about before you came here the first time?" asked Cooper.

Bob thought for a while. "Well, I don't know what it means – but feathers," he said.

"Feathers?"

"Yep. Feathers. Loads of them. Everywhere. All around me."

"Hmm – feathers – and then?"

"Nothing," said Bob "After that it's a complete blank. How long have I been here?"

They all turned to Beebop. "Search me," he said. "He's been here as long as I can remember."

Cooper started pacing up and down.

"What's he up to?" asked Beebop.

Cooper stopped pacing and they all turned to look at him.

"Show me your back," said the priest to the skinny man.

"I beg your pardon?"

"Show him your back," barked Azriel, with such ferocity and power of command that the man immediately spun round so that all gathered could take a close look at his naked back. Cooper walked up to the man until his face was no more than a few inches from the man's shoulder blades.

"What are those?" he asked, pointing to two lumps on the man's back.

"What are what?" asked the man.

"Those lumps on your back."

"Never seen them before in my life," said the man.

"Well of course you haven't, they're on your back, stupid" said Beebop.

"Emm – shoulder blades?"

"Nope, they look more like nobbly joints to me."

"Joints?" Now the man sounded frightened.

"Yep. Joints."

"Where you going with this, Sherlock?" asked Azriel softly.

Cooper looked at Azriel. "I think he used to have wings."

"Wings?" shrieked the man.

Azriel's eyes narrowed. He looked at Cooper, then the lumps. "Are you saying what I think you're saying?"

"I think he's an angel," said Cooper, nodding. "Or was."

"You think a lot," said Azriel.

"It's a curse, I know, but it makes sense," said Cooper. "Zaphir stashes *The Eye of God* in the Vatican where nobody can get it, then picks one of his feathered friends, works his magic on the poor bugger and makes him the only one who can tell us how to reverse the process and shove technology down the pecking order and religion back up where it belongs, when the time comes. Then wipes his memory and stashes him in Purgatory so nobody can find him and steal the information. Only problem is, Zaphir suffered a convenient little memory loss himself. Too convenient, if you ask me." He spread his hands wide and looked to Azriel for a reaction.

"I'm an angel?" asked Bob.

Azriel's eyes sparkled bright, "Yeah, and he pops up out of thin air as soon as we get to Purgatory? Come on Sherlock, it's too easy!"

"Well," said Beebop " if you'd got here yesterday you'd have had the Devil of a job finding him. Bloody billions here there were. Standing room only, far as the eye could see."

"And it only took you a day to clear Purgatory?" asked Cooper, obviously impressed.

"Nope. Not even that! Never saw anything like it. Some of them were backlogged, but most weren't even due for relocation. Then some fancy Joe from upstairs comes and says 'Shift them all out, you've got an hour and a half', bloody cheek! Personally, I think there's something fishy going on."

"I'm really an angel?" repeated Bob.

"Yes, you're really an angel. Maybe. Get used to it," said Cooper, impatiently. He turned back to Beebop. "Fishy like what?"

"Well, like somebody pretty powerful wanted somebody pretty hidden to be found pretty quickly. Maybe."

Azriel frowned. In all his existence, he had never questioned the motivations of his boss, and he wasn't about to start now. On the other hand – what if God had nothing to do with this. What if somebody else wanted Bob flushed out so he could get to *The Eye of God.*

"I don't like this. Everybody move now," he said, moving towards the door to Purgatory. "Three in, four out, Beebop."

He turned to Cooper. "We need to get back to *The Eye* with our friend Bob here. If he's *The One*, then the sooner the two of them get together, the sooner this whole mess gets sorted out. Agreed?"

"What *One*?" asked Bob.

Cooper nodded. "Agreed."

"I don't think it's going to be as simple as that," said MoMo. "I have another feeling."

"*What One*?" insisted Bob. The angel ignored him. "Where to Sherlock?"

"I have an idea," said Cooper.

Thirteen

At roughly the same time as the quartet were leaving Purgatory like bats out of Hell, a small ceremony was taking place on top of a rock, in the southern part of the Northern Territory, in central Australia. It wasn't an ordinary ceremony. But then again, it wasn't an ordinary rock.

Sunset was approaching, and the sandstone rock was beginning to take on a stunning red glow. Its name was Uluru, and near its highest point, 863 metres above sea level, a small blanket was spread on its surface. Sitting cross-legged on the blanket was an elder from the Pitjantjatjara people, traditional owners of this world-famous and sacred landmark. The elder's name was Jacob Crow and he was talking to the sky.

His body was scarred and painted and he was having a conversation with an old friend. Someone he had been waiting for since he had been a young boy. Someone who had been on walkabout in the stars and was now coming home.

As the sun began to sink below the horizon, Jacob stopped speaking, nodded a couple of times and smiled. He closed his eyes, breathed deeply and remembered an old man and a young boy. They were both sitting on the ground at the base of Kata Tjuta, known as The Olgas, about 30kms west of Uluru. Taller than Uluru, it was the place where the old man came to talk with the sky.

It was his place and his name was Tom Freeman.

After a while, the man looked down at the boy and put a hand on his shoulder. "Time you walked on your own now mate. I can't teach you anymore. You got the seeing. Somebody else gonna teach you now."

Jacob Crow looked up at his old friend, stood up and walked away. He didn't look back. It was Tom's time and he knew it.

Now, many years later, Jacob nodded, stood up and prepared to leave Uluru for the night. Below him, at the foot of the rock, sitting in a beat-up Land Rover, was a young Aboriginal man. His name was Nipper, or at least that's what his uncle Jacob called him, and he was waiting.

For Nipper, the thought of waiting for Jacob Crow never entered his head. It was just something he did. Something he'd always done. It was as natural a thing to do as breathing and he couldn't imagine doing anything else.

An hour or so after dark, he heard the sound of Jacob approaching the vehicle. He knew the only reason he heard the old man was because the old man wanted to be heard. It was his way of announcing his presence. Nipper smiled.

He got out of the driver's seat, walked to the other side of the Land Rover and opened the door.

Jacob Crow halted before getting in. "He won't be long," he said.

Fourteen

"I don't even know if time exists in Purgatory, but what time is it in Rome?" Cooper asked Azriel. He had stopped wearing a watch years previously.

"Just after midnight."

He tried to think of somewhere safe inside the Vatican where they wouldn't get interrupted. "Any chance of dropping us inside the private apartment of Cardinal Alfredo Bonetti? He'll be at Midnight Mass."

"No problem," said Azriel, turning to Bob. "Right, you do exactly as I say. Close your eyes and hold your breath." Cooper and MoMo did the same.

As they felt the tingling sensation, they vaguely heard Beebop shouting, "Now don't be strangers. Come back any time!"

The priest waited for Azriel's voice telling him to open his eyes, but it didn't come.

Carefully, he opened one eye and peeked at the surroundings. They were in a bedroom, presumably Bonetti's. Azriel was nowhere in sight and Bob was kneeling on the floor, throwing up on a very expensive-looking Chinese rug.

Bonetti was standing in front of them, wearing pyjamas and holding an unlit cigarette in one hand and a personalised Vatican Zippo lighter in the other, looking slack-jawed at MoMo.

There was a digital alarm clock on a bedside cabinet. The time was 1.30am. Midnight mass was done and dusted and the sound of Azriel's voice was a faint echo in Cooper's head.

Back soon, shapeshifter," he said.

MoMo rested a large friendly hand on Bonetti's shoulder. "You need to mind your step," he said, as the Cardinal dropped his cigarette and lighter on the floor in surprise.

"Oooraaaaghhh!" spluttered Bob again, as he deposited another hefty load, this time with half-digested ex-wriggly things, at the Cardinal's feet.

"What the –" Bonetti yelled and moved quickly to avoid the slippery pool of angel puke. Instead, he lurched wildly off balance, falling heavily on the floor, temporarily winded.

MoMo shook his head slowly from side to side. "I told him. 'Mind your step' I said."

"Perfect," said Cooper in disgust. "Absolutely perfect!" He manhandled Bonetti into a fireside chair. One of the Cardinal's slippers had come off and was now nestling comfortably in the puke puddle. He was dazed and gasping for breath.

Just then, there was a soft knocking sound. Instead of wondering what to do next, something inside Cooper seemed to take over and, without hesitation, he stood up and walked towards the door.

Halfway there his image seemed to shimmer and in the space of two steps he went up in the Vatican hierarchy, changing into a perfect facsimile of Bonetti, complete with pyjamas.

As Bob hoisted himself upright, wiping the dregs of puke and spit from his mouth on his naked hairy arm, Cooper reached the door and opened it slightly.

"Didn't I say I wasn't to be disturbed?" he asked a perplexed Father David Monroe, standing on the other side.

"Emm – no, your Eminence. You actually said you wanted to see me after mass and here I am. I got here as soon as I could." As far as Monroe was concerned, he was not only looking at, but also listening to, Cardinal Bonetti.

Cooper nodded. "Well, I can see you very nicely, thank you. Now off you go to bed!" And with that, he shut the door, locked it quickly then crossed himself.

"So, I'll just go to bed then, shall I?"

"Absolutely. See you in the morning."

As the sound of Munroe's footsteps faded, the real Cardinal groaned in the chair. In a second or two the priest was at his side looking suitably concerned.

Bonetti's eyes shifted from Cooper, to MoMo, to Bob and back again to the priest.

"Did I see what I thought I saw?" he said, trying to get up from the chair, only to be pushed back into it by a gentle nudge from MoMo.

Cooper looked innocent. "Why? What do you think you saw?"

"Spill the beans," said the Cardinal.

"What, all of them?"

"Every last one."

"Fair enough." Cooper handed the Cardinal his fallen cigarette, flicked the Zippo into fiery life – and watched as Bonetti sucked in a long, calming nicotine hit. As he blew the smoke out, the Cardinal nodded to Bob. "Who's he?"

"He's Bob, we think he might be an angel," said Cooper, and proceeded to tell the Cardinal everything that had happened since he entered the White Room. About Azriel, MoMo and Beebop.

"Purgatory? Holy Mother of God."

"Excuse me," said Bob, pointing to his loincloth. "Do you think I could have something to wear? I'm freezing."

"You're smelly, too," said MoMo, who, without being asked, had decided to clean up Bob's mess. Even kneeling down he was tall.

At first Bob looked hurt by the remark. Then he looked embarrassed as he realised he couldn't remember the last time any water had touched any part of his body.

"There's a bathroom through there," said Bonetti, indicating a white door. "It has a power shower. On second thoughts, maybe a nice soak in the bath would be better."

Bob looked suspicious. "What's a bath?"

"Maybe I better help," offered Cooper, who led Bob through to the bathroom. He returned a few minutes later smiling. "I think he's fallen in love with the shower. You might have to have it completely sanitised when he's finished."

"You've done well," said Bonetti. "The Holy Father will be pleased."

"Still seeing those dead people?"

"Unfortunately yes. He's also deaf now."

"What?"

"As a doorpost."

"Don't forget his bowels," added MoMo.

"How did you –? "

"Oracle powers," said Cooper, shrugging. "Who knew?"

"I did," said MoMo.

"Well – thank God he can still speak."

"Don't speak too soon."

Twenty minutes later, Bob, dressed in a spare pair of the cardinal's pyjamas, came out of the bathroom smiling and a few skin tones lighter. "I don't suppose there's anything to eat," he asked, hopefully.

Cooper glanced quickly at the puke stain on the rug. "I don't think that would be a good idea."

"Probably just throw up again anyway," said MoMo.

"Don't blame me," he whined. "Blame that other fella."

"Azriel?"

"That's him. Hold your breath, he said. Close your eyes, he said. Never said nothing about a queasy gut-churning feeling." Bob looked genuinely apologetic.

Bonetti softened. "It's ok, Bob. I think we could all use some sleep." He looked at Cooper and MoMo. "First thing tomorrow, I think we should introduce Bob to *The Eye* and see what happens. That okay with you two?"

"Sounds like a plan," said the priest.

"Right," said the Cardinal. "Out the door to the right you'll find some spare guest bedrooms. The sheets are clean. I suggest you all try to get some shuteye. I'll have someone wake you about 8.30." He looked MoMo up and down. "I'll get some blankets. I think the floor is the only bed big enough for you."

As they left, Bonetti looked up to the ceiling, crossed himself and softly murmured The Lord's Prayer. The smell of evicted Bob's stomach contents still emanated from the rug and assaulted the room. So he dragged his expensive circular floorcovering into the bathroom, dumped it in the bath to be dealt with in the morning, and closed the door firmly behind him. Exhausted, he slipped beneath the sheets and drifted off to a sleep disturbed by the kind of dark dreams that, thankfully, he would never remember.

Fifteen

At 9.30 sharp the following morning, Bonetti, Cooper, MoMo and Bob were standing outside the door that led to the *The Eye of God.*

Bonetti knocked twice. Nothing happened.

"Brother Carlos – Brother Roberto – open the door," he commanded.

A croaky, ancient voice from the other side of the door said, "Who is it?"

"Cardinal Bonetti," said the Cardinal, impatience in his voice.

"I was just going to go for a pee," Brother Carlos said, as the door was unlocked from the inside.

Without hesitation, Bonetti walked in and indicated the other three to follow. They all walked past a very uncomfortable looking monk, smiling at him each in their turn.

When it came MoMo's turn to enter, Carlos's understanding of how big any two-legged humanoid should be decided to exit. His mind simply refused to believe anyone could grow that big – and it reduced MoMo's size accordingly to a more believable height. Then it told him to smile and close the door.

Brother Roberto was sitting in the chair in front of the glass case containing *The Eye of God*, his eyes firmly fixed on the crystal.

"We've brought someone to look at the crystal," said Bonetti, walking over to the old monk and patting him gently on the shoulder.

"Well it hasn't been doing any of that looking back nonsense since the last time," said Roberto.

"This is Bob," said the Cardinal, indicating the skinny newcomer, who was heading for the vacant armchair. Bonetti grabbed him by the arm and half dragged him towards the case. "Why don't you have a nice look?"

The angel tentatively stepped closer until his nose was almost touching the glass. "It's very nice, but I've never seen it before in my life. Is it supposed to do anything?"

72

Bonetti looked surprised.

"You mean it doesn't ring a bell anywhere in that slightly warped head of yours?" chipped in Cooper.

Bob tapped his head. "No bells, no alarms, no ringing."

Bonetti turned to Cooper. "You sure he's *The One*?"

"Why do you keep calling me *The One*?" asked Bob. "I don't even know who this *One* fella is. I'm very happy being just plain old Bob, if that's okay with you."

"Well, we *think* he's *The One*," said Cooper. "He was the only one left in Purgatory. All the others had been relocated and Bob was the only one who came back. It's a process of elimination. He has to be *The One*. Probably."

Bonetti sighed and poked Bob in the ribs. "Take another look," he said. "And closer this time."

"If you want me to take a closer look I'll have to take it out of the box," said Bob.

"You mean he gets to hold it?" asked Roberto, his voice thick with jealousy. "Over fifty years we've guarded it and not even so much as breathed heavy on it – and he gets to hold it!"

"Tell him," said Bonetti.

"We think he's an angel," said Cooper.

Roberto promptly fainted and Carlos prostrated himself at Bob's feet, kissing them repeatedly and muttering something in Latin.

Bob smiled. "It tickles," he said. "Never had my feet kissed before."

Cooper dragged Carlos away from Bob's feet and steered him towards Roberto. "See if you can wake him up."

Meanwhile, Bob slowly reached out, almost afraid to touch the box. "You sure about this?" he asked Bonetti.

"Yes!"

"Okay, open the box."

Bonetti turned to Brother Carlos, who was still trying to wake up Roberto, and held out his hand.

The monk's right hand went to the neck of his habit, to where a small key was attached to an old leather cord. He pulled the cord over his head and grudgingly handed it to the Cardinal, who walked with it to the box.

It was then that they all noticed for the first time the small lock fashioned into the front left hand edge of the box.

It was almost as if the contents of the box had rendered the mechanism invisible, only to become visible in the vicinity of the key. Bonetti inserted the key, turned it to the right and gently pulled. The whole front face of the glass case swung open on unseen hinges.

Bob put both hands into the box and gently lifted out the crystal, bringing it as close as he could to his face. There was complete silence in the room.

"Well?" asked Bonetti.

"Never felt better in my life, thank you," said Bob.

"Very nice, but can you *feel* anything?"

"Wait – I can feel something," said MoMo, who was rubbing the bump on his forehead again.

"You?"

"Oh yeah. I can feel tingly all over. I think I better sit down." With that, the large Oracle's legs gave way and he promptly sank to the floor, closing his eyes. His 'middle eye' bump was glowing."

Bonetti's eyebrows rose in surprise.

Cooper looked at Bob. "Can *you* feel anything yet?"

"Funny you should say that. I do feel a bit of a tingling round about my shoulder blades."

"Quick. Take your shirt off and turn round."

As they looked at Bob's naked back, they could see the stumps of his removed wings begin to glow and grow.

"Well that's something you don't see every day," said Cooper, poking one of the stumps gently. It felt warm. "I think maybe his wings are growing back!"

"What?" yelled Bob, almost dropping the crystal in alarm.

This time it was Brother Carlos who swooned with religious fervour at the angel's feet, who obviously wasn't sure whether he liked the idea of a couple of extra appendages growing at a rate of knots out of his back, precisely where he couldn't keep an eye on them.

Cooper saw his distress and patted him on the shoulder. "Don't worry," he said.

"Alright for you to say," said Bob. "You're not the one with a new set of feathers!" Suddenly a new thought crept into his head. "Hey, you think this means I can fly?"

"Not yet, superman. I'd wait a bit with the wing thing till they're all grown back. See anything in the crystal yet?"

Bob looked even closer at the lump of twinkling rock in his hands. He examined every facet. Stared as hard as he could and then loudly proclaimed, "You sure this is the genuine article? Because all I see is a piece of rock with a wooooaaah! The damned thing looked at me!"

"At last!" exclaimed Bonetti.

"There's an eye in there."

"We know. It's *The Eye of God.*"

"Well, it's making me feel all queasy," said Bob. "I think I need to sit down" and with that he reeled to one side and slumped to the floor, the crystal nestling comfortably in his lap.

Bonetti looked exasperated. "Oh for Heaven's sake, he better not puke again!"

On the armchair, Brother Roberto was coming awake. As he opened his eyes his first sight was of the empty crystal case. "Thief!" he shouted. "Sound the alarm. Somebody's stolen the holy crystal!" Then the memory of what had just happened came crashing in on him as he saw Bob sitting on the floor, awake but looking a little white, with the crystal on his lap. He crossed himself quickly.

"Don't worry my son," said Bonetti. "It's not every day you see a real, live angel."

"Complete with wings, of the short and stubby kind," said Cooper.

The monk started to shake. "Angel?"

"His name's Bob, the same as yours, sort of."

The monk gasped and crossed himself again. "I think I'll go make some tea," he said, grabbing Carlos and dragging him, protesting, into the kitchen.

Cooper nudged the still asleep MoMo, whose middle eye bump was still glowing a soft red. On the second nudge, MoMo woke up, the bump popped open, looked at the priest and slowly closed again. The Oracle mumbled "YouTube".

"YouTube?"

"Yes."

"What about it?"

"Haven't a clue. The Oracle powers don't come with a rulebook or explanations. That's all I got. YouTube."

Meanwhile, Bonetti had helped Bob up from the floor and steered him in the direction of the eye again. This time, the closer the angel got to the crystal the stronger the attraction got.

He felt as though he was actually being pulled into it, surrounded by a swirling cloud of muzziness, with tiny lights flickering around here and there and a curious aroma of garlic permeating the air. Suddenly the feeling vanished and he was back in the room.

"Well, I managed to get a bit of a funny feeling for a second or two," he said "but it seems to have gone now. Sorry."

"You've been staring at the crystal for two and a half hours," said Bonetti, clearly annoyed. "We tried shouting at you, but it was like you were in some kind of a trance."

Bob's eyebrows did the 'well bugger me' kind of upwards arch thing. "Two and a half hours?" he yelped.

"Yes," said Cooper. "You were mumbling as if you were talking to someone. And once you laughed your head off for about thirty seconds."

"And then there was that thing you kept saying, over and over again," said MoMo.

"What thing?"

"'When you need him, he will come'."

"Who will come?" asked Bonetti.

"Buggered if I know," said Bob, who was trying to figure out how two and a half hours worth of anything could be squished into a couple of seconds of Bob time.

"Can't you remember anything about what happened while you were off wherever you were?" asked Bonetti.

Bob frowned and looked at the crystal, trying hard to concentrate. After what seemed like a second or two, he said, "Nope. Sorry!"

"There. You did it again!"

"Did what again?" yelled Bob, trying desperately hard not to look guilty, or worried, or needing to go to the toilet.

"You've been babbling again for another hour and twenty minutes," said Cooper.

"Someone's coming," said MoMo.

"*Stop!*" yelled Bonetti and Bob froze. So did everyone else in the room. It was as if time itself had stood still which, in a way, it had. But not for him.

"Okay, that's not what I meant."

"Be careful what you ask for," said a disembodied voice.

"Azriel?" asked Bonetti, recognising the voice.

76

"Sorry about this, I'm a bit inter-dimensional at the moment."

The air in front of Bonetti shimmered and the angel appeared. "There. That's better," he said.

The Cardinal looked worried. "You're very literal, aren't you," he said. "Kindly undo whatever it is you just did."

Azriel touched Cooper, MoMo and Bob lightly on the head and all three unfroze. Cooper and MoMo grinned widely when they saw their recent travelling companion. Bob's grin was narrower and less spontaneous.

"So, let's see what all the trouble is about," he murmured, walking the few paces over to Bob and peering down at the skinny angel, who reluctantly opened his hands to reveal *The Eye of God*, nestling protectively in his palms.

Cooper told Azriel about Bob's message. "Is that you? Are you *The One* who's going to come when we need you?" he asked.

"No," said MoMo.

"No," said the angel. "But it might be Junior."

"Junior?" asked Bonetti and Cooper, simultaneously turning and looking at Bob.

"What you looking at me for?" asked Bob, whose eyebrows were doing the up and down thing again. "I don't know any Junior. Never heard of him!"

"Oh, you know Junior alright," said Azriel. "Trouble is, your memory's been so fried you wouldn't know your own face if you saw it in a mirror."

"Excuse me. But who's Junior?" asked Bonetti.

Azriel was about to speak when there was a cough from the darkness at the far end of the room. The kind of cough that's discrete, polite, yet at the same time has that 'now every bugger shut up' kind of quality to it.

Azriel smiled. "Aaah, Junior, there you are."

"I was told that my services might be needed again," said a soft voice. Not a weak voice. Just one that simply didn't have to try hard to make itself heard. Almost as if just by existing, it beat the crap out of any other sound in the universe that even dreamed of existing at the same time.

There was a small sigh and a figure moved out of the dark. "Ok, whose bright idea was this, then," said the voice.

"I think maybe I had something to do with it. But only in the 'knowing what was going to happen next' sort of way," said MoMo.

"Well, well, well – if it isn't the blimp," said Junior. Long time no see.

Bob shrieked. *The Eye of God* was glowing red hot and pulsing. He flung it up in the air away from him as if it were molten lava. The figure, now completely visible to all, reached out a hand and caught it effortlessly. There was no glow, no heat and no pulsing. It was almost as if, merely by landing where it did, it decided that this was where it was meant to be.

In all but three things the catcher was completely unremarkable. One was his voice. The other two were his eyes. Well, to say that they were eyes was like saying the sun was just a blob of bright hot red stuff in the sky. Put together, these three things gave rise to possibly the most remarkable religion the world has ever seen. As for the rest of him: early thirties, medium height, average looks, a bit on the thin side with a spot of acne here and there – and ears like jug handles.

"Well held," said Azriel.

Junior walked towards the gathering, throwing *The Eye* up in the air and catching it with all the confidence of a professional baseball player or cricketer.

"Are you –?" breathed Bonetti, leaving the question hanging in mid-air.

"Am I what?" asked Junior. "Hungry? Absolutely. The bringer of glad tidings? Well, I'm not really in a comfort and joy frame of mind at the moment."

All eyes turned to *The Eye of God*, bouncing up and down.

"In that case it might be an idea if you give *The Eye* back to nice Bob here," said Azriel.

Junior threw the now normal looking crystal back to the angel, who fumbled the catch and just managed to grab hold of it before it hit the tiled floor. "Who are the two stiffs in the kitchen?" he said.

"Stiffs?" asked Bonetti, puzzled.

"Yep. Of the very rigid variety," said Junior.

"Of the very dead variety?" asked Cooper, alarmed.

"Hard to tell."

"Oops," said Azriel, who waved a finger and suddenly the sounds of the now unfrozen Brothers Carlos and Roberto could be heard coming from the kitchen, making tea.

"Ok," said Junior. "Let's fast forward to the bit where somebody asks me just how much I know about what's going on."

"Fine. How much?"

"Well," said Junior, stuffing his fists into the pockets of a very stylish pair of designer jeans. "For starters I know you're all in some deep shit. And I know that you got a Pope here who's a teensy weensy bit shy of being a total veggie burger because of the whole dead people thing and the physical deterioration stuff. And I know that yours truly is supposed to extricate everyone out of the soft and stinky. How am I doing so far?"

"Perfect," said Bonetti, who now had an apostolic glint in his eyes.

"Oh I wouldn't go that far. Nearly perfect will do for now."

Cooper's ears did a double take. How the Hell could they manage to stuff an ego this big into a body this ordinary and build a world-changing religion around him?

That's easy, said Azriel's voice in his head. *All we did was perform a little hocus pocus, brought in a top PR outfit, gave the kid that voice and those eyes. We call them his Holy Mojo. The rest, as they say, is history and, curiously enough, geography, too. Unfortunately we couldn't do much about the ego.*

"You know," said Junior, "I was having a real nice nap before I got the wakeup call."

"Is that blood on your hands? You cut yourself?" remarked Bonetti.

"Oh, shit," exclaimed Junior in surprise and promptly fainted.

Azriel caught him before he hit the floor, and dragged him into the vacant armchair. "He absolutely hates the sight of blood, especially on himself. One little drop and off he goes."

"Very understandable," said Cooper.

The angel was looking worried now. He was examining the blossoming red bloody marks on Junior's wrists closely and mumbling in a strange language. "Anybody got a bandage? Or even some plasters?"

"Hang on a minute. Aren't you lot supposed to be immune to physical injuries and emotional trauma?"

Bob bristled. "That's a bit strong. We higher beings have feelings, too, y'know. And blood and other bodily fluids."

"How would you know? You can't remember anything!" hissed Bonetti.

"Ahaah!" exclaimed Bob, almost triumphantly. "That's where you're wrong. I *can* remember! Well, I'm beginning to. Bits and pieces here and there. And some bits that were never there in the first place and got shoved in whether I wanted them or not." He glared at *The Eye of God* and began throwing it between his hands faster and faster. "It's like someone just shoved a garden hose up my nostrils, turned on the tap, rinsed out my brain and expanded my memory!"

"For instance, I remember that bastard angel Zaphir holding something bright and shiny up in front of my eyes, and the shiny thing making me feel kinda weird." he continued.

Now he was slamming *The Eye of God* from one hand to the other with a fierceness that made even Azriel wince. "And I remember him holding a massive pair of secateurs and asking me to turn around and saying, 'Don't worry, this won't hurt'."

Bonetti looked elated. "Now we're getting somewhere. What else do you remember?"

"All I know is that there are some things I know and some things I don't. Then there are all the other things."

"Other things?" asked Cooper.

Bob looked uncomfortable. "Bees," he said.

Cooper looked confused.

"Angels have a hive mind," explained Azriel, "which means we all know what each knows, or is thinking. Well, part of us does."

"And the other part of you?" asked the priest.

"That's personal. Everyone needs a little privacy. So some of our feelings and knowledge are locked away from the hive. A bit like 'on a need to know' basis. That way, every angel is linked and yet still completely unique."

"That's all very nice," said Junior, groggily, " but what you want me to do?" He had come out of his blood-induced swoon and was looking at Azriel wrapping his wrists in bandages.

Bob stopped throwing *The Eye of God* around. He straightened his back, a feat that added about six inches to his height, and walked over to Junior sitting in the chair.

"Newsflash from *The Eye*. Your mission," he said, "should you choose to accept it –"

"And we all sincerely hope you do," added Bonetti.

Bob glared at the Cardinal, then turned back to Junior and continued. "Your mission is to discover who *The One* is, help shove technology back down the pecking order and pull good old fashioned religion back up where it rightly belongs!"

"*Ask him about the catch*," said Azriel in Cooper's head.

Cooper inwardly replied. "*You ask him!*"

"*He knows I already know about it now. You need to ask him so he knows that you know about it. It's all to do with the passage of knowledge and the chain of evidence.*"

"*Do you have any idea how stupid that sounds?*"

"*Just ASK!*"

Cooper sighed. "What's the catch?" he asked Bob.

"He's only got 147 days to do it!"

"*Whaaaaat?*" yelled Bonetti.

Junior's countenance changed to one of grim determination. "Right. Odds stacked against me. Time running out. I love a bit of a challenge. When do we get started?"

"Drinks anyone?" announced Brother Roberto, returning from the kitchen carrying a large tray full of steaming mugs of brown liquid. Following on behind him, Brother Carlos was struggling under the weight of a massive plate of sandwiches.

"I hope you're all hungry," he said. He saw Azriel, and began to slow down, surprise all over his face. Then he saw Junior, looked in his eyes, felt the merest touch of the Holy Mojo, and dropped the plate.

"Get the food," yelled Azriel and Cooper dived for the plate, catching it, with all its contents intact, about six inches from the floor.

"Get the monk," yelled Bonetti, thinking the old man was about to do a repeat performance with the rubber legs and the unconsciousness thing that he did before.

"Get off me!" yelled Brother Carlos as both Bonetti and Cooper grabbed him and manhandled him into the vacant armchair.

Junior looked at Brother Roberto and switched on the Holy Mojo. The monk nodded, pulled a protesting and confused Brother Carlos back out of the armchair and dragged him into the kitchen, where the two stood in silence in front of an empty dishwasher.

"Why 147 days?" asked Cooper. "I mean why not 500 or 1000? What happens in 147 days?"

"Two things. First, if the balance of power carries on shifting the way it is, in 147 days the number of people who believe in technology will be more than the number who believe in God and The Devil – and we won't be able to reverse the process. And when that happens *The Eye of God* will disappear taking with it everyone in Heaven, Hell and Earth. Second, the asteroid known as Homer is due to arrive in 147 days, so even if we do manage to turn the tide back in religion's favour, we might still be up the creek without a paddle. Unless we manage to somehow stop the rock!"

The silence was so overpowering, you could have heard a pin going through the thought process of preparing to drop itself from a great height.

Junior broke the spell. "And you expect me to play the hero, kill the dragon, save the damsel and spread the holy word to everyone on earth. Oh, and if I've got time, could I think of a way of taking care of that nice little space rock. That about cover it?"

"Don't worry Wunderkid, you don't have to do everything," said Azriel. "All you need to do is light the blue touch paper and then retire back upstairs for the duration. Just like you did the last time."

"A hundred and forty seven days!" whispered Bonetti, shaking his head slowly, early onset panic beginning to invade his face.

Junior began rubbing his wrists and looking worried. "Last time? Last time? Nobody said anything about this time being even remotely like last time! Services needed, they said. Help out, they said. Moral support, they said. Maybe use the voice and eyes a bit here and there, they said."

Azriel, who had thought about taking up temporary residence in the vacant armchair, decided against it and instead walked over to where Junior was standing, rubbing his wrists even harder now. "If I remember correctly, we did actually send in a fast-response unit to extract you before any real damage was done."

"Real damage?" Junior hissed. "They killed me!" There was a distinct touch of panic creeping into his voice.

"Yes, maybe. But you also got fabulous press and a whole lot of fans. Eventually."

The angel reached out and held Junior's wrists, which had started to seep blood again, in an effort to keep the dark stains out of view. Junior stared into his eyes, which had the immediate effect of calming him down.

"So he's not the only one with mojo eyes," said Cooper, impressed.

"We all have them to some degree. Just not to his degree. This teeny bit of memory loss should help with the panic. But be warned – it won't last long."

"Listen," said Bonetti, "I don't mean to be the harbinger of doom and gloom, but Junior here has 147 days to save our world. Does anyone have the slightest idea how he's going to do it?"

"Sorry," said Bob, shrugging. "Don't shoot me, I'm only the messenger. I only know what *The Eye* told me. I don't even know how I know I know it. What's more, I don't want to know. Call it plausible deniability or whatever. As for all that saving stuff – a miracle might just do it. So – anyone here any good at miracles? Very big miracles?"

They all turned and looked at Junior.

Bob smiled. "Looks like it's down to you, Wunderkid."

Junior, who still hadn't noticed the bloody wraps on his wrists, had calmed down and was murmuring "Wunderkid" slowly, savouring every letter. He paused and a vacant look passed over his face. "What was I saying? Hmm – it's gone. Anyway, before we get started, we need to sort out some serious ground rules. Agreed?"

"Like what?" asked Azriel.

"Number one –" he said and pulled his wrists from Azriel's grip, held his left hand up to count off on his fingers. Then he saw the blood and performed the collapsible hero dance again. This time, nobody caught him before he met the floor in a tangled heap.

"Great!" said Bonetti. "If he pulls this off it'll be the biggest miracle in the history of the world!"

Azriel, who was leaning over the unconscious Junior, suddenly stopped and cocked his head to one side, listening intently. "Sorry," he said, glancing upwards. "Small matter to attend to. Back as soon as I can. Have fun. I'll send reinforcements." And with that, he seemed to go from kneeling on the ground to leaping into the air, before disappearing completely.

"Now that's what I call a great exit!" said Bob.

"Naaah," said Cooper. "A great exit is Humphrey Bogart saying 'Louis, I think this is the beginning of a beautiful friendship' to Claude Rains in Casablanca.

About half a second later he realised that the Heavenly member of the team was AWOL, Junior was out for the count, and he had no idea what to do next.

"*Need some help?*" asked a familiar voice in his head.

"Gabriel! You're the reinforcements?" Cooper blurted aloud.

"Give that guy a coconut!" said a small, gruff voice, followed rapidly by the appearance of an equally small tubby body, dressed in a slightly wrinkled robe.

"Small world," said the priest, looking down at the little angel and smiling. He was the only living being that could even mention the angel's diminutive size without incurring his wrath, either physically or verbally.

"Clear the way folks – very impressive VIP angel coming through," said the new arrival, as he barged his way towards the unconscious Junior.

The surprise on Bonetti's face was compounded by the realisation that angels had a sense of humour. "You're –" he began to say.

"If you say what I think you're gonna say –"

"You're –"

Gabriel stopped by the side of Junior, who by now was beginning to stir. He turned, looked up at Bonetti towering above him, frowned and said, "I see. You want to know how I got to be so tall, right?"

"Don't worry. He'll be okay in a minute," said MoMo.

The little angel looked up at the large Oracle. The difference in sizes between the two was almost comical. At full stretch, Gabriel's whole body was as long as one of MoMo's whole legs. This, however, didn't stop the angel from grinning widely and hugging the Oracle's left knee. "Hiya big boy. How's the bump?"

MoMo looked down and tried hard to smile. Instead, all he could manage was a sigh.

"I knew you were going to ask that."

Bob was standing scratching his head and looking at Gabriel. "Do I know you?" he asked. "I've got the strangest feeling we've met before."

At their feet, Junior groaned, "Awww – not again!"

Gabriel looked at Cooper. "The blood thing?"

"Yes. Saw some and keeled over. Does it always affect him like this?"

"Mostly. Especially if the red stuff is his. He had a bad experience. Developed a natural aversion to being stabbed by sharp objects."

Bonetti was rooted to the spot. As his mouth repeated the one word he uttered when the little angel first appeared, his mind went back in time and stayed there for approximately two seconds. Despite his age, however, the Cardinal was the proud possessor of a fast-moving mind. And mere seconds had a habit of seeming like mere decades.

He was a boy again.

Sixteen

Even before he reached his teens, Cardinal Bonetti, or, as he was known then, Alfredo Bonetti, had one dream. To become a priest in the service of Our Lord and the Holy Mother Church. He became an altar boy at the age of eight, much to the delight and pride of his parents, Maria and Franco.

Over the next few years, before he was accepted into the seminary, he read every page of his precious, leather-bound Bible over and over, almost fanatically, until there was no part he was not intimately familiar with. Father Giuseppe Falco, the ageing priest who saw something special in the boy and wrote his letter of recommendation to the seminary Vocation Office, gave Alfredo a small book showing the names and hierarchy of the angels.

He learned their names and ranks all the way from the Seraphim, Cherubim and Thrones, through the Dominions, Powers and Rulers, to the Archangels and Angels. They became his heroes. His inspiration. And chief amongst those heroes was Gabriel.

Now, as an ageing Cardinal, seeing his boyhood angelic hero in the flesh, albeit in such a small package, was all too much for the emotional constitution and ability to speak of the ageing Cardinal.

"You're –" he repeated, rubbing his eyes and still coming to terms with the reality of the encounter.

"Don't say it," said Gabriel with a warning tone in his voice.

"You're–"

"I really would take his advice," said Junior, who was back on his feet and wondering vaguely what the mild sinking feeling was in the pit of his stomach. "He tends to get a little annoyed when people mention his height. Look – I'm normally very anti-violence, but needs must. Maybe this will help." He raised his right hand and slapped Bonetti hard across his left cheek.

The act immediately brought the Cardinal out of his trance. He blinked, rubbed his cheek hard and finished his sentence. "You're older-looking than I imagined."

"Hang on – you think I look old?"

"Let's say not completely young."

"Oh, right. And you don't have any problem with my immense height?"

"Absolutely not. Size is all relative anyway," said Bonetti, looking down at the little angel.

"Good. In that case, let's get this show on the road."

"You mean let's get *my* show on the road," said a voice from the background.

"Junior," exclaimed Gabriel. "I wondered when they'd pull you into this."

MoMo's voice intruded into Cooper's mind. *"You know what Gabriel's nickname for Junior was?"*

"I thought Junior *was* his nickname," the priest replied mentally.

"Oh no. That's his real name. Well, one of them. But Gabriel used to call him Brains!"

"Because he was clever?"

"Because he wasn't very bright. At least that's how he was in the beginning, before they fiddled around with him. Now he's better. Sort of."

"Sort of?"

"He's work in progress. Still thinks he's God's gift to mankind. Or was it the other way around? Well, he probably is. But–"

"It's okay. I get the picture."

Cooper switched to speaking aloud. "So, what's with Azriel?" he asked Gabriel.

"Family business," said the little angel, shaking his head. "He's having a few words with his cousin Zaphir."

"Azriel likes words like bruise, cut, pain and suffering. He might be a while," said Junior.

Gabriel nodded his head. He knew what the big angel was capable of and pitied anyone he was going to have any words with.

"So, going back to me being a Wunderkid, and given the fact that that if we don't act soon, everything we know and love might end shortly –"

The angel looked directly at Junior. Well, more like directly and up. "You know, first time around, we never thought you'd be such a smash hit."

He shrugged. "We thought a hundred, two hundred years at a stretch. Maybe three tops. In fact we already had plans for your replacement. A very smart guy called George. Good looking too. But then something strange happened.

"Before we knew it, you had a bunch of followers, every one of them with that religious zeal in their eyes. Then there were more. And more. And soon they were spreading the word and writing stories about you.

"By then there was no way we could stop the rollercoaster ride. So we thought, 'okay, make the best of it. Go with the flow.' Now I know what you're thinking. Did we turn you into the hero of the greatest story ever told on purpose? Or was it all just one big happy accident? Well, to tell you the truth, in all this excitement, I've kinda lost track. But me being Gabriel, the most powerful angel in my height and weight division in the history of Heaven, and could kick your ass from here to Armageddon, you've got to ask yourself one thing. Are you going to call me 'shortly' ever again? Well, are you?"

Under normal circumstances vertically challenged intimidation didn't work on Junior. However, the little angel's veiled threat nudged open a door that had only recently been closed and a niggling feeling in the pit of his stomach began to grow.

"Oh! I can see something," said MoMo, frantically rubbing his middle-eye bump and diverting attention away from the niggling feeling.

"How can you see anything? You've got your eyes closed," said Bonetti.

The Oracle stopped rubbing and the middle eye popped open and looked around the room.

"Wow – déjà vu all over again!" said Bob, staggering back from the group and falling backwards into the vacant armchair. "Keep that bugger away from me. I don't want to go all woozy like before. Me and funny-looking eyes don't get on very well."

MoMo still had his two normal eyes closed, but his middle eye stopped looking around and stared at Junior. "Save the babies," he said.

"What babies? Where?" asked Cooper, slightly alarmed.

MoMo's towering frame slumped to the floor. Siting down he was now the height of the priest, who grabbed hold of the Oracle's shoulders and shook them as hard as he could. They hardly moved. Instead, his middle eye closed, the ones on either side of his nose opened and he mumbled, "I saw darkness and babies."

Azriel's disembodied voice cut through the drama. "Darkness and babies. Right. Good start. Anything else? Anything less vague? A clue would be good. An explanation would be better."

MoMo frowned, leaving the bump in his forehead looking like a perfectly oval-shaped island in the middle of an ocean of wrinkled flesh. "Nope. Don't have any of those. I got a headache, if that's any use."

"Azriel! That didn't take long!" exclaimed Cooper aloud, looking around and expecting the angel to appear amongst them. He didn't. He also looked for Gabriel and instead found the space that the little angel had occupied mere seconds ago.

"What didn't take long?" asked Bonetti, wondering if he should look around the room, too. "And where's –?"

"The little guy?" Azriel, who now appeared standing next to Junior, finished the Cardinal's question. "Special assignment. I could tell you, but then I'd have to kill you." There was a look in his eyes and Cooper wasn't sure if it was humour.

"But he's only been here five minutes."

The angel shrugged. "You say five minutes – we say a microsecond. Or maybe a year or two. Time's very flexible."

"It's not the length of time you're here that's important. It's what you do with the time you have," said Junior. "Gabriel can do more things in less time than is physically possible. In fact he has been known to do an amazing amount of things with absolutely no time at all. But enough about him. Let's talk about me again."

"MoMo's middle eye did something," Cooper said, possibly just delaying the inevitable.

Azriel closed the distance between him and the priest without seeming to move at all, until their eyes were inches apart. "Was it anything to do with opening and looking around then shutting?"

The priest nodded once. "All of that. Then he said something."

The angel's right eyebrow rose slightly. "Was it anything to do with darkness and saving babies?"

"It was everything to do with that. What does it mean?"

"Who knows, but if it has anything to do with *The One* and Homer, then it has everything to do with us. We need to figure it out. No, let me rephrase that. You need to figure it out."

Bob decided to wag a warning finger in everyone's direction. "Nothing good ever comes of trying to figure out the meaning of something that nobody knows the meaning of," he said.

Everyone paused and looked at Bob. "You know, the more I know you the less I believe you could ever be *The One*," said Bonetti.

"Hey – did I ever claim to be *The One*?" Bob replied angrily.

Cooper shrugged. "Well, no."

"And at any time did I ever say anything about saving anyone?"

"Not in so many words."

"Enough about *The One*. Let's talk about me again," insisted Junior.

The words massive and ego crashed into Cooper's head and he sighed. "Do we really have to do this?"

Azriel's gaze was steely. "We have no alternative. We ran multiple scenarios for finding *The One* and the same answer came out every time."

"You've had time to run multiple scenarios?"

"No. Gabriel's had time. He's the head of our multiple scenarios division.

"You have a division for multiple scenarios?"

"We have divisions for everything."

"Never mind that," interrupted Bonetti impatiently. "What was the answer?"

"If you want to find *The One* – ask Bob."

Everyone looked at Bob, who wasn't where he was 0.000001 seconds previously. Instead he was halfway across the room heading for a large, comforting shadow in a corner.

The hastily retreating angel had almost reached the shadow when the sound of Azriel's voice stopped him in his tracks. "Going somewhere?" he asked. It wasn't a question.

"This is a very pressurised situation," said Bob. "I don't respond well under stress. I think I need to lie down, preferably in a dark room."

The angel walked to the shadow and stood between it and Bob. "Who's *The One*?" he whispered in his ear.

Azriel's voice coming from a few feet away could be intimidating enough. But when it came softly from immediately behind either of your ears and you could feel his breath setting off every alarm bell between your scalp and the soles of your feet? That was a whole different bag of warnings.

Bob let out a long, resigned sigh. "Okay. The question isn't really just 'who?' It's also 'where?'" he said. "And before you ask, I really don't know the answer to either."

"I do – possibly," said Cooper.

"You do?" Bob's eyebrows pointed to Heaven. There was relief in his voice and he walked away from the edge of the dark corner towards the others.

A presence within the darkness cursed out of earshot. "Dammit – nearly had you!"

A second presence, not nearly as important or terrifying as the first, offered a few soothing bon mots in the hope of making the first presence feel better. "Shit boss, is that the best you can do?" The darkness engulfed the sound of a smack and a muffled cry of pain.

Back in the room, Bonetti's feet were aching. "If you're going to go into some long-winded explanation, I'm going to sit down," he said, making himself comfortable in the armchair recently vacated by Azriel. He gestured to the priest with his right hand. "Go on then."

Cooper held court.

"Well first the 'who'. What message did *The Eye* give to you?" He looked at the Cardinal.

"That's between me and the Holy Father," said Bonetti, glaring. "It was for his ears only." Suddenly his seat didn't feel so comfortable.

"Not any more. A certain compact angel just happened to be incognito in the room at the time and he and I have what you might call a close and personal friendship. He heard the message, told it to me, now it's for all our ears."

Bonetti paused. Cooper was right. Time was running out. There was no point keeping the confidence any longer. He took a deep breath and spoke. "*The One* will save you."

"Right," said Cooper. *The One* will save you. Think about it. *The One* is a saviour. Who do we know who's a saviour?"

Everyone looked at Junior. Junior looked at the ceiling. Suddenly the door in his mind that Azriel managed to temporarily close was flung open – and the niggling feeling in the pit of his stomach turned into a volcanic eruption of memories.

The panic returned.

"Wow – wait a minute – me? *The One*?

Azriel saw the danger signs and grabbed Junior's wrists again. "Why not? It's not as if you haven't done it before."

It was too late.

Junior was approaching full-blown 'let's get the shit out of here' mode. "Sure, and if I remember correctly it involved a fair amount of physical and emotional pain and suffering. Being healthy and being *The One* don't go well together. I don't mind getting involved in an advisory capacity. Say, as a technical consultant or something. But it's someone else's turn to be *The One*. Maybe I can be *The One's* sidekick, like *The Two*?"

Cooper had a thought. A very fast one. Not one that had anything to do with lightbulbs or eureka moments. More like one that was sneaky, wore dark clothes and a ski mask and came in the back door without making a sound after picking the lock. He turned to the others and shrugged his shoulders. "Okay, my mistake. Maybe he's not *The One*. Anyone called *The One* would have gonads the size of melons. Anyone called *The One* wouldn't be afraid of a little physical discomfort. Anyone called *The One* would have camped out overnight in the freezing cold to be first in line to do grievous physical and emotional violence to anyone who even dreamed of doing harm to the beautiful planet where he grew up!" He gasped for breath.

"Hey – I had a near death experience," yelled Junior, who was unsuccessfully trying to forget certain very important details of his first time on Earth as *The One*. "In fact it was so near, it got bumped up to a complete death experience. In my book that's about as grievous as you can get."

"Yes, but it wasn't exactly permanent, was it? Anyway, that was then, this is now."

There was a pause. "Meaning?"

"Well then you were a wandering nobody with a handful of hippie followers. Now you're a heroic somebody with a fanbase in the billions."

"Yes. And the best heroes are the ones who die a memorable death and get stories and songs written about them."

"Meaning?"

"Meaning I go back to being *The One* again and, love me or not, somewhere along the line, my loyal followers will find another excuse to bump me off. It's in their nature and I have natural hatred of death. Especially if it's mine."

There was another pause. "So – I guess you're not interested in being the kind of hero that every one of those people will fall in love with all over again. The kind of hero who *doesn't* suffer any pain or torture and *doesn't* get killed. The one who saves the world. Again. And rides off into the sunset – a hero with no scratches." He let those tasty morsels hang in the air for a second before shrugging in disappointment. "No? Okay. We'll look else –"

"Whoa there Trigger!" blurted Junior, slowly returning from the shadow. "Hold your horses. Who said anything about not being interested?" There was a smile on his face but his wrists were behind his back, out of sight and out of reach. "You said saving the world with no death involved?"

"Absolutely."

"No pain or bruising or spilling of any of the red stuff?"

"Not a drop. Now will you stop being such a wuss and live up to your reputation? You know, that one where everyone thinks you're a credit to your father and a real stand-up guy."

There seemed to be a shimmer in the air all around Junior and a slight increase in his stature. Also a visible relaxing of the shoulders and a small puffing out of the chest. In the space of a heartbeat his whole demeanour altered and he became once again the wuss-free Junior who Cooper had known for most of his life. The Junior who was now staring directly into the priest's eyes.

"*Nicely done, Sherlock,*" said Azriel in Cooper's head. "*I think we have lift-off. By the way, don't look at his eyes.*"

The priest quickly looked away. "So, what's next?"

"*That's MoMo's speciality. He's the one who can switch on his Oracle powers and take a peek into the future, before it becomes the present.*"

"About that," said MoMo, still sat down. "I think we might have a teeny problem with the whole peeking into the future thing."

"How come you didn't see that coming?"

"I did."

"You mean you foresaw that you wouldn't be able to foresee any more?"

MoMo struggled to move his large bulk but eventually managed to stand up with Cooper's help. "You're stronger than you look," he said, surprised at the priest's strength.

Azriel, standing nearby, didn't even attempt to help. "Where our Shapeshifter here is concerned, looks can be deceiving."

Cooper saw the worry on MoMo's face. "Balance of power getting worse?"

MoMo nodded, tentatively touching his forehead bump and shook his head slowly. There didn't seem to be anything happening under the skin.

"What about the 'where?'" asked Bonetti.

"What where?"

"You said finding *The One* wasn't just about who, it was also about where. So where is he, or she, or it?"

Cooper smiled. "Answering the first question also answers the second. If the 'who' is Junior, then the 'where' is here."

"I don't like it," mumbled Azriel. "It's too simple. I don't trust things that slot nicely into place without any effort. It doesn't smell right."

"You'd rather it smelled better?"

Azriel touched Cooper's nose gently with the tip of his right index finger. "Lesson number one," he said. Then he stuck out his tongue and licked the air. "No matter how good you think your sense of smell is with that," and he tapped Cooper's nose, "ours is roughly a billion times better with this," and he tapped his tongue.

Then he touched the priest's stomach with his finger. "And no matter how good you think your ability to know when something feels wrong with this is," and he tapped his own stomach, "our guts tell us unimaginably more than yours ever could."

"Okay," Cooper conceded. "So what are we missing?"

"You tell me."

The priest took a deep breath and closed his eyes. The room and everyone in it faded away from conscious thought and all that remained was a single point of light in the middle of a sea of darkness. The light expanded until it was all around Cooper and he felt a presence. And a voice.

"You're the Changin' Man," said the voice. "You need t'get yer arse in gear mate. There's not much time left, so listen up."

Cooper opened his eyes and he was back in the room.

Bonetti was now the one sitting in the armchair. MoMo was sleeping sitting up against the wall behind him. Junior was sitting cross-legged in the middle of the room. Eyes closed.

"How long?" he asked, looking at Azriel, who was standing immediately in front of him.

"Your time? About an hour and a half. Our time? You don't have a number small enough. So – figured out what we're missing yet?"

The priest looked around the room. "It's not just a what. It's a who and a what."

Bob was nowhere in sight. Neither was *The Eye of God*.

"Okay, where is he?"

"He who?" asked Bonetti.

"He Bob!"

Junior opened his eyes and let out a long, slow breath. "Last time I saw him he was standing in the corner next to the kitchen door looking at *The Eye* and giggling."

"I have a bad feeling about this," said MoMo, awake but still on the floor.

Cooper shrugged and looked at Azriel. "Can't you use that angelic hive mind thing, or a locator spell or something and find him?"

The angel frowned. "Something's blocking the signal," he said and disappeared, reappearing seconds later looking less than happy.

"Well?" asked Bonetti.

"Not really. Bob's off the grid. He's no longer linked to the hive, so we don't have a clue where he is."

"Woah!" exclaimed Brother Roberto in alarm, rushing in from the kitchen. "Holy Mother of God. Something invisible just brushed past me. I felt it touch my arm!" His pasty face had turned pure white and he was blessing himself with the sign of the cross, over and over again.

"And I heard Bob's voice," added Brother Carlos, following on behind him.

"What did he say?" asked Cooper.

"He said, 'Who the Hell are you?' and then there was a bit of a strangled sound," said the monk.

95

"That feeling I had just went from bad to very bad," said MoMo, who had now opened his eyes.

"Bob – show yourself!" demanded Bonetti. The room remained Bobless.

Cooper looked to the ceiling. "How many more creeks do we have to be up before *somebody* decides to give us a paddle?"

Seventeen

"Got you this time!" said a voice from the darkness. "That's a nice little bauble you have there. I think I'd like a bauble like that. In fact, I think I'd like *that* one!" The voice was very familiar, and not in a pleasant way.

Bob's grip on *The Eye of God* tightened. "Oh, you again! Where am I this time?" he asked the darkness. There was a soft, low laugh. The kind of laugh that has nothing whatsoever to do with fun and happiness and everything to do with running away very fast and hoping you don't get caught.

"So that's the famous *Eye of God*, eh?" said the voice, now a little nearer, and behind him.

The angel couldn't grip the crystal any tighter with his right hand, so he added his left one to the grip, for extra security.

There was a long, drawn-out sigh. "It's a lot smaller than I imagined," said the voice, now to the left of Bob and so close he could very nearly make out a shape. Then it receded into the darkness, leaving the distinct smell of garlic. "You think maybe I could – hold it for a minute or two?"

Bob got the distinct impression that if he handed over the crystal it would be the last time he ever saw it. He also got the impression that it would be the last time anyone ever saw him. So he decided to decline, as forcefully as he could, under the circumstances.

"The phrase 'bugger off' comes to mind," he said. "You ain't gonna get it. Not unless you prise it from my cold, dead hands. So up yours!"

There was that laugh again. "You always were a bit on the feisty side Bob. But don't worry. You're safe, for the moment anyway. And so is your little bauble. I just want you to give a certain tall, dark friend of yours a message, that's all. You think you can do that?"

Bob felt a reassuring surge of courage. "I got so many tall, dark friends. Which particular one do you mean?"

Suddenly the image of the angel Azriel appeared in the darkness. "How about this one, eh?"

Bob's grip on *The Eye of God* relaxed a little and he noticed, rather embarrassingly, that his buttocks unclenched slightly. "I don't suppose it would do any good if I said I've never seen him before in my life, would it?"

A slight chuckle came out of the darkness.

"Nice try, but no."

"And that's all you want?"

"That's all. For now," said the voice.

"And there's no pain involved?"

"No pain."

Bob relaxed. "Okay. What's the message?"

"Tell him, 'Watch your back'."

"That's it? Watch your back?"

"Believe me, that will be enough."

Bob was about to ask him who the message was from when he began to feel a little queasy, the darkness faded away, and he found himself back in the room with the others. "Yaaaaaarrrough!" his vocal chords protested, as he threw up on the floor.

"Oh no – not *again!*" protested Bonetti, looking down at the contents of Bob's stomach, splattered not only on the stone slabs of the room, but also on the soft uppers of his expensive Italian leather shoes. "Are you going for some kind of puking record or something?" he pleaded.

As he apologised profusely, Bob looked around and saw a mixture of smiles, mild annoyance, and surprise on the faces of those around him. Brother Roberto was holding onto Brother Carlos, who had decided that now might be a good time to faint again.

Junior, who had a beaming grin on his face, was slow handclapping. "Now *that's* what I call an entrance," he said.

Cooper walked over to Bob and gave him a handkerchief to wipe his mouth. The angel nodded appreciatively, stood up straight and took a deep breath. "I got a message and I think it's for you," he said, looking at Azriel.

He spent the next minute telling everyone what had happened while he was in the darkness. Finally he got to the message and he looked directly into Azriel's dark eyes. "The voice said to give you this message and he said you'd understand."

"I'm all ears," said the dark angel.

"He said, 'Watch your back'."

The effect on the angel was instant. His eyes narrowed and a sharp hiss of breath escaped his lips. His face contorted into a sneer that was full of anger. He growled, said something in a language that Cooper had never heard before – and vanished.

Cooper was the first to react. "Wow – what was all *that* about?" His brain was in overdrive, frantically trying to image what could possibly throw the normally ice-cool angel into a murderous-looking rage.

MoMo was shaking his large head from side to side. His eyes were widening and the lump on his forehead was beginning to glow. "I just got another feeling," he said, almost on the verge of panic. "Houston, we got a problem!"

"It's the voice, isn't it," said Cooper. "You know who it is."

The Oracle seemed to come to a decision. He looked at everyone in the room and his gaze finally settled on the priest. "It's Spike," he said.

"Spike?" asked Bonetti, wondering what kind of creature could set alarm bells ringing for both angels and demons.

"You might know him by his real name. Apollyon."

"As in Apollyon The Destroyer?" The name and title clawed their way up into his consciousness from the angelic studies of his boyhood.

"He's not very nice."

It was Cooper's turn to interrupt. "As in the *angel* Apollyon?"

"As in the twisted sociopath Apollyon. And he's really, *really* not very nice!" emphasised a familiar disembodied voice.

Gabriel appeared standing next to Cooper. He wasn't smiling. "Spike is the nastiest piece of work that ever grew wings. He's evil incarnate with feathers. Black ones. After the Great War of the Angels, he and his band of followers were thrown in The Abyss – and yes, before you ask, there is such a place. It's not the Hilton Hotel and there's no way out. We think."

"You think?"

"Azriel is checking. Let's say they have a special relationship. Or had. And the message was for him so – "

"Okay, what happens if this Spike has managed to get free?"

The look on Gabriel's face told him everything he needed to know.

Eighteen

The darkness contained two voices.

"So – you got my message, then?" asked Spike.

"Loud and clear. What do you want, Spike?" answered Azriel.

"Can't a guy have a pleasant chat with one of his old brothers in arms?"

"Not if the guy's you."

"You know – you can be very hurtful at times. There was a time when we were best buddies. Always at each other's side. Always had each other's back."

At the mention of the word 'back' Azriel growled, almost animal-like. The imprisoned angel's voice became almost confessional in tone. "Okay, let's say I like the idea of watching you all squirm."

"Let's say the feeling's mutual. Now again, what do you want?"

There was a sigh. "How about a move to a minimum security facility? I've been a very good boy, for a very long time."

"You're up to something and it's got nothing to do with being a model prisoner," said Azriel. "The only reason I'm here is to make sure that you're still here and you stay here."

"My – aren't we the good little jailer," sneered Spike. "Tell me – how *is* your back these days, by the way?"

The dark angel felt a twinge travel along the giant scar shaped like an 'S' along his spine. A present from Spike before he was defeated and sentenced to an eternity in The Abyss. The memory was like an open wound. A reminder that, had it not been for the timely intervention of Gabriel, the scar would have cut much deeper.

"Bye Spike," said Azriel, with a hint of grim satisfaction in his voice. He was the visitor, not the detainee.

"Bye brother," said Spike, reminding him exactly how close the two had been before greed and ambition had forced them apart. "Oh, and take good care of that bauble, by the way."

Aaaah, so now we come to it, thought Azriel. *The Eye of God.* "How did you manage it?" he asked.

"What, the spiriting away of poor old Bob, complete with bauble, all the way to here and back?" asked Spike, almost lightheartedly.

"That, yes. But mostly how did you manage to join the hive mind again. In here you're supposed to be completely cut off from all contact."

"Oh I didn't join it. I suppose you could say I developed the ability to listen in, without being listened to. You have no idea how liberating that is. And how much fun."

"And that's when you learned about *The Eye of God*," said Azriel, with a growing sense of alarm.

"Let's say I heard a rumour or two. And as for Bob and his disappearing act, well, I still had a few powers left when I was put in this beautiful five star accommodation. Over the aeons I've merely put them to good use. They're parlour tricks mostly, but recently I find I can muster up some real juice. I just wanted to see if the bauble was real, that's all."

Azriel realised the danger and instantly moved all thoughts of the balance of power between Heaven, Hell, and Earth, plus the threat of Homer, into the 'private' section of his mind, out of the area linked to the hive. But it was too late. The echo of the clear and present dangers remained for Spike to pounce on.

"Aaah," said The Destroyer, "so it *is* true? There I was wondering why I was beginning to feel a little more powerful every day. I thought maybe, somehow, The Abyss was losing its grip. Maybe the old guy wasn't the God he used to be."

"Careful–" warned Azriel, but Spike was oblivious to the tone in the dark angel's voice.

"I kept hearing about this mysterious crystal. Just little bits, now and then, like trying to see something clearly through a fog. I knew it had power, but every time I tried to find out more about it, the fog would just get thicker."

"You're way off track," said Azriel, but the look on his face told Spike that he was too damned close for comfort.

Spike's voice rose almost in wonder. "So all this time I thought I was being clever and spying into the hive mind, that was just the balance of power getting weaker and weaker – just like the power of The Abyss."

"The Abyss is still strong enough to hold you."

"For now maybe. But for how long?"

"You'll never get out," snarled Azriel. "Now that we know about your little parlour tricks, we can nip them in the bud. In fact I had a quiet word in the ear of the boss on the way here. You remember him?"

"I don't forget."

"Neither does he."

"And what happens if all your efforts to restore the balance and stop the asteroid fail?" asked Spike, softly.

Azriel paused for a second. "If we fail, which we won't, then none of this will matter anyway. Neither you nor I will be around to see the consequences. Either way you lose."

"Oh I wouldn't be too sure about that, brother."

Azriel felt a large wave of sadness wash over him. "Bye Spike!"

As the darkness receded and he left The Abyss, he heard the faint sound of laughter. The same laughter that he'd heard as Spike was carving the 'S' into his back so long ago. It was still echoing in his ears as he appeared back in the room where the others were waiting.

"Just how dangerous is this Spike?" Bonetti was asking Gabriel.

Before the little angel could answer, Azriel popped into full view of everyone. "Don't worry. He's no threat. As long as we put right the balance of power and stop Homer, he'll rot in there for all eternity."

"He was very interested in *The Eye*," said Bob. "He wanted to see what it looked like, up close."

"Well why didn't he just take it?" asked Bonetti. "Why would he kidnap Bob and show interest in *The Eye of God*, if all he wanted to do was pass on a message to Azriel."

Cooper started pacing. Gabriel, instead of disappearing, paced alongside him. The priest's hands were animated as he spoke. "How did Spike even know about *The Eye* in the first place?"

"We told him," said Azriel. "Not intentionally, of course. *The Eye's* case is its guardian as much as the monks are. While it's in there, it's safe from any unholy prying eyes, plus any attempt to steal it or interfere with it in any way – human, angelic or demonic!"

"So," said the Cardinal, "as soon as Bob took it out of the case, Spike could sense it and that's why he grabbed him?"

Cooper nodded. "I think he sensed it before that, but he had to be sure. So he used what powers he had to kidnap Bob to see it in the flesh, so to speak. He gave him a message to pass on because he knew that Azriel would immediately go to The Abyss to check up on him. He wanted to know what Azriel knew."

"And now he does," growled Azriel. "I was stupid. My guard wasn't up and now he knows the truth about the balance of power and about the threat from Homer," said the angel. "I tried to hide it but I was too slow."

"The question still is – why didn't he just grab it when he had Bob?"

Azriel smiled grimly and walked over to Bob. He grabbed Bob's closed hands and tried to prise *The Eye* from his grasp. It refused to move. No matter how hard he pulled, the gem seemed stuck to Bob's hands. "The thing you need to understand about *The Eye* is that it has a very determined personality. It's extremely strong-willed. In a sense, it has 'bonded' to Bob a bit like a baby bonds to its mother. To snatch it away would probably take more power than Spike has at the moment."

"And then there's good old revenge."

"I don't get it," said Bonetti.

"I do," said Azriel, realisation dawning on his face. "He finds out what *The Eye* can do and knows that he might never have enough power to grab it before we put things right, so he does the next best thing."

"He shows his hand," added Cooper. "He lets us know that he wants it and we'll be so busy trying to figure out how to stop him that we'll get distracted and we won't be able to stop Homer."

"End of planet...end of people...end of everything! The Boss goes back to the drawing board and Spike, even though he's not around to enjoy it, gets to throw the biggest damned spanner in the works in the history of creation!" growled Gabriel.

"If I was in full Oracle mode I would *definitely* have seen that coming!" said MoMo, trying to appear helpful and proactive. "Maybe if I give my bump another rub."

Bonetti patted as near MoMo's shoulder as he could reach. "You're doing fine, my large friend."

"I'd do better if I had something to eat," said MoMo, as the rumble of a large, hungry digestive system decided to make its presence known.

"I can have some food sent to my apartment. At least there we can sit down and talk. We still need to discover what MoMo meant by saving the babies and darkness."

"Sounds like a plan," said Cooper.

"You want me to bring this with me?" answered Bob, hopefully, holding up *The Eye.* "I'll take very good care of it, promise!"

Bonetti's eyebrows shot up. "Absolutely not. Put it back in the case where it belongs."

Reluctantly, Bob walked over to the glass case and placed the crystal gently back on the spot it had occupied for almost 600 years. Bonetti then locked the case door using the key he had taken from Brother Roberto. Once secured and the key removed, the lock disappeared from sight, leaving no clue as to how the case could be opened.

The Cardinal turned to the two aged monks who had guarded the crystal so faithfully since they were young and in their prime. He handed the key to Roberto who nodded and pulled its leather cord over his head, letting the priceless, almost magical object hang around his neck and under his robes, next to his heart.

"Not long now," said Bonetti, "then you can rest."

That brought smiles of relief to the faces of both guardians and, as they went back to their sacred duty, Bonetti and Cooper made their way via corridors and stairs to the Cardinal's private apartment.

Gabriel, Azriel, MoMo and Bob all disappeared into thin air, three of them reappearing moments later in the apartment. Gabriel was conspicuous by his absence.

Bob, to his credit, managed to stop throwing up. He did, however, silently break wind and emit a foul stench. By the time Bonetti and Cooper arrived, the stench had been downgraded to a slightly unpleasant odour that, although uncomfortable, wasn't unbearable.

The dining room in Bonetti's apartment had a table big enough for everyone to sit round comfortably.

All except MoMo, who decided to ease his way into a nearby two-seater leather Chesterfield sofa that was sufficiently well built to hold his bulk and weight without too much protest.

Bonetti picked up a nearby phone receiver and pressing a single button. After two rings the call was answered by an elderly male voice.

"Bring me the guest buffet for ten," the Cardinal said looking at MoMo. How long?" The voice answered and Bonetti frowned. "Half an hour? In that case make it the 15 minute version."

There was no protest. His Eminence had spoken. Time was flexible. Minutes could be squashed.

Ten minutes later two kitchen staff wheeled in the small mountain of sandwiches, cut meats, pies, rice, cakes and various other tasty edibles, and looked around the room expecting to see a reasonable sized gathering of hungry people. The confusion was palpable on their faces seeing only Bonetti and Cooper.

However, true to the tradition of kitchen staff the world over, they kept their opinions to themselves, placed the food where they were told, and left without saying a word.

Azriel sat at the table but looked on as the others ate.

"Not hungry?" asked Bonetti, through a mouthful of pork pie.

"Don't need to eat," said the angel.

The Cardinal looked confused. "But – what about Bob, and MoMo? How come they need to eat?"

"Oh we don't need to eat, either," said MoMo, happily munching his way through a complete jam sponge. "We just like to."

It wasn't long before the only evidence left of the recent arrival of food was a few crumbs here and there and a series of appreciative burps.

In an excellent piece of timing, the burps were followed by the return of a frowning Gabriel. "Just popped back to tell you that Homer's a lot closer than we thought." He turned to Bonetti. "Your telephone will ring in a minute. Good idea if you answer it personally. You need to know about Daisy Roper."

"Daisy who?"

The little angel vanished.

Nineteen

Homer 3421F really was a handsome devil. In the world, or rather cosmos, of asteroids he was practically a drop dead gorgeous male model. Not the pretty boy, no-brains variety, but the rough, tough, chiselled good looks sort. He was an asteroid's asteroid.

Had circumstances been different, he might have been formed somewhere nice and cosy, like the warmer inner solar system between the orbits of Mars and Jupiter a few billion years ago. But they weren't. And he wasn't. However, throughout his vagabond life he had done his fair share of wandering about the galaxy, sowing his wild cosmic oats. Now he'd decided it was time to settle down.

So, in the grand tradition of male asteroids, he searched amongst the stars for a suitable home and, after a while, he spied a sight that, if he'd had any, would have taken his breath clean away.

Even though she was millions of miles away, she shone like a jewelled beacon in the darkness, all blue and white and radiant. Homer was instantly smitten. There was something vaguely and tantalisingly familiar about the sight – but the thought went as soon as it came.

He could tell that she was big. Vastly bigger than him. But then, Homer had always preferred the company of large females. They made him feel warm and comfortable and welcome. And they always seemed very grateful for his affections. In truth, it was he who was always very grateful for theirs.

Of course, he'd never actually been near enough to one to do anything. Somehow the whole confusing mish-mash of angles and trajectories, orbits and gravitational fields had always come between him and the ultimate act of cosmic consummation.

He was, sadly, very alone.

Once, he'd come agonisingly close. About three hundred thousand years ago a mere 15 million miles had separated him from a bit of surface-to-surface action.

Unfortunately it might as well have been 500 million miles. He didn't even receive a quick peck on the cheek, as he shot past his intended and off into the wide black yonder, never to see her again. The pain of rejection was almost too much to bear.

Still, this time would be different. He could feel it in his rocks. The trouble was, this new object of his affections was a very long way away and it would probably take a century or so before he could reach her. Not a great passage of time in the life of an asteroid. But Homer, like all males, was impatient. Very impatient.

As he tumbled unerringly through cold space towards his home-to-be, almost urging himself on faster and faster, he wished, in fact prayed, for something or someone to make his journey shorter.

His prayer did not go unheard.

In the blink of an eye, Homer 3421F went from being very far away from the big blue and white planet, to being very, close to it. Then very, very close.

The kind of close that makes buttocks clench of their own accord with no prior warning. The kind of close that extremely good brakes and extremely loud screams were created for. The kind of close that makes easily excitable individuals say things very loudly. Things like: "Holyfrigginmoly! Where the smeg did that come from?"

Curiously enough, those were the exact words that came from the mouth of a shit-scared, geek-type person called Wingnut who, right at that moment, was on the big blue and white planet, browsing the sky on his PC screen, which was linked, possibly illegally, to some very powerful offworld telescopes pointing into deep space.

One minute he was looking at lots of space with no Homer in it. Then suddenly there was lots of Homer and a lot less space. It's at times like these when a person either really discovers what they're made of, or needs to go to the toilet very quickly.

Wingnut, who didn't know a holy from a moly even on a good day, pointed at his PC screen and turned to his co-worker, a tall, cute young woman called Daisy Roper. They were both Night Watchers at the Falling Sky Foundation, a privately funded organisation that constantly monitored the skies for Near Earth Objects, meteors or comets about 1 kilometre or more in diameter, which threatened to either collide with earth or pass close enough to make the human race very, very nervous.

"Where did *what* come from?" asked Daisy, turning to him, annoyed that he had taken her attention away from the "Big Bang' magazine article she was engrossed in.

"We got a new NEO. Just came right out of nowhere, and it's so close it's practically knocking on the front door!"

Daisy sighed, "You know we got every NEO heading our way over the next hundred years down on file, thanks to dear old NASA and that nice little LINEAR programme of theirs we peeked into."

"Not this one," said Wingnut, pointing to his screen. "See for yourself."

Reluctantly, Daisy closed her magazine and casually dropped it onto her desk. "If this is some kind of a joke, I might consider breaking one of your fingers," she said, frowning.

Wingnut's head was shaking slowly from side to side, "No joke," he said.

Daisy looked at his screen. "What the–?" she said, slowly.

"I think the term 'shitalmighty' might have been a tad better!"

Daisy ignored him and began typing rapidly on the PC's keyboard. The screen view changed and was replaced by four mini-screens. One a reduced version of the previous screen showing Homer in all his glory, and the other three filled with ever changing numbers, calculating the size, speed and trajectory of the space rock.

After a couple of minutes the calculations stopped and a constantly updating figure appeared.

"Holy shit," said Daisy. "It's Homer."

"What – Homer 3421F?

"Yes!"

"*Your* Homer?" asked an incredulous Wingnut.

Daisy was typing furiously again. "This is all wrong," she said.

"Wrong as in bad news wrong?" said an alarmed Wingnut.

"He's not where he should be."

"So where *should* he be?"

"About a hundred years away from even being near us. And even when he does get near us, he should miss by about 25 million miles."

"This is one of those 'but not any more' moments, isn't it?"

"Yes. According to this update, he's headed straight for us. And he's not a hundred years away."

"How long, then?"

"Well – according to these figures, he sped up and about an hour ago, he was 147 days away. Then about five minutes ago, he was about 30 days away, give or take!" said Daisy.

More alarm and panic combined to do a temporary remodelling of Wingnut's facial features. "He can do that?"

"He just did!"

"Tell me we have things that can stop this. Large explosive things."

"How the Hell should I know!" said Daisy, " I'm a Night Watcher. I look for things in the damned sky. I'm not a blow-things-up expert-type person. Hell, I'm a vegetarian for God's sake!"

They both looked at the red phone sitting on Daisy's desk. Under normal circumstances, their first act would be to contact Harlan Quinn, Falling Sky's on-site Director. Quinn would then take the news upwards to the Foundation's owners.

However, the Director was somewhere in Australia's outback on walkabout in a very expensive 4x4. The irony didn't escape her. So, Daisy was, to all intents and purposes, 'it'. As senior Night Watcher on duty, it was now her responsibility to be 'it' in either a 'first contact' or emergency situation. Homer qualified by at least 50%.

She reached over to the red phone and picked up the receiver. There were no buttons or dialling wheel, but as soon as she put the handset to her ear, she could hear a ringing sound. After four rings it was answered.

"Yes?" said a man's voice. Very calm, very flat, and with a slight American accent.

"Who am I speaking to?" asked Daisy.

There was a pause and the man asked, "Who do you want to be speaking to?"

Daisy was about to answer when she heard a woman's sleepy voice in the background. "Who is it, Charlie?"

"It's ok, honey," said the man. "You go back to sleep. It's business."

There was another pause, the sound of rustling clothes and footsteps and eventually the man came back on the line.

"Ok," he said, breathlessly. "This is General Charles Parker. This better be damned good. Who the Hell are you?"

"How about if it was very bad?" asked Daisy, now clearly annoyed. She then proceeded to tell the general everything that had happened from the moment that Wingnut discovered Homer on his screen.

When she finished, the General said, "Anyone else know about this?"

"Not yet. I've checked on the NASA and EURO systems and they don't have a clue he's coming."

"So, we were the first to see it?"

"What difference does being first make when you're about to be squished, sir?"

"Who said anything about being squished?" asked Parker, a worried tone creeping into his voice.

"Look. Homer's a very BIG boy. And he's gonna land in England. And if he doesn't break up on the way down, he'll land in West Yorkshire. Not just a bit of the county. Not just a bit of vacant moorland. Here. Right on us!"

"What's the problem? We could evacuate the facility in 30 minutes never mind 30 days," said Wingnut, joining the conversation that Daisy had put on the conference speaker.

"You couldn't evacuate your bowels in 30 days," muttered Daisy to Wingnut.

"How many of you are there?" asked Parker.

"In West Yorkshire? Oh...about..."

"No!" said the General, impatiently. "In the facility."

"Just the two of us. We're the Night Watch."

"Right, here's what we do. Send a flash report to NASA with all the details. And make sure The Falling Sky Foundation gets the credit."

Daisy sighed. "You don't get it, do you sir."

"Don't get what?"

"Homer won't just squish us here in West Yorkshire."

"You mean this could affect the whole country?" said the General, his irritation now changing to alarm.

"You mean the country that's there until Homer lands? This is bigger than the UK. Bigger than Europe. Bigger tha–"

"How big?"

"Sir," said Daisy. "When I said Homer was big I mean he's a bloody giant in the field of asteroids. He's around 15 miles in diameter. So we're not talking about a large hole in the ground.

"Remember that itty-bitty rock that wiped out about 75% of life on earth about 65 million years ago?" said Wingnut. "Including all those big scary things with large, sharp teeth?"

"That was a Homer-type rock?" asked the General, alarm in his voice. His mind began to think of collateral damage and earthquakes and floods...all very quickly.

"Yep. Now THAT one packed a punch about a billion times more powerful than the atomic bomb that flattened Hiroshima. Homer is a little bit bigger."

There was silence at the other end of the line.

"Sir?" said Daisy into the silence.

"Hey General!" yelled Wingnut.

"I've got to make a phone call," said Parker.

"Okay" said Wingnut, "who you gonna call...Asteroid Busters R Us?"

"My boss. Meanwhile, you two sit tight and keep watching the rock."

"Oh, don't worry," said Daisy. "We won't take our eyes off Homer for a second. Besides, he's an old friend."

"What?" exclaimed a puzzled General, wondering how a planet threatening space rock could be regarded as even remotely friendly.

"Well...I kinda discovered him," said Daisy, with more than a little pride in her voice.

"You did?"

"Yup. Just over four years ago. Been keeping an eye on him ever since."

"In that case," said Parker, "I guess you know this damned rock better than anyone else. I got some people to talk to. Meanwhile, you keep a good eye on that baby of yours. I'll get back to you."

The phone went dead.

Daisy and Wingnut both looked at each other, not wishing to speak aloud their own personal fears, and then began their new task of monitoring and tracking Homer.

Meanwhile, the General dialled a number committed to memory many years ago.

"Yes?" said a male voice. Parker thought he recognised an Italian accent.

"This is Parker."

"Yes. Good to hear from you General. It's been a long time. I was expecting your call."

"You were?"

"Absolutely. As a matter of fact, I have been sitting here eagerly anticipating your news about our celestial visitor."

Parker was feeling decidedly spooked. "You know?"

The man laughed softly. "Oh we know many things. And generally, we know them way before anybody else. Tell me, how is our dear Daisy?"

Parker was surprised. "She's – fine," he said.

"Good, good. Now, what's the latest on Homer?"

"When did you find out?"

"Oh, we've known about him for quite some time. In fact we've started working on how to deal with him already."

Parker immediately felt a sea of relief wash over him. After he brought them up to date with Daisy's report, he said, "So what happens next?"

"Well," said the man, "NASA will probably think of throwing everything they have at our visitor from the stars. No doubt try to blow it out of the sky before it gets much closer. Now – you've done your bit. Tell Daisy and her young companion to keep an eye on Homer for us. I'm sure everything will turn out okay."

"Yes, and miracles really happen," said the general with more than a hint of sarcasm in his voice.

"Stranger things have happened."

In an office at Castlegandolfo, the Pope's summer residence in the Alban Hills, about 35 miles southeast of Rome, the man on the other end of the phone ended the call.

The residence was the headquarters of the Vatican Observatory and home to the Astrophysical Research Centre. It was also one of the oldest astronomical research institutions in the world. The fact that the Holy Church had an observatory was in no way contradictory to its fundamental belief in God and the miracle of Creation. Off the record, it agreed more with the scientific community about timescales than was generally known.

The fact that it had not one but TWO observatories, the other in Tucson, Arizona, was seen by many within the church hierarchy as simply promoting the public face of the 'Church Scientific'.

The man, who a moment ago had been speaking to General Parker, picked up the phone and dialled a number he had known for almost 30 years. After the second ring, the call was answered. "Hello," said Cardinal Bonetti.

"Alfredo, it's Julio," said the Observatory Director, in a voice that was elderly and soft, but had the kind of strength that could bend nails. "I think we need to talk."

"Aaah, so you've spotted our large flying friend, then?" asked Bonetti. "I might have known."

There was a long sigh as Julio Stassinos once again marvelled at the ability of his old friend to surprise him. "You know about Homer?"

"I have friends in high places," said the Cardinal. He liked the Jesuit's plain speaking manner and his obvious lack of anything remotely resembling ignorance. The man had a fine mind and a wit dry enough to suck a mouthful of moisture from a dried-up prune.

"And did your friends also tell you that the rock will be paying us a visit?" There was an infinitesimal amount of triumph in the Director's voice. Surely Bonetti didn't have *that* juicy morsel.

"My friends are very knowledgeable," said the Cardinal.

"So they've told you about Daisy, then?"

"Only vaguely," Bonetti lied through the tiny gap between his two front teeth. "Tell me more."

Aaah, so you *don't* know, then, thought Julio, pouncing on the only piece of new information that he could give to his dear friend. Theirs was an old game. For as long as they had known each other, they had taken great enjoyment in the gentlemanly art of verbal sparring. There was no malice, no animosity, no crude and unworthy jealousy. Just a continuous and long-standing exchange of information from giver to receiver, with an unspoken 'well done' awarded to the giver of any new information. This time, the award went to the Director, along with the traditional and to outsiders, baffling, acknowledgement.

"Marco," said Julio.

"Polo," said Bonetti, with an audible sigh and a grudging smile in his voice.

"Daisy Roper is a brilliant astrophysicist and an ex-NASA infant terrible," said the old Jesuit.

"She's quite cute, utterly pigheaded and, for the past three years, she's been working as a Night Watcher at the Falling Sky Foundation in the UK. It's one of our quieter projects. Two years ago, she discovered our flying friend and named it Homer 3421F. She's been keeping a close eye on it ever since."

The surprise in Bonetti's voice was undisguised. "So, you've known Homer was coming our way and you didn't think it was important enough to pick up the phone?"

"Now don't get your pants in a twist," replied Julio. "We didn't think he was ever going to be a threat. He was just moving through space, bothering nobody and *definitely not* pointed at us – when all of a sudden he changed direction and sped up."

Bonetti didn't trust himself to say anything about hands of God or eyes. "So what did you do?" he said softly.

"What do you think I did? I knelt down right there on the spot and prayed! That's what I did. Then I checked my figures again, and again." There was a pause.

"And?"

"Asteroids around 100 light years away aren't affected by prayer. I can now say, without fear of rebuttal, that this is a scientifically proven fact," said Julio, with a touch of both discovery and defeat in his voice. It was as if one side of his face was happy and the other was sad. "But that's not the worst news," he added.

Bonetti's heart skipped a beat.

"Then less than an hour ago I received a phone call to say that the Homer was now only 30 days away. Can you believe it?"

The Cardinal's heart relaxed. "Who called you?"

There was a pause on the other end of the line. "Where is your surprise Alfredo? Where is your shock? There's no panic in your voice. You damned well knew this already! Who's giving you this information?"

"I'll tell you one day over a nice Merlot," said Bonetti. "Meanwhile, tell me who called you?"

Julio told him about the call General Parker had received from Daisy Roper, and the Cardinal began to regard the young astrophysicist as not just a valuable source of information, but also a potential extra member for the team from Earth.

Who better to act as an early warning system on the 'human' team, just in case Homer decided that 30 days was too long to wait?

Who better to set the alarm bells off if that 30 suddenly turned into 20 or even, Heaven forbid, 10. Angels were one thing. But Bonetti liked the idea of a flesh and blood backup Plan B.

"Julio – does Daisy know of our involvement?"

"Not in the slightest," said the Director.

"Let's keep it that way, at least for the moment. Push her in the direction of the Americans and see what she does next. And keep me updated."

The cardinal put the phone down. "So what now?" he said, turning to Azriel.

"Now we let Junior and his mojo loose – and make that sure all the technology designed to blow Homer out of the sky doesn't work."

"I don't want to appear defeatist or anything, but if we don't blow Homer out of the sky or fail to nudge him so he misses the planet, doesn't that mean we end up signing our own death warrants?"

Azriel smiled. "Remember the asteroid that wiped out the dinosaurs and three quarters of life on earth sixty odd million years ago?" Cooper looked worried. "You're not telling me you tried to stop that one, are you?"

The angel was still smiling. "Oh no, we let that one through."

"What?"

"We had to, so we could get the really big one following on behind it. We had one shot, so we figured, better to have somewhere we can start again, than nowhere at all."

"What he means, said MoMo, "that his Boss and my Boss joined forces and politely persuaded it to destroy itself before it destroyed the planet – and it took both of them to do it."

Cooper had a small lightbulb moment. "So that's why the joining up of forces this time round?"

"Exactly. Except my force doesn't seem to be very strong in me at the moment," the Oracle said, disappointment heavy in his voice.

"He's not the only one, either," said Azriel, with a worried edge to his voice. "We have Boss trouble."

"You mean that God and The Devil are actually physically affected by this lack of belief?"

"Oh they'll be fine," said Azriel, unconvincingly. "They always are. Even when it happened the last time."

"There was a last time?"

"Three, actually," said Azriel, casually. "What is it you say – if you want to make the perfect omelette, you have to break a few eggs?"

Bonetti slapped the table. "So the whole act of creation, from Big Bang until now, was just a matter of trial and error until you got it right?"

The angel looked genuinely surprised. "Oh I see. You believe in the Big Bang? Not very creationist of you, is it?"

"Just because I believe in a scientific explanation for the birth of the Universe, doesn't mean I don't believe in God's involvement in it."

Their debate was interrupted by MoMo. "Tweet tweet," he said from the sofa.

Cooper looked confused. "What?"

"Faces and books!"

"Eh?"

"And tubes."

"Pardon?"

"Is your Oracle power back up again?" asked Azriel softly.

"Don't have a clue," said MoMo, scratching his bald head. "Voice in my head said 'Faces, books and tubes.' And when an Oracle hears voices, he listens to them. That's one of an Oracle's top ten rules. Ask any of them."

"You're the only one left."

Cooper's brain was now racing. "Faces, books, tweets and tubes,' he repeated under his breath. His fingers were drumming on the edge of the table as he said the words softly, almost like a mantra. "Faces, books, tweets and tubes – faces, books, tweets and tubes."

Suddenly he stopped drumming and a smile slowly crept across his face. "Social media," he said, looking at the others. "That's the answer," he said. "Facebook, Twitter and YouTube.

"Don't you see? It's the fastest way to get whatever miracle we cook up out to the rest of the world – and we don't actually have to do anything. Anyone with a cell phone or a laptop or a tablet will spread the word for us! In fact, even The Holy Father's on Facebook."

"He is?" asked Bonetti.

"Absolutely. Got his own page. Even got a Twitter account, too!"

"He tweets?"

"You didn't know? Oh he's very progressive in communicating with the world. He's a founding member of the Vatican Twitterati. Of course, he's a bit inactive at the moment for obvious reasons."

Bonetti made a mental note to 'friend' and 'follow' his immediate boss at the earliest opportunity. Then another thought wriggled its way into his thinking process. "What about those who wouldn't know social media if it came up behind them and bit them on the bum?" he asked Cooper. "How do we get the message out to them?"

"You ever heard of Larry Black?" interrupted Azriel.

The Cardinal closed his eyes thought. After a few seconds of mental file searching, he came across the one he wanted. His eyes opened and he frowned. "You mean the American television guy?"

Cooper sighed and shook his head slowly. "That's like asking if Satchmo was the American trumpet playing guy. Larry Black is probably the most watched chat show host on the face of the earth."

"Well, unless we figure out how to get the balance of Heaven and Hell back to normal and stop Homer in his tracks, there won't be any faces left on the face of the earth. So – what's the plan?"

It was the kind of question people asked when they had no answers. The kind of question that made every head, except one, turn round and look at the head that remained motionless. The head that, in this case, had a nice gleaming white dog collar sitting around the neck underneath it.

Somewhere inside the priest's mind three thoughts were about to beat the Hell out of each other to see which one was left standing. One thought was, 'Now might be a good time to turn my head, look at everyone else very quickly and plead the Fifth.' The second thought was, 'Maybe if I turned myself into a chair they wouldn't ask me any more questions.' And the third thought was, 'Plans? I love it when a plan comes together. Especially the ones where I can solve the case, get the Hell out of Dodge and go back to being an Eagle."

The third thought, being the sneakiest, won without even throwing a punch. "Right. The plan –"

"Hospital," interrupted MoMo.

"Pardon?"

"Pardon what?"

"You said 'hospital'."

"I did?"

There were nods round the table. "Why did you say 'hospital'?" asked Bonetti. "Is it a clue?"

Cooper stood up and walked round to the sofa filled with MoMo. "It's something to do with saving the babies, right?"

MoMo looked worried. "I don't know. Did my middle eye open?"

"Nope."

The Oracle touched the bump on his forehead, checking to see for himself. It was shut tight. "Sometimes I get images coming through on Half Oracle Power. It's like the door's closed but the store's still open for business."

Cooper suddenly had an image come crashing into his brain without so much as an invitation. "These babies you saw – were they in a hospital?" he asked.

MoMo's normal eyes widened. "How did you –?"

"I know what we have to do. Azriel, you need to get us to Los Angeles quickly. Junior, how do you feel about being a worldwide multimedia sensation? There may be a miracle or two required."

A voice came from the floor where Junior was now sitting, his legs crossed at the ankles, his back against a wall. Cell phone in hand. Logging on to a Twitter account. "Are you absolutely sure there won't be any physical or emotional pain?"

"Promise."

A few seconds later a short tweet from someone called @juniortherealdeal hit the Twitterverse through the desktop and mobile devices of hundreds of millions of registered users. At precisely the same time, all over the world, their accounts received a tweet which simply said: "I'm back in business. Expect the unexpected!"

Technology and systems and all the planning for worst case scenarios sometimes simply take it into their heads to do what they're not supposed to do. Twitter wasn't meant to open its arms to millions of tweets in the space of a few seconds. But it did. Millions of tweets weren't meant to hit the Twitterverse at the same time without crashing and burning the site. But they did.

Twitter, no doubt for its own good reasons, decided to do something not just totally unexpected, but technically impossible.

It kept going, allowing the original tweet to be retweeted at a rate of re's and tweets that caused minor global repetitive strain injury on an unprecedented level.

The word didn't just get out – it snapped its chains, bent its bars, broke free of its cage and ran down the road laughing with glee.

Of course if you'd asked any one of the retweeting millions what the original message meant, they wouldn't have had a clue. All they knew was that they were overcome with a sudden and irresistible urge to pass the message on till their fingers begged for mercy – and watch out for something monumental happing soon.

Then the loveable, social media colossus known as Facebook joined the party with a billion users and a hunger to pick up the word and run with it that bordered on the messianic. They, also, didn't have the slightest idea what was going on – only that if it was good enough for Twitter, it was damned well more than good enough for them. Whatever it was.

In total, from Junior logging on to Twitter, flexing his thumbs, sending his tweet – and Facebook waking up and breaking the speed limit for contacting, well, everyone – 15 minutes had passed. Under normal circumstances, those minutes would have grown into hours, maybe even days, or weeks.

But then again, under normal circumstances, the universe and everything in it would have taken billions of years to create and fiddle with – instead of six days, with a holiday on the seventh for a few beers, a hog roast and a bit of a rest. The passage of time was flexible – and simply depended on which side of the fence you stood.

While the magic of social media was lighting the blue touch paper and retiring to a comfortable distance, Cooper was explaining his reason for the team's relocation to The City of Angels.

It went something like this.

Los Angeles was where The Larry Black show was filmed. The show was seen all over the world and had viewing figures in the billions. It was ten minutes from possibly the most famous children's hospital in the western hemisphere. Holy Trinity General.

The hospital that had combined reality TV and maternity wards and come up with the most riveting piece of weekly television ever conceived – "Born Winners". All they needed was a miracle scenario – and they could figure that out when they got there. But it had to be big and it had to be dramatic and it had to involve Larry Black and saving babies.

Cooper took a break for breath and looked at everyone in the room, waiting for some reaction. The pause was as pregnant as the mothers at Holy Trinity were just before they gave birth.

Azriel was the first to react. "So, we save some babies, big deal. How does that stop *The Eye of God* from disappearing and the rest of us with it? And even if we manage to pull that off, how does it save us from Homer?"

MoMo, in an unexpected defensive movement that bordered on the suicidal – glared. It was the kind of glare that involved staring at someone through squinty eyes and with murderous intent – although it had all of those attributes. It was also the kind that came out of left field, out of character, sudden, unexpected and from a great height.

"He's not finished. It might be a good idea to shut up," his glare said. His voice, not wishing to feel left out, repeated the glare.

The fact that it was directed at Azriel who, just by coincidence, happened to be The Angel of Death, made it impressive enough. The other fact that the angel gritted his teeth, stood his ground and returned the gaze without blinking put it in a whole new category of 'everyone run for cover'.

Showing what some might have said was great bravery – and others immense stupidity – Cooper interrupt the tender moment before blows were struck.

"I was thinking we need to put the babies in danger, then remove the threat in a way that science can't explain. Maybe a small but perfectly formed miracle would be good. Then we need to do the same with the Homer problem. Only on a bigger scale. Much bigger."

"Hey, now that I'm a real, bona fide angel, does that mean I can do miracle stuff?" asked Bob, who was staring intently at a jug of water. The water stared back, determined not to change into anything even remotely alcoholic.

"Why are you still here?" asked Azriel, who had decided that saving babies might be a good idea and had transferred his stare from a large, immovable object to annoying skinny individual. "Don't you have to go somewhere and finish growing some wings?"

Bonetti, despite Bob's penchant for throwing up anywhere near him, decided that it might be a good idea to keep him around. *"The Eye of God* has spoken to him. Who knows what it planted in that addled head of his. He might come in useful."

Bob, who seemed oblivious to the argument for and against his presence, had now taken to grimacing at the water jug and making signs in the air with his fingers in the hope that a miracle would occur. The water, thinking this highly amusing, decided to play along and changed in an instant from transparent to a nice fruity Beaujolais. Bob screamed in surprise, pushed himself away from the table and fell backwards over his chair. "It's a miracle!" he yelled. "I changed water into wine. Look!"

As he scrambled to his feet, heart pounding with excitement, he pointed at the jug and saw clear water. His joy turned to confusion. "But – but –"

"You were saying?" drawled Azriel slowly to Bonetti.

The Cardinal merely lowered his head and shook it slowly from side to side.

Cooper, on the other hand, seemed unaffected by the slapstick interlude. "Los Angeles, Azriel. We need to go now."

"I can arrange a plane," said Bonetti.

"No need. We have our own transport," said the priest. "I'll keep in touch."

He nodded to Azriel and felt a slight muzzy sensation that cleared moments later. He was no longer in the Vatican. Instead, he was sitting in the leather upholstered back of a limousine.

"Welcome to Hollywood, Sherlock," said Azriel, from the driver's seat. MoMo and Bob were nowhere in sight. Outside, the second most populous city in the US got on with its life and not one of its 4 million inhabitants, give or take, gave a damn whether the priest in the limo was alive or dead. One inhabitant, however, shortly would. His name was Larry Black. And he was about to show the world what a sure-fire miracle looked like.

Only he didn't know it yet.

Twenty

Larry Black lived in the kind of home that a staggering proportion of the world's population could only dream about, and would probably cook and eat their relatives to possess.

Nestling snugly in over 100 acres of prime Californian land, complete with its own vineyard, orangery, outdoor swimming pool and original ancient Indian graveyard, it was Larry's little piece of Heaven right here on earth.

The day he bought it he promised himself that nothing, absolutely nothing, would take it away from him.

Determination ran in Larry's family. So did alcoholism and premature baldness. However Larry had what he liked to call 'friends in high places' and left it mysteriously at that. Larry's special friends watched over him, took care of him and in return, he would do the odd favour for them whenever they came calling.

Mostly of the time he just helped people. Gave them the chance to tell their story, get a little heartache off their chest and generally discover that it was okay to like each other. It normally involved lots of shouting and crying, some sporadic violence from overweight angry folk and a few pearls of wisdom.

Sometimes the help involved favours of a more profound nature. Like the time one of his show guests mentioned that the town she came from was being terrorised by two rival gangs and the kids who refused to join either gang were being used for target practice. Rather than arrest the criminals, the local police turned a blind eye. The way they figured it, anything that resulted in a little teenage population control and contributed to their own police benevolent fund had to be a good thing. Rocking the boat wasn't a profitable move.

Within 24 hours of the show's broadcast, the police and the criminals had mysteriously disappeared off the face of the earth and the town was able to return to the normality of neighbourly bickering and family squabbles. But at least they could do without the threat of extreme lead poisoning.

Larry loved his job and his life. More importantly, his audience loved him. Ratings for his primetime talk show were at an all-time high and life was good. The ideal time for mysterious friends to come calling again.

About the time Cooper found himself in the limo with Azriel, Larry was sleeping like a baby at home in California, in an outrageously large bed, between silk sheets and wearing silk pyjamas – all black, naturally.

It was 6.35am and his brain was deep in REM sleep.

"Hello Larry, time to wake up," said a voice.

Larry's ears were also deep in REM sleep.

"LARRY – WAKE UP!"

Larry woke up, leapt out of bed, tripped over a slipper, took a nosedive, and yelled in panic as the floor inconsiderately refused to move out of the way. A hair's breadth from making contact with his Persian rug, his forward momentum suddenly became a backward momentum and he found himself hoisted from nasal calamity and placed roughly back in his bed.

His confused mind, unable to put two and two together on the same planet, never mind in the same bedroom, grabbed onto the most rational explanation.

"I'm still dreaming, right?"

"That could be one explanation," said Gabriel, now sitting on the bed next to him. "Another could be that you're wide awake, sitting on your bed next to a pretty important individual who's about to ask you for another favour."

"Gabriel?"

The angel feigned hurt. He bum-shuffled closer, reached up and put a hand on Larry's shoulder, patting it and letting out a long, weary sigh. "You never write. You never call. A person could get the feeling that you didn't care anymore!" he said.

Larry didn't know whether to be delighted and enthusiastic or penitent and slightly confused. He decided that the latter combination might be safer. "I'm – I'm – so sorry. I thought you were the one who was going to get in touch when you needed another favour doing."

"What? You mean two old friends can't have a coffee and a chat every now and then?"

"Sure. It's just that – well, the last time we had a coffee and a chat you persuaded me to bring together, on live TV, Carlos Roberto Moreno, a highly homophobic Mexican drugs cartel leader and his highly gay, youngest son Geraldo."

Larry's mind had a flashback to the show. Carlos loved being a big celebrity and couldn't resist the invitation to be on it. Geraldo loved Carlos' money but wanted to be as far away from him as possible when he outed himself publicly to his family. It was a good job that 'daddy dearest' was only there via live satellite feed. Things turned very ugly very quick. Great TV.

"Remind me what happened," asked.

"His own people weren't too impressed at the large dent in their leader's masculine reputation – and, by association, their own reputations. The next morning they found Carlos' head in a box, in a gay bar in Mexico City. The authorities said it set the cartel's operations back ten years. Good old paranoid Carlos had all the passwords to all the cartel's bank accounts locked away safely inside his head. Before they realised this essential little fact, they had separated his head from the rest of his body. How's that for irony!"

"You saved a lot of lives that day."

Larry looked down at his feet. "Funny. I felt like I was just delaying the inevitable. The thing about throwing spanners in works is that sooner or later somebody else always comes around to take the spanner out and carry on the good work. I never found out what happened to Geraldo."

"And neither did his father's old friends," said Gabriel, leaving the explanation hanging mysteriously in mid air like so much dirty washing, cleaned and flapping in the wind.

"Is he safe?"

"Aaah. Now see – there's the problem. If you do this little favour for us, he could be as safe as houses for the rest of his long and happy life."

Larry's heart skipped a beat. "I can feel a 'but' coming."

Gabriel didn't see any reason to tell him about *The Eye of God* and the threat it held. But he did tell him about Homer and the fact that, if the space rock wasn't stopped, the Human Race was doomed. One annihilation of everyone and everything in the universe was enough bad news for the day. Two was possibly an Armageddon too far.

The little angel continued. "Imagine that there was only one way to stop Homer and that was on your show!"

"I'm not in a very imagining state at the moment, sorry. I can do a very good panic state if that will help" Larry said, frantically trying to understand what in Heaven's name he could do to help stop this catastrophe. "Anyway, what about all those nuclear warheads we've got lying around doing nothing?"

"What if I told you that relying on technology will get you all killed."

"But we've got the best defence network the world has ever seen," said Larry, trying to be defensive. "We had a general on the show once who told us that you couldn't shit in space now without our monitoring devices hearing it and our armaments blasting it to Hell and back!"

"So what do you do if you flick the switch and press the button and nothing happens?"

Larry thought for a moment. "Pray for a bloody miracle, I suppose," he said softly.

"Exactly!" exclaimed Gabriel. "And that's just what the world will get. A miracle. Courtesy of you, and the biggest guest anyone could ever have on any show."

"Like who?" said Larry, as a Rolodex full of famous names fluttered in front of his brain. You believe in God, don't you Larry" he said.

"What?" Larry's panicometer registered off the chart. "I'm having *God* on my show?"

Gabriel thought for a microsecond and shook his head. *"Never gonna happen,"* an internal voice said. It wasn't his.

"Yeah – right. Dream on. I can however, arrange to have the next best thing. How d'you fancy interviewing His Son?"

The panicometer needle twitched and pulled back from self-destruct just slightly.

"Emm–"

"See," said Gabriel, looking and talking skywards. "I told you he'd love the idea!"

Larry's brain was experiencing the mental equivalent of palpitations. "But – but –

"Outstanding. It's all set, then. We'll get in touch later on today and set up a lunch or something."

Larry closed his eyelids tight, hoping than when he opened them he would be in bed and all this would have been a bad dream. He woke instead to the insistent trill of his cell phone, complaining loudly on his bedside cabinet. He reached over, grabbed it, pressed the green answer button and shoved the phone to his right ear. "Hello?" he asked, still slightly groggy from sleep.

"Mr. Black?"

"Yeah?"

"My name's Cooper. Father John Wayne Cooper–"

Larry was suddenly wide awake. "Father, as in priest?"

"Well yes, I was given to understand you were expecting my call," said Cooper.

Larry's mouth did some stalling while his brain caught up. "I was?"

"We have a mutual friend."

"We do?"

"Gabriel."

Larry's brain caught up pretty damned quickly. In fact it couldn't have caught up quicker even if it had a red cape and wore its pants on the outside.

Every part of the previous night's dream came crashing into his memory and the whole episode did a fast rewind, beginning to end, in about 10 seconds.

"Mr. Black?" Cooper said into the silence while Larry's tape was running.

"*Larry!*" Cooper shouted. That did the trick.

"You're the, the – Him?" asked Larry softly with about two tons of awe in his voice.

"What? No, I'm not the Him. I'm the Me. Simply a companion. The Him needs to meet with you as soon as possible. How about lunch?"

Larry heard himself saying, "Lunch? How the Hell can I take the Son of God to lunch?"

"It's okay Mr. Black," said Cooper calmly, sensing Larry's growing panic. "He looks just like any normal person. No long hair. No robe. No crowds of followers. Any other day, you wouldn't look at him twice. Hell, he's got ears that you could hang your jacket off!"

"And he's the –?"

"Son of God? Absolutely," said Cooper. "The genuine article. The Big Cheese. Well – Son of Big Cheese more like!"

"So the dream?"

"Wasn't a dream at all. Larry, you're going to have to get into the habit of finishing your sentences," said Cooper.

Larry's head was stuffed full of questions. "So how the – I mean where the –?"

"Larry – listen to my voice very carefully."

"Okay."

"*Finish your sentences!*" yelled Cooper.

"I think I'm –"

"Ready?"

"More like just about to pee myself."

"Good. We'll come by in about an hour and pick you up in the limo." Cooper put the phone down, dialled a number and spoke to Cardinal Bonetti. "We're meeting Larry Black in about an hour. I'll call you afterwards."

"Is Junior okay?" asked Bonetti.

"Well, he played around with his Holy Mojo on the way over and we had to strap an air stewardess in her seat to stop her trying to wash his feet. But apart from that, no problem – so far."

"Where is he now?"

"We're in the hotel. He's in the next room," said Cooper.

"What makes you think he won't turn the Mojo on you?"

Cooper laughed. "Don't worry, everything's under control."

It was the kind of thing you always regret saying, thought Cooper, as soon as he said it. "By the way," he added. "Where are the others?"

"Disappeared into thin air after you left. Didn't even say goodbye. One second I was talking to Gabriel about how to get sick out of Persian rugs, the next I was having a conversation with an empty chair. I got the distinct feeling they had to be somewhere else.

"So don't be surprised if that somewhere else is wherever you are! Stay in touch," said the Cardinal and hung up.

Cooper looked around his bedroom in the penthouse suite of the exclusive Starlight Hotel, visited at one time or another by a bucketful of A-list movie stars and at least three Presidents of the United States, if the photos on the walls were anything to go by.

It had a vast living area off which were two bedrooms, each with its own en-suite bathroom. He decided that his bedroom was about the size of the average basketball court.

He was sitting on the side of a bed that wasn't so much king-sized but more Emperor or maybe even World Conqueror size. The rest of the room was sparse, but ultra stylish.

The priest had begged Bonetti to book them into somewhere a little more private and a lot less luxurious. The Cardinal, however, disagreed. "Look," he said, "if we're going to do the whole 'Son of God' thing with Junior, we really need to put on a show this time. We failed miserably the last time."

Cooper had tried to argue that, maybe the rise of Christianity was precisely the result of it's humble beginnings, and maybe booking into a swanky hotel wasn't exactly a great idea.

Bonetti had politely invited him not to get his knickers in a twist – and go with the flow.

His moment of good old Catholic guilt over, Cooper decided to check in on Junior, who, when they arrived, said he needed a little personal time and disappeared into the other bedroom.

He knocked twice on the bedroom door and waited. No answer. He knocked again, louder and more insistent this time. Again nothing. Bugger this, he thought, opening the door slowly. The room was dark. He searched the wall nearby for the light switch and was about to flick it on when a soft voice interrupted the act.

"Just because I didn't answer, doesn't mean I didn't hear you," said Junior.

"Something seems to be wrong with the light."

"The light's fine. We had a friendly conversation and it decided to go for a break. I just like thinking in the dark. It gives me a different perspective. You should try it some time."

"Been there, done that," said Cooper, remembering his time spent as a large, male Bengal tiger, lying in the dark in the long grass, near a Sal tree in the Chitwan National Park in Nepal – thinking intently about the fact that he was seriously hungry, yet unwilling to kill to eat. It was a morale dilemma unknown to other predators, except one. Those who walked upright and learned to hide their nakedness knew it only too well.

"Aaah yes – Nepal," said Junior. "I forgot about your fascinating talent."

The priest paused at the doorway. The fact that Junior knew about his unique ability wasn't surprising. It was an open secret to many, if not all, in Heaven or Hell – and a select few on Earth. Looking into the darkness, he had no idea where Junior was in the room. It was as if the space within the walls had denied any visual access, except to those it chose. Even light from the lounge outside the bedroom stopped at the doorway, unable or unwilling to intrude any further.

The thought of shapeshifting into something nocturnal entered his head, looked around, and quickly vanished. "I think I'll have a shower, then we should get started," he said. "Been there, done that," said Junior, mimicking Cooper's voice and appearing through the darkness, walking towards the priest. He stopped when he was about four feet in front of him, the darkness falling back politely to allow at least some light into the room. He was barefoot, dressed in a pair of skinny-fit black jeans and an oversized black t-shirt with a slogan on the front. The slogan said: Heaven Help Us.

Cooper looked at the words. "Nothing like a bit of optimism to start the day."

"Or a nice, strong coffee."

"You like coffee?"

"As long as it's hot, black, wet and strong. I'm sugar-free and lactose intolerant."

"What about green tea?"

"What about it?" asked Junior, turning round and walking back into the darkness.

Cooper grunted and made for his en-suite. "We roll in twenty," he said as he walked away. Two minutes later he was being pummelled by a masochistic power shower. The kind that blasts your skin's outer layer away, taking with it all the aches and cares of the day and leaving you a crumpled, happy heap on the shower cubicle floor. He relished the moment. Bliss was an infrequent visitor to Coopertown.

Exactly one hour and fifty minutes later, after a short drive from the hotel, the white limousine carrying the priest and the Son of God drew up outside the grand entrance to Larry Black's mansion. Larry was outside the front door, pacing back and forth, mumbling and oblivious to the car's arrival. It was only when Cooper opened the door, climbed out and said "Mr. Black?" that Larry's attention returned to the here and now from wherever it had been.

"Father Cooper?"

"Please, call me Cooper. Everyone else does."

"Is he–?"

"Yes, he's here."

Larry looked startled, "Oh holy crap."

"Don't worry," said the priest, taking Larry by the arm and guiding him towards the open door of the car.

"Yeah, how hard could this be? Talk show host meets 2,000 year old Saviour of the World –right?"

"Right," said Cooper as they both got in.

Larry sat down in the limo's plush leather back seat, his eyes adjusting to the dimly lit interior. A figure sat opposite him.

"Larry," said Cooper, settling himself into his seat next to the TV host, "I'd like you to meet Junior."

Larry looked closely for the first time at the other figure and saw an unremarkable young man. On the surface, nobody to write home about, or use as the basis for the world's largest religion.

Cooper saw the confusion on Larry's face, but before he could say anything, Junior leaned forward and clasped both of Larry's hands in his. Then he switched on the Holy Mojo, looked into Larry's eyes and spoke.

"So, you're Larry," he said, in a voice filled with warmth and comfort and soft, gooey happiness.

"I am?" asked Larry, speaking as if in a trance.

Junior smiled. "It's nice to meet you."

"It is?" asked Larry, gently. 'Those eyes' he was thinking as he looked at Junior. 'Where have I seen those eyes before?' Then, literally like a bolt from the blue, a memory surfaced which had been buried since childhood. He was 9 years old and an altar boy at St Joseph's Roman Catholic Church in Scotland, two years before he emigrated with his parents to America.

It was his third Sunday in and he was learning the ropes from Ewan Roberts a big-boned 15-year-old farmer's son with wiry red hair and ruddy cheeks.

The church, although small and fairly simple in design and ornament, had one item that many a grand cathedral would have given up its saints' bones to possess. It was a beautifully carved, full-sized figure called Our Saviour On the Cross. Stunningly realistic. In fact it was so realistic that even non-believers would visit the church simply to look at it.

This particular Sunday was supposed to be his 'initiation' into what Ewan called the Brotherhood of the Boys of St. Joseph. Those who served the priest and Our Lord before, during, and after every mass.

So the boys went in an hour early for the 8am service, when they knew Father Duggan was busy elsewhere. They were the only two in the church.

"Right," said Ewan, after making sure the coast was clear, "folla me."

Both went into the vestry at the side of the altar where the altar boys and priest put their robes on and Ewan made straight for the oak cabinet where the altar wine was kept.

"What ye doin'?" whispered Larry, nervously looking around, half expecting Father Duggan to walk in on them.

"Shut it! Stop pissin' yer pants and get me the chalice, quick!"

"The chalice?"

"Ye cannae drink oot the bottle. That's no allowed. It *has* tae be the chalice. Now go'n get it!"

Being that Ewan was much bigger than him, and that this *was*, after all, his initiation, Larry obeyed, fetching the large, golden altar chalice from its silk-lined carved wooden box that was sitting on a small table under the room's only window.

Meanwhile, Ewan opened the wine closet and took out a half-empty bottle of the distinctively sweet, liqueur wine that was used by the priest at every mass to serve as a reminder of the blood of Our Lord.

"C'moan quick," said Ewan and he walked, Larry trotting on behind like an obedient lamb, out the door and up to the front of the altar, hanging behind which was the life-sized crucified figure stared at in awe by so many.

As he was standing there in front of the figure, Larry realised for the first time that he hadn't really looked at the man on the cross. Oh, he'd viewed it casually for years, but it always seemed just part of the church furniture. A part that didn't warrant closer inspection.

Now here he was standing in front of it. Dwarfed by it.

"Right," said Ewan. "Haud oot the chalice."

Larry did as he was told and Ewan uncorked the wine and poured a large mouthful into the golden cup. His face took on an earnest expression as befitted a serious ceremony.

"Larry Black," he said in a half whisper. "You have been chosen tae serve Our Lord and the Priest of this Parish as a member of the Brotherhood of The Boys of St. Joseph. Do you promise to be a damned good boy and honour the big man and his mam and dad and be a good Catholic always and never become a Protestant?"

Pride surged through Larry and even through the chalice was shaking in his hands, he was careful not to spill a drop of the precious wine. "I do!" he whispered.

"Good man, Larry," said Ewan. "Now, here's the important bit. Raise the chalice up towards the cross and say, 'Here's tae ye, big man', then down the lot in one gulp!"

So that's just what Larry did. He held up the chalice, made the toast, and drank the wine.

Then his eyes looked at the figure as if for the very first time. He saw the torture, and the wounds, and the blood. And then Larry saw the eyes. He would remember those eyes as long as he lived.

Well, truth be told, he forgot completely about them for about 40 years.

Then he looked at Junior's face and saw the same eyes staring back at him. Then he knew, really knew. Here, sitting in front of him was the man – *the man*!

Okay, the body was a bit smaller, and the ears a bit bigger. But things can look different when you're 9 years old and shit scared. And it didn't matter a frig that his name was Junior. You can't have that effect on somebody and not be the genuine article, Larry thought.

So he leaned over, threw his arms around Junior and hugged him tightly. "Nice t'see you again," he said softly into Junior's ear. "Boy," he added, "wait till the world sees *you*!"

"Ok – enough!" said Junior, struggling to break free and succeeding only when Cooper hauled Larry by the scruff of his jacket back into the seat beside him.

"Right," said the priest, "now we're all acquainted, why don't we go for a bite to eat, eh?"

"Well," said Larry, energised and excited. "How does everyone feel about Italian? I know a lovely little restaurant, very clean, very private. The chef is a personal friend. They have the kind of fresh seafood Tag –"

"Actually," interrupted Junior, "I really fancy a large chili dog with onions and a diet coke."

"Or we could have that."

"How about over there?" asked Cooper, pointing to a busy hot dog stall parked outside a movie theatre on the opposite side of the street. He knocked on the glass separating them from the driver. "Hey driver, pull up by that hot dog stand over there."

The driver turned round and smiled. "You know, it must be ten years since I had a chili dog. I can still taste it," he said, emitting a large burp that filled the driving cab with the stale odour of meat and burnt onions. He shrugged apologetically. "Better out than in, eh?"

"Azriel!" exclaimed Cooper, smiling.

"Scuzbucket!" said Junior.

"Who?" asked Larry, thoroughly confused.

"Long story," said Azriel, doing a u-turn through traffic, miraculously missing every vehicle or causing a single crash, bump or scrape. As they pulled in just behind the hot dog stand, the dark angel, who was wearing an immaculately cut black suit, white shirt and black tie, turned his head and said, "This one's on me." Then he got out of the car and went to fetch lunch.

The stand had a sign which said *Smokin' Sam's Red Hot Chili Dogs. Made with Genuine Red Savina Habaneros – one of the world's hottest chilies! WARNING: We got directions to the local hospital!"*

Azriel soon returned with five steaming chili dogs and five standard cokes. "He said if anybody went into convulsions or started foaming at the mouth, drink this." Smiling, he produced a quart of milk from a bulging pocket and squeezed into the back of the limo to join the others.

They say you can tell a lot about a person by the way they react to eating a very, *very* hot chili pepper. There are those who, after years of eating fiery late night currys after heavy drinking sessions, bite into one, simply notice a slight increase in body temperature, and carry on chomping away enthusiastically.

There are those who, afraid to admit to their fellow munchers that they have absolutely no strength of character and a palate like a newborn baby, suffer the fires of Hell from their lips right through to their backsides, and still refuse to admit defeat.

There are those who, for reasons best kept to themselves, delight in inflicting the most horrendous pain on any part of their body.

And for these pathetic individuals, there is no better gastronomic turn-on than a murderously evil Red Savina Habanero Chili.

Then, lastly, there are those poor demented fools who, having never experienced Death by Chili, bite into their first ever Red Chili Dog and instantly feel like removing their heads with the nearest available sharp – or even blunt – object.

Cooper was one of the latter.

"Gaaaaaaaaaaaargh!" he yelled, frantically lowering the car window and spitting the contents of his mouth onto the sidewalk. He grabbed the milk and drank the entire contents in one go, moaning in between gulps. "*Holymotherofgod!*" he gasped, as he tried to stem the flow of tears from his eyes.

"You never had a real chili dog before, have you?" said Azriel.

Cooper glared through tear-filled eyes, feeling the milk beginning to calm the all-over body burning sensation. Larry was sweating profusely and the look on his face was halfway between determination and pain.

The angel nodded towards Cooper's mostly uneaten chili dog. "Are you going to finish eating that?"

The priest handed the offending item over to the dark angel. "I've heard they put all kinds of meat in these dogs."

"Could even be dog meat!" said Azriel.

"Or rat."

Larry's face went white. "You're kiddin', right?" he said, as he was just about to swallow his last mouthful. He looked at the others, alarmed, "he's pullin' my chain – right guys?"

"Maybe," said the angel through a large mouthful of indeterminate flesh.

"I think I'm gonna be sick." Larry opened the door window quickly. Seconds later, the others heard the sound him throwing up.

Azriel smiled triumphantly. "Mmmmmm – I love the smell of vomit in the morning."

Cooper decided it was time to get serious. "Right – that's enough fun for today. We need to talk about the show."

"What is there to talk about," said Larry, who had pulled his head back inside the limo and was wiping bits of food from his chin. "The next show's Friday and Junior here is the guest of honour."

Cooper looked surprised. "You mean we don't have to clear it with anyone else?"

"Like I said, it's my show and the only one who picks the guests is yours truly. Of course my producer is gonna go apeshit when I tell him who we got for the show. He'll think I've finally signed up for the funny farm! So we gotta give him something, like a mini-miracle.

"Nothing too big or showy. Just something we can maybe catch on camera. Then we do the interview live and exclusive, and syndicate the repeats."

"Hmm," said Azriel, "a mini-miracle, eh?"

"Absolutely. Something that couldn't easily be explained by technology or science or stage magic or even computer generated images."

Junior smiled. "In that case I might have an idea."

Twenty One

On what used to be a swampy wasteland, a stone's throw from the Potomac river in Washington DC, sits the largest and probably most famous office building in the world. To those who work there – around 30,000 people, civilian, military and non-defence support – it's unofficially known by a variety of nicknames. The Puzzle Palace is just one of them. The rest of the world knows it by its official name – The Pentagon.

"So, what do you think?" asked the man in the military uniform, whose name was General Ellis P. Crumb. Crumb was the Chairman of the Joint Chiefs of Staff, the principal military advisor to the President of the United States, the Secretary of Defence and the National Security Council.

"Well, between you and me," said NASA Assistant Administrator George McHale, sitting across the desk from the general, "we're way deep in bear poo!"

"And is that your official, scientific conclusion?"

McHale frowned and shook his head slowly. "No Ellis, that's a bare-faced fact."

The two were in the general's office in the Pentagon complex in Washington DC. McHale had just arrived for a special briefing with the Joint Chiefs, following the discovery that the asteroid called Homer 3541F was suddenly very close to, and heading directly for, Earth.

They were both drinking strong, black coffee and the General was feeling the after effects of too much brandy downed the night before at a dinner held in honour of a visiting politician. A pot-bellied pain in the butt from a country that Crumb couldn't even remember the name of, never mind find on a map.

He was contemplating an unlit cigar he wasn't even allowed to smoke within the confines of the Pentagon buildings any more, due to the new anti-smoking clamp down. Pretty damned soon a fella wouldn't be able to fart indoors, he thought.

Crumb was a champion of the free-thinking good old American pioneering spirit that, damn it, was being flushed down the toilet these days. "What the Hell do we tell them?"

"There's always the truth," said McHale, shrugging.

"Ah yes," said Crumb, "the truth. We could waltz in there and tell the Joint Chiefs of the Army, Navy, Air Force, Coast Guard and Marines that we have a rock the size of Gibraltar due to hit us in about 28 days and that with all the technology at our disposal, we never saw it coming. Just sorta popped up outa nowhere. That's one helluva truth, George."

McHale blushed slightly and began to feel the sweat under his collar. "Well –"

Crumb was beating his cigar like a drumstick against his desktop. The cigar was losing. "Oh and by the way guys, at precisely 8.30 this morning, Eastern Standard Time, every piece of military armament we have capable of blowing this damned rock out of the sky ceased to function because every computerised system inside every rocket and warhead we can throw into space is fried. Coffee anyone?"

"Or –" said McHale, desperately thinking of options.

"Or what?"

"Or we could pray for a damned miracle," said McHale, softly.

An intercom buzzed on Crumb's desk and a female voice said, "They're all here sir, except Admiral Davies." Davies was Chief of Staff of the US Coast Guard and at present he was in traction in hospital after his staff car hit a patch of oil on the road, lost control and overturned.

Davies was lucky...if you can call two broken legs and minor internal injuries lucky. The driver, sadly, was a whole lot luckier...his massive injuries wouldn't bother him any more.

"Thank you, Eileen," said Crumb. "Do we have a stand-in?"

"Rear Admiral Dobbs," said Eileen. "He's already with the others."

"On our way," said Crumb, flicking the intercom off, standing up and reaching for his jacket hanging over the back of his chair.

A few minutes later, McHale and Crumb walked into a hi-tech meeting room in the Pentagon where 6 other men were sitting round a table waiting for them.

The Joint Chiefs of Staff – plus one stand-in – as well as Harold Bright, the Secretary of Defence.

After saying their hellos, General Crumb turned to McHale and said, "Okay George, I think it's time we brought these gentlemen up to date."

McHale left his seat and went to the far end of the table, pressed a button on a panel on the wall and half the wall slid aside to reveal a large plasma screen.

"All of you, I presume, are acquainted with the term NEO or Near Earth Object?"

There were nods all around the table.

"Okay. Well, in conjunction with organisations and tracking stations throughout the world, we're constantly monitoring space to check on any comets or asteroids that could pose a threat to us. We're looking in particular for asteroids of 1 kilometre in diameter or more and to date we've discovered and catalogued about 100 of these big boys. We think there may be as many as 1600 out there."

At that last figure, General Sam Lowther, Air Force Chief of Staff let out a long, high pitched whistle. Lowther was a tall 61-year-old Texan with a permatan and prematurely silver hair.

Crumb liked him instinctively the first time he met him. It was an opinion that hadn't changed in nearly 25 years.

"I hope you got some sharp eyes out there, son," said Lowther.

"Well, General," said McHale, "we thought we had, until we had an unexpected visitor yesterday afternoon at exactly 4.17 EST." He pressed a button on the remote control on his hand and the screen blinked to life. On it, in sharp focus, was the picture of a large rock floating through space.

"Gentlemen," said McHale, "I'd like to introduce you to Homer 3421F."

There were mumbles from around the table as, on the screen in high definition colour, Homer in all his computer-enhanced and artistically-impressioned glory tumbled towards Earth.

"Jeez...he's one ugly son of a bitch," said General Lou 'Pug' DaCosta, Army Chief of Staff, proving conclusively that in life it really does sometimes take one to know one.

"Ah, but beauty's in the eye of the beholder," said McHale. "And right now, Homer thinks that this old planet of ours is the most beautiful thing he's ever seen. So much so that he's headin' straight for us at about 50,000 miles an hour."

"Two questions," said Brigadier General Bryce Stone, the large Marine Chief of Staff sittting about three feet away from him. Looking at him was like looking at John Wayne and The Incredible Hulk's little brother morphed into the one body. "How big is it...and how do we stop it?"

McHale took a deep breath. "Homer's about 15 miles in diameter, near as we can tell. And as of this moment, there's not a damned thing we can do to stop him."

"Now just what the Hellfire do you mean by that, son," said the Texan Lowther, whose voice cut right through the babble of protest generated by McHale's announcement.

"And how come he's right up our ass without so much as a decent damn warning?" added the short, stout DaCosta.

McHale wished he was elsewhere, doing the things every red-blooded male would do given the news he had less than a month to live. Instead he held up his hands in mock surrender.

"Okay, okay – look, why don't I tell you all I know without you shouting at me, then you can shout at me and tell me what you think I should be doing?" He looked to Crumb, who nodded at him and said, "Boys, let's hear what he has to say." The voices calmed down and gradually stopped and all eyes were again on McHale.

The NASA man continued, "Naturally everyone's talking to everyone else on this. Lowell, Arecibo, Goldstone – even the space research boys at Langley. We got the guys at DARPA and the LINEAR program at White Sands in Socorro. We got Joe Buscami from the NEO centre in the UK, Spaceguard in the UK, plus a bucketful of space agencies including Canada, France, Germany, Japan and Sweden." He paused.

"And?" said Crumb.

McHale looked at them in that 'don't kill me I'm only the messenger' kind of way and said, "The general consensus of opinion seems to be that if we had a year it might just be long enough. At this moment they're running around like crazy trying to pluck a damned miracle out of a hopeless situation. And I don't know about you guys, but miracles seem to be in damned short supply these days."

"You mean all our planetary defence strategies are long-term?" asked DaCosta, incredulously.

"Well, General," said McHale, choosing his words very carefully, "the tracking and monitoring systems we have are designed to spot any potential NEO way before it's a threat and give us years to put any plan we decide on into operation."

"But this time we fucked up? Is that what you're saying, son?" drawled Lowther.

"No sir," said McHale, "we didn't fuck up. Two very strange things happened and as of right now we have no idea why they happened or what we can do about it!"

"And they are?" asked Crumb, taking control again from the head of the table.

McHale pressed his remote control again and the scene on the screen image was replaced by a hazy, pixelated image of darkness speckled with indistinct light spots. One of these spots was circled in red.

"What you're looking at is an image of Homer taken last week by the radio telescope at Arecibo, Puerto Rico. Roughly translated, it shows Homer where we expected him to be. Light years away and not even due to come anywhere near us until 2086." He pressed the remote control again and another image filled the screen. This time, the asteroid seemed much larger.

"This was Homer's position as of sixteen hundred hours yesterday afternoon," said McHale, pausing and letting that fact sink in.

Lowther was the first to respond. "Just how damned close is that bastard?"

"At his present speed of about 50,000 miles an hour, Homer should collide at 6.15am our time on the 17th of next month."

"Twenty five days?" gasped Chief of Naval Operations Admiral Shaun Taggart, speaking up for the first time.

Then McHale added the bit about their non-existent defence capability, something he expected they already knew about.

"So," said DaCosta, "somehow this damned rock sneaked past every damned telescope we got and magicked itself from the other side of the galaxy to our own back yard in the space of a monkey fart – and we don't even have jack shit to throw at it?"

"Nothing that works," said McHale. "And nothing that, even if it did work, would either nudge the damned thing away in time, or blow it up into small enough pieces to burn up in the atmosphere on the way down."

"You say Langley is workin' on it?" asked Lowther, stroking his wild-west moustache. "Jeez, Ellis," he said to General Crumb, "those sons of bitches got more black projects on the roll than fleas on a hound. I bet they got somethin' spinnin' round up above us right now that could blast the Hell outa this damned thing."

"Wishful thinking, General," said McHale.

"Wishful my hairy ass," said Lowther. "They're a damned dangerous and resourceful buncha people, son."

"Mister McHale," said Taggart, rubbing the sweat off his bald head, "how in tarnation did we ever get to the spot where all the damned computer hardware in *all* our armaments went down at the very same time? I mean, doesn't the word '*sabotage*' pop up in anyone else's head? I think we're talkin' about terrorism here, gentlemen."

"Of course, Shaun," said Crumb, "why the hell didn't I think of that! And how did they manage the rock? Who brought that here for them – Captain James T. damn Kirk?"

Taggart's mouth opened, but no sound came out.

Crumb held up his hand in apology. "I'm sorry, Shaun," he said, "but the fact is that the more time we spend looking for folk to blame, the less time we got to figure out how to squeeze ourselves out of this mess with our balls intact."

He turned to McHale. "George, who's our Homer expert?"

McHale thought for a second and said, "Well, I suppose that would be the person who discovered him. Daisy Roper."

General Crumb sat bolt upright in his seat. "Daisy? What – *our* Daisy? My *niece* Daisy?"

"The very same," said McHale.

Crumb's smile was full of pride. "Dammit. I never knew."

'Yeah, there's a lot about your Daisy that you don't know', thought McHale. "I've been keeping a discrete eye on her," he said. "She's working for some maverick, privately-funded asteroid-hunting outfit in the UK. Call themselves The Falling Sky Foundation. They're good at what they do. The trouble is they're just too good at it to be doing it on their own. They've got help from somewhere, I just haven't figured out where, yet."

"You think she knows what's happening?" asked Crumb.

"Oh no doubt about it," said McHale with a slightly crooked smile. "If I know Daisy she was probably the first one to see it happen. Homer's her baby."

"Right," said Crumb, "here's what you do. Get in touch with Daisy and get her on the team, unofficially, of course. I don't care what the Hell it takes, have a word with her superiors at this Fallen – whatever."

"Falling Sky Foundation."

"That might be difficult. Harlan Quinn, their Director is a hard man to find. I'll call Daisy direct."

"Whatever," said Crumb. "We need to know if she knows anything we *don't* know!"

"I know what you mean," said McHale.

"And give her my love," said Crumb.

"*I'd rather give her mine – again*", thought McHale.

"Ellis," said Brigadier General Bryce Stone, "if it's all right with you, I think I might have a quiet talk with them boys down at Langley. See if I can incentivise their asses."

Crumb didn't envy *anyone* who Stone had a quiet little talk to. But if anyone could scare the living shit out of spooks, it would be the large marine commander.

"Okay boys," said Crumb, "I'm gonna see The President now. I hope to Hell he's in a good mood before I start, 'cos he's sure gonna be in a damned bad one before I finish."

Twenty Two

"You're gonna *what*?" yelled Father Cooper, in a voice that reverberated round the inside of the limousine where he, Larry Black, and Azriel were discussing the finer points of miracles and the making thereof. The limo was in the open top deck of a multi-storey car park with the highly tinted windows down.

Junior shrugged. "All I said was that maybe doing something like making the sun disappear might be a good way to get peoples' attention."

"Well personally I think it's a great idea. Very imaginative," said Larry, giving Junior the thumb's up sign.

Cooper's voice went up an octave. "*You cannot be serious!*"

Larry threw his hands up and shook his head at the priest. "See, there you go again with the shouting thing. If you want to catch peoples' attention, you need to think *BIG!*"

Cooper glared at him. "I just think it's very drastic. Anyway, people will just say it's an eclipse."

"Not if the sun's not there anymore they won't," said Junior.

"Did you say 'if the sun's not there'?"

"Sure," said Junior. "I mean if they can't find it *because it's not there anymore*, then I think that would make them sit up and take notice, eh?"

"Nope," said Cooper, his voice getting increasingly louder again. "I think that would make them *fly off the planet!* See, no sun, no orbit for the earth and all the other planets in our nice little cosy part of the solar system. *"*

"Hmm, I see your point."

"Okay boys," said Azriel, "How about this then. What if all the nice, dry, hot and sunny places in the world suddenly became wet, cold and horrible? And all the wet, cold and horrible places became dry, hot and sunny. Then after oh, say a couple of hours, it all went back to normal again. That would freak them out, eh?"

"Naaah," said Larry. "The only thing freaky about it would be the freak weather conditions they'd blame it on. What we *really* need is a small but highly impressive event. Something that will get you on the show fast as 'the guy who did that thing'."

"Then Junior here can work his Mojo."

"Hell," said Cooper. "At this rate it will be a miracle if we even *think* of a miracle!"

Suddenly Azriel started laughing. Not a hearty, belly laugh, but a slow, soft weird kinda laugh. The kind that, when you hear it, you *know* that somebody's just thought of something really cool. Something that nobody thought of before. They all looked at the dark angel.

"Hospitals," he said. "Everybody needs hospitals. They're full of sick people either dying or annoyingly getting better. But what if at *one* hospital the power went down, then the emergency power went down – and somehow the juice kept flowing to those machines keeping all those sick people *and new-born babies in those incubator things* alive. Now *that* would be a pretty impressive miracle, wouldn't it?"

"I like the sound of that," said Larry.

Cooper joined in. "Don't forget smartphones," he said.

"Eh?" replied Larry.

The priest reached into a pocket of his jacket and pulled out a smartphone. "Imagine how many people saw a miracle happen, took a photo of it on their smartphone – or even a video – then uploaded it to Facebook or some other social media website. Before you could say Hail Mary it would be halfway round the world, seen by millions!"

There was a pause as all three looked at each other. Cogs were turning. Synapses were firing. Pennies were dropping all over the place.

Eventually Cooper looked at Junior. "You could do this?"

"Barley loaves and fish," said Junior, smiling and nodding confidently.

"Eh?"

"Water and a lovely red wine."

"He means of course he can!" said Azriel.

"In that case timing's the key," said Cooper. "We have to be at the hospital ready to keep the juice flowing the moment the back-up generators fail. Junior here has to be seen to be making it happen. And there can't be any delays with life support machines, right?" They all nodded.

"Hey, I know the very hospital," said Larry. "It's big, it's local, it's community focused – and it's got the perfect name. Holy Trinity. How about *that* for a recipe for a miracle, eh?"

After much nodding of heads Azriel hopped back into the driving seat and they set out for Holy Trinity. Ten minutes later they pulled into the crowded hospital car park. Leaving the limo in the only space left, which was reserved strictly for hospital staff, they headed for the entrance.

"Can't we be a bit less conspicuous?" said Cooper, wondering if he should change into a doctor or a nurse or maybe an ambulanceman. The ambulanceman felt right. "How about a drink in the hospital coffee shop. At least there we can hang out there and nobody will bat an eyelid."

"A man with a cunning plan," said Azriel, leading the way into the hospital and following the signs for a coffee shop called *The Lite Bite*.

"Okay," said Junior shortly afterwards, sitting at a pastel-coloured table next to a plastic plant display and slurping the dregs of a Quadruple Strong Espresso. "That hits the spot! Now it's time to get to work. Anyone know where the maternity unit is?"

"Follow me," said Cooper, now a tall, beefy ambulanceman with a slight tan, shaved head and a pierced left ear. Nobody in the small party could remember the exact time or place that the priest had changed into the ambulance crew member. One second he was Cooper, the next he was Stanley Boone, or so his name badge said.

Three corridors and two flights of stairs later, they were outside the doors to the hospital's maternity unit. No signs were necessary, although there was one. The sound of tiny lungs and vocal chords being exercised was all the indication they needed.

"Okay folks," said Junior, "it's Showtime," he said, looking upwards. "You ready?"

"Ready," said the disembodied voice of Gabriel – and suddenly the lights went out.

"Welcome to my world," said Junior to the others, and he led the way through the door into Maternity Mayhem.

The first thing they realised when they entered was how dark a hospital could be, even in broad daylight, when there are no windows and no lights on. The second was how many people there were running about in the darkness yelling and screaming for the power to come back on again.

They could just about make out the reception desk where what sounded like an extremely agitated woman was shouting into a cell phone. "Yeah honey, you could say I'm a little upset! The damned power's down and the back-up hasn't come on and I got babies up here in incubators – and God help you if you don't the get the power back on NOW! Uhuuh – uhuuh – what? You mean the whole hospital's out?"

The light from torches, grabbed by fumbling hands from cupboards, began flooding the large, open-plan area. Someone ran past them and a young man said to the receptionist, "What they say, Sadie?"

"They say the whole hospital's out and the back-up ain't snapped in. We need power, Charlie – ma babies need power."

Charlie begged to differ. "No ma'am – we need a damned miracle is what we need, if we want to save them babies!"

"Well God better be listenin' now. What the –?"

Her sentence was cut short when she saw Junior who had suddenly started glowing. All around him was a bright, white light. The blue of his eyes had grown even more intense and the enveloping glow moved with him as he walked slowly towards the receptionist.

"He always hears you Sadie," said Junior, his Holy Mojo up and running.

Suddenly, the flash of cell phones illuminated the scene. All around, camera phones leapt into life, held by dozens of hands, eager to capture images of the glowing man and send it to their respective YouTube and Facebook accounts. The snowball was rolling. The blue touch paper had been well and truly lit.

The woman backed away, wide-eyed and fearful. "You – you get away from me you hear?" Then, all of a sudden, she stopped moving and the fear left her face.

"Give me your hands," said Junior, reaching out and allowing her to place her hands in his. The glow that was around him spread to surround her and from the room where the incubators were, a woman screamed, "Sweet Mother of God, they're back on."

"I don't understand," said Sadie, suspiciously. "What you just do?"

"It doesn't matter," said Junior, softly. "Your babies are safe now."

"But they said the power wasn't on," she added, incomprehension creeping into her face.

Junior smiled at her. "Theirs isn't the only power, Sadie. Theirs isn't even the greater power."

A spark of understanding entered Sadie's eyes and she pulled her hands away and crossed herself. She looked down at Junior's t-shirt and the words "Heaven Help Us". "God bless you," she said and she cried softly. "God bless you."

"Go tend to your babies, Sadie," said Junior. Then he turned to Ambulanceman Cooper, Larry and Azriel and said, "Right, I think another one of those delicious coffees is in order," and marched off in the direction of *The Lite Bite* coffee bar. Larry, who was standing rooted to the spot, slack jawed with a look of wonder on his face, had to be dragged from the scene by Cooper. As they left the unit, the power mysteriously returned to the hospital and the lights blinked into life.

They had been in the coffee bar about 10 minutes, when Sadie, accompanied by two large security guards and a conveniently arranged television camera crew burst into the coffee bar. Sadie pointed to Junior and yelled, *"That's him! That's the man who made a miracle happen and saved my babies. That's him sat right there!"*

The TV reporter and cameraman rushed ahead of the others. "Sir," said the young female reporter, "were you responsible for saving the lives of 25 babies in this hospital's maternity unit just a short while ago?"

Around the small team, more camera phones jumped into life, eagerly capturing the unfolding event. The world of social networking had a brand new hero – and déjà vu would never be the same again.

Before Junior could open his mouth to speak, Larry Black interrupted. "Ladies and gentlemen, you may know me, my name's Larry Black. This gentleman here is a personal friend of mine and he will be telling his story exclusively live on my show tonight at 9 on Channel 78. Until then I'd just like to say on behalf of this remarkable man that he's delighted he just happened to be here when the unfortunate power cut hit the hospital.

"And he's glad he was able to help bring the power back on, especially for those beautiful little babies. Now, if you'll excuse us, please." With that, he grabbed Junior by the arm, hauled him out of his seat and guided him towards the exit with a large ambulanceman and a grinning limousine driver following swiftly behind.

"Right," said Larry as they headed for the parking lot and the limousine. "Guess who won't have *any* trouble being the solo guest on my show now!"

"I have to hand it to you," said a smiling Cooper, patting Junior on the back. "That's some Holy Mojo you got there."

As they entered the limo, Cooper once again assumed his true form and, sitting down, wondered how far the health of the Pope had deteriorated. He kept his thoughts to himself, or so he thought.

"*Let's just say we better wrap this thing up quickly,*" said the voice of Gabriel in his head.

Azriel glanced at Junior and nodded. "Nicely done," he said. He seemed to stare blankly into space for a second or two, then he looked at Cooper. "Good news and bad news, shapeshifter."

"Bad news first!" said Cooper.

"Okay. Technology worship's still on the up. All those Facebook posts and Twitter tweets and YouTube videos that have exploded all over the social network about a miracle, have had the ironic effect of boosting the power of technology, instead of pulling it back!"

"Well won't the same thing happen when we go on Larry's TV show?"

"That's where The Boss's Rule number 204 comes in."

"Okay, suppose for a minute I had the faintest idea what the other 203 Rules were, let's presume I temporarily forget what 204 was."

"God has Rules?" whispered a genuinely surprised Larry.

"Of course. You think creating the universe and everything in it – and expecting it to run like clockwork – would be possible without a handy list of do's and don'ts?"

Cooper's mind was racing. "How many of these Rules are there?"

"Oh millions. Billions, maybe. Nobody knows. We think that He either makes them up as He goes along, or they were all there nicely made up right from the beginning. Hard to tell."

"You mean Rules like the Ten Commandments?" asked Larry.

Junior smiled. "Make that 95."

"There are 95 Commandments?"

"Give or take. You only got the Top Ten. Anyway, Rule 204 states: Just because something happens once, doesn't mean it will ever happen again."

The TV show host, used to thinking on his feet, immediately replied. "It also doesn't mean it won't happen again, either."

"True. That's Rule 205. Now, want to hear the good news?"

"Fire away."

"This will all be over sooner than we thought."

"Meaning what?"

"Meaning that instead of having 25 days before Homer collides, we now have 15."

"That's the GOOD news?" shrieked Larry.

"Hang about," said Cooper slowly. "I'm beginning to smell a Heavenly rat here. You mean Homer got faster all by himself – or somebody gave him another helping hand?"

"Haven't a clue. All I know is all I know. So we need to get very, very urgent about things. That okay?"

They all looked at Junior, who seemed to be deep in thought.

"No pressure, then, kid," said the angel.

Twenty Three

Nestling comfortably in the countryside, about 10 miles south of The Falling Sky Foundation in the undulating county of West Yorkshire, England, there was a small, friendly village called Castle Green. It didn't have a castle, neither did it have anything resembling a village green. In fact nobody living in the village knew why on earth the place was called Castle Green at all. Of course that left all kinds of creative options open. For instance, it could easily have been called Carpenter's Ford, because it didn't have either of those.

The village had one main street, two facing rows of proudly kept terraced houses, a sub-post office that doubled as a Buyrite Mini-Mart and senior citizen travel agency, a fully functional classic red public phone box, and a picturesque thatched cottage with a very tall radio mast in its back garden.

The cottage was appropriately enough called 'The Cottage'. The previous occupant tried various names ranging from: The Mansion (they had a sense of humour), and The Small White House, to Chez Higginbotham. But as everyone else in the village kept referring to it as 'The Cottage', they renamed it that and promptly moved.

Four hours before Junior was due to appear on the Larry Black show in California, Daisy Roper, the cottage's owner, woke up and began to get ready for her Night Watcher duty at the Foundation. She was in the shower.

It was precisely at this moment that her cell phone inconveniently decided to bleep into action. All cell phones are taught to do this since birth. Not when you have them in your hand or conveniently nearby. But when you're either on the loo, or being blasted breathless by pulsating water jets, or at the far end of the garden, or dancing to loud music, or at the checkout in the supermarket, or shouting to your mates in a crowded bar, or snoring your head off in a drunken stupor.

Daisy's cell phone delighted in catching her out and was proud of doing so more times than she ever caught *it* out.

150

"This better be good, Wingnut," she said, looking at the caller ID.

She heard her shift partner snigger and reminded herself mentally to do something painful to him at the next available opportunity. "In the shower, or the loo?" he asked.

"Being groped by the local vicar, actually," said Daisy, with feigned excitement. "Now what the Hell is it that can't wait until I get there?"

"Think you better get here quick, then. Somebody's been calling you. American accent."

Tiny little alarm bells started ringing in Daisy's head. "This American accent got a name attached to it?"

"Yup. McHale. Says he's an old friend."

The tiny little bells suddenly got a whole lot bigger and very noisy. They were so loud that Daisy could hardly hear her brain go into overdrive as her emotions bumped into each other with lots of heavy clanging.

"Daisy? You there?" asked Wingnut into the silence outside Daisy's head.

There was a sigh and a soft curse. "His name is George McHale and he's NASA's Assistant Administrator and before you ask we used to have a thing," said Daisy.

"A thing? What kind of thing?" asked Wingnut.

"*A thing!*" said Daisy forcibly. "You want me to spell it out?"

"Spelling it out would be good," said Wingnut, feeling a fantasy coming on.

Daisy slammed the phone down. Fifteen minutes later she was in her dark blue, beaten up, B registration VW Polo travelling the 10 miles between the cottage and the Foundation along winding country lanes at death-defying speeds. The only thing really impressive about the car – more impressive than the fact that it still ran – was her sound system. As she drove, it blasted out her favourite Def Leppard track at a volume loud enough to startle pregnant cows in the field nearby so much that they considered giving birth prematurely.

After the call from Wingnut, she decided to wait until she was at work before calling George McHale. She didn't want him to have her address, cottage landline telephone number, or cell number.

Relationships like the one they enjoyed, based half on lust and half on something to do with handcuffs and leather, had no business trying to extend themselves into full blown love after everything drooped and eventually shrank away into the sunset. That was her story and she was sticking to it, for now anyway.

There was only one thing that he could be calling about and it wasn't her! It must be Homer. But why the hell ask her about something they already knew. They probably already had most of the data she had. The only thing they didn't have was Daisy's intimate knowledge of Homer. Aaah! There was the little jasper. There was the wriggly worm that George 'tattooed bum' McHale wanted to use to hook her. Well, he could pucker his ass and train it to whistle Dixie!

By the time she'd sorted out all that in her head, the Foundation complex could be seen up ahead, brooding moodily on Sutter's Crag, the highest point for miles around. It was also just about the loneliest point, too, which meant no prying eyes or local nosey parker wondering what went on.

For those who idly wondered what it might be like to take a quick peek, there was the razor wire. For those of a more inquisitive disposition, there was always Samson and Delilah.

Samson and Delilah were two of the largest Rhodesian Ridgebacks ever to walk the face of the Earth. Not only did they scare the shit out of anyone who didn't know them, they helped evacuate the bowels of lots of people who *did* know them, too.

Medium tan coloured, with the distinctive dark ridge running down their back, from which the breed took its name, the dogs had been brought to Falling Sky when they were six months old by Harlan Quinn.

Quinn also happened to be a bit of a self-professed expert when it came to animal behaviour, and consequently his training ensured that Samson and Delilah grew up to be the Foundation's protectors. They made the man-killing Hound of the Baskerville seem like a cute little puppy. Or so he thought.

In reality, both dogs were experts in completely fooling Quinn. Whenever he was around, they behaved like the vicious devil dogs he wished them to be. As soon as he left the building, however, they did the doggy equivalent of relaxing and having a few beers.

Actually, thanks to Wingnut, they really did relax and have a few beers. He was their secret Alpha master and they worshipped him with all their canine hearts. Second to him in their affections was Daisy, who always brought them large bones to gnaw on. Probably the remains of the poor cows who died after giving birth prematurely when they heard her in-car music.

Falling Sky was Samson and Delilah's home and everyone in it their family. They regarded it not simply their job, but their lifelong duty and pleasure, to protect their family by giving strangers two things.

The first of these was the pair's highly sneaky 'Bark of Death'. This was very similar to the famous 'Vulcan death grip' in its effect on those unfortunate enough to experience it.

Like the grip, the 'Bark of Death' was so vicious and effective that it rendered its victims completely unconscious for at least half an hour. This, naturally, led to the question 'why the word death?' This always led to the answer, provided by Wingnut, of, "Mind your own damned business."

The second thing Samson and Delilah gave strangers was a deep and lasting understanding that, should anything nasty happen to their family as a direct or indirect result of their visit, then large parts of their bodies would be removed without anaesthetic and with the aid of very large canine teeth.

This second gift was obligatory and happened with every stranger. The first gift, however, could be circumvented by the simple means of an introduction to the two dogs by a trusted member of their Falling Sky family. Even then, the lucky visitor always had the distinct impression that wherever they went, two pairs of large yellow eyes followed them at a discrete distance.

The dogs were also lifelong car enthusiasts. In previous lives they may even have been motor mechanics. Their knowledge was so finely tuned that they could recognise the make and engine capacity of a car before it even came into sight. Sometimes, when the wind was a bit iffy, and if they were bored, they would make side bets as to the make and occupant of the next car to come into sight. More often than not Delilah won. Of the two, her hearing was the better. When it came to smell, though, Samson was king.

So it was no surprise to them when Daisy's car stopped at the electronic entry gates and buzzed security to open up.

It was also no surprise that, on driving through the gates, Daisy lowered her driver's window and threw out two large bones fresh from her fridge.

Using their greeting bark reserved only for very special friends, the two dogs acknowledged the gifts, sniffed the bones then trotted away with them in their mouths, salivating and wagging their tails.

Daisy parked in her usual night duty spot – the one marked H.Quinn in large white letters. The Director was always either away at conferences, away on holiday, away meeting the owners of Falling Sky, gone home by the time she normally arrived or, like now, at the other side of the world.

She liked the tingly, usurping feeling that parking in a forbidden spot gave her. Two minutes later, after sliding her pass card through three security doors, she arrived at the office she shared with Wingnut – a 30 feet by 20 feet box filled with monitors, keyboards and a whole stack of computerised measuring equipment. There was a large barred window, a meeting table and four chairs, plus a chair each for Daisy and Wingnut at their usual monitoring stations. Then there were the plants.

The sign on the door said 'The Jungle' and that just about said everything. Apart from the other things that Daisy and Wingnut had in common, like dangerous space debris and a love of very loud rock music, they also shared a passion for potted plants. Not small, weedy things with a few green leaves and the odd bit of colour, but very large-leaved exotic things that would have felt more at home in an Amazonian rainforest, plus one or two suspiciously mutated growths that twitched enthusiastically whenever human flesh came near.

Wingnut was conspicuous by his absence and by the scrawled note on Daisy's chair that read 'on coffee patrol'.

Daisy dropped her bag on the floor next to her chair and looked at the red voicemail indicator light flashing on her phone. It had been two years since she'd heard George McHale's voice.

Two years, during which she had finally exorcised the ghosts of a very failed relationship and made a home for herself in a new country, with a very well paid job and the prospect of intermittent sex with hairy young Yorkshiremen.

"Oh hell," she thought, "let's get this over with," and she picked up the receiver and pushed the message button.

"Hiya Daisy," said George McHale. "Long time no see. You're probably wondering why I'm calling, right?"

"Stop trying to be nice and get to the point George," she said aloud to the recording. Almost in answer, George continued.

"I need to talk to you about Homer. I think by now you know what's happening. What would you say to a little collaboration? A little NASA/Falling Sky joint operation, so to speak. I'll call again at 7pm your time. Daisy, this is real important. Speak to you in about an hour and a half."

The call ended and Wingnut walked in with two steaming cups of coffee. One white with four sugars for him and one black, no milk no sugar for Daisy.

"Ah," he said, "so you've listened to Captain America then. Sounds a bit on the wet side, if you ask me. Not the sort of rough, unshaven bricklayer you'd normally go for."

Daisy glared in mock anger, picked up the cordless phone, thought for a second or two then punched in McHale's number from memory.

Wingnut spoke to a nearby potted fern. "What does it tell you about a woman when she can immediately recall her ex's phone number *two years* after they break up, hmmm?" The fern listened and, with the aid of the draft from the wall-mounted fan, nodded its leaves sympathetically. Wingnut was fluent in all dialects of fernese.

Daisy ignored him and waited as the US dialling tones fell into place. After about three seconds a man's voice answered. "Yeah?"

"Hello, Mac," said Daisy, instantly recognising his voice and wondering if he would recognise hers unprompted.

"Hello, cupcake," said George McHale and in her mind's eye she could see his face break out into a large grin. It was one of the things that instantly attracted her to him. The other was his inability to halt or hide his blushes.

"Thought I stopped being a cupcake a couple of years ago. Round about the time I started being a stale tart," she said.

"Ooooh," whispered Wingnut. "What a comeback. Stinging, but stylish."

Daisy heard a small, sad little sigh at the other end of the line. Part of her wanted to punch the air in triumph and the rest of her wanted to slap herself silly for being such a bitch.

'*You can't even last two minutes without kicking him in the nuts, can you Daisy,*' she thought. So she decided to be nice. Well, as nice as possible, given the fact that he broke her heart and for two years she fervently wished she could break all his bones.

Her voice softened and took on an interested tone. "So, you want to trade insults, or talk about Homer?"

"The latter, if it's okay with you," he said.

"What's the matter? Can't figure out what he's doing, or how to stop him?"

"We're working on it," he said which, to Daisy, was as good as saying, 'Nope, haven't got a damned clue.'

There was a short pause on the line, then McHale added, "You don't know, do you?"

"Know what?"

"When was the last time you looked at Homer?"

"Yesterday around midnight," said Daisy, suspicion growing in her voice.

"I think you better take another look– like now."

"Why?"

"I'll call you back in half an hour," said McHale and hung up.

Daisy put the phone down, her mind starting to race. She turned to Wingnut. "What's the latest on Homer," she said.

Her partner shrugged. "Same old same old, far as I know."

"I don't get phone calls like that if it's same old same old," she said. "I think some kinda shit's just hit some kinda fan. Let's see what he's up to."

Two minutes later they were looking at an update of Homer's latest position and estimated time and place of collision.

"Fanshit time?" asked Wingnut, seeing the concern in Daisy's face.

"Yup," said Daisy. "He's done it again!"

"Done what again?" said Wingnut.

"Jumped. From where he was before to where he is now, and I don't know how the Hell he did it! What's more, neither do NASA."

"But – but – asteroids don't jump. They don't have jumpability. It's a bloody rock. It doesn't have legs or a propulsion system."

Daisy was frantically punching computer keys. Rows of numbers came up on her screen. "*What?*" she shrieked.

"What *What?*" shrieked Wingnut back at her.

"He hits in 15 days, if we don't hit him first," she said softly, as if saying it any louder would make the asteroid hit sooner.

Wingnut reached out and pulled open the top drawer of his desk. "This is very bad news," he said. "Very bad." He reached in and pulled out a pack of cigarettes. He hadn't touched a cigarette in two months, but kept a stash in the event of a physical or emotional emergency.

He grabbed a lighter from the drawer, got up from his seat and headed for the door. "I'll be back," he said in a grotesque impression of Arnold Schwarzenegger.

Smoking was allowed in the grounds of Falling Sky, but not in the buildings. Wingnut headed for the Foundation's small, courtyard garden with his nicotine comforter.

As soon as he went out the door, Daisy decided to jump the gun and call McHale, but before she could the red hotline phone rang, making her do the jumping. She'd never heard it ring before.

"Hello?" she answered nervously.

"Miss Roper, this is General Parker. How's the situation with our friend Homer?"

"I just got a call from George McHale at NASA," she said. "Homer suddenly got a lot closer and they don't know how he did it. Neither do I."

"How much closer?" asked Parker.

"Well, I've just run the numbers and we're now only 15 days away from the end of everything as we know it. I don't know whether to laugh, cry, or kiss my ass goodbye!"

"But – how?"

"Don't ask me that, I don't have a clue. One minute he was 25 days away and the next he got ten days closer."

"Listen," said Parker, "from now on, I'm placing you in direct charge of keeping an eye on Homer every minute for the next 15 days. I don't give a shit about bloody Harlan. As of this minute, you're calling the shots, understand?"

"But –" protested Daisy.

"No damned buts, Miss Roper. You just got shoved up the peckin' order. Now, you call me every day with an update. And if that damned rock decides to play silly buggers again you shout, y'hear?"

As the general hung up, Daisy sighed, "Loud and clear." She picked up her own office phone and dialled McHale's number. He answered immediately.

"Well?" he said.

"If you knew for sure that you were going to die," she said, "what's the last thing you'd want to do before the end came?"

There was a pause. "You and me in the back seat of a cinema with coke and popcorn watching Casablanca," he said.

"No sex?"

"Naaah. Can't beat a damned good grope in the dark," he said softly.

Suddenly Daisy knew. "You can't stop him, can you," she said.

"Nope. Can't blast him to hell or nudge him off course, cupcake." He then proceeded to tell her about the failure of all the planet's anti-Homer defence systems. His voice sounded sad and tired.

"I was wondering," he continued, "you being the planetary expert astrophysicist on Homer and all, if you had any ideas up your sleeve."

"I'm the expert on Homer, Mac. Not on how to get rid of him. The last time I looked that was *your* job. You're the ones with all the rockets and explosive-type stuff and experts in blowing things up in space and saving the world in the nick of time. Don't you have a Plan B?"

"We got plans coming out of our ears. But none of them are worth shit. We don't need a plan, we need a goddam miracle. I don't suppose you have a spare one lying about, do you?"

"Hang about," she blurted. " I'm not the 'save the world' type, Mac. I'm not heroine material and I have a very healthy disregard for blood and pain of any sort.

"I know about Homer and that's it. I know what he's probably made of. I know roughly how big he is. I know how fast he's travelling and where and when he'll land. Or at least I thought I did. But that's it! Nothing more. Zilch. Nada.

"You want a miracle? You're knocking on the wrong door. Try the damned Vatican. But don't hold your breath, Mac. Miracles don't grow on trees."

She slammed the phone down and cursed silently.

"My grandmother went to Lourdes once," said Wingnut, who had returned, nicotine comforted.

"Where?"

"You know, Lourdes. The place where the Virgin Mary appeared to that girl."

Daisy, whose head was full of Homer, was desperately trying to figure out what Wingnut was talking about.

"What girl?" she said.

"The girl that had the vision of the Virgin Mary!"

Daisy sighed as the story fought its way out of her memory banks and into her conscious thinking. "Okay, I know the story. Nineteenth century France. Girl called Bernadette starts seeing the Virgin Mary. Then people started getting cured and the next thing you know she's a saint. What's your point?"

"Well, maybe miracles only happen if you believe in them enough. Like, how many times have you heard of people praying hard enough for something and then, out of the blue, their prayers are answered."

"Coincidence," said Daisy.

"Bollocks! My Gran had arthritis of the spine before she went."

"And she was cured?"

"Of the arthritis yes. If she hadn't developed double pneumonia and died six weeks later she'd be alive today and fit as a fiddle."

Daisy considered throwing something at him. "So what you're saying then, is that if we can't destroy Homer or nudge him out of the way, everyone in the world should join in prayer and use the holy 'force' to persuade him to bugger off somewhere else?"

"You got a better plan?"

"My head hurts," said Daisy. "I need a large, strong coffee and a little social media escapism. Let's see what's on Facebook and Twitter, eh?"

"Righty ho. I'll be mum," said Wingnut, grabbing his laptop and loading up the sites. It didn't take long. Top-notch equipment was one thing the Foundation wasn't short of.

"Holyfrigginmoly!" he exclaimed 1.5 seconds later. "Something big's happening. Everything's off the charts. Look at these posts. Shit Daisy – I've never seen anything like it before."

Daisy was watching, slack-jawed and wide-eyed.

The world's social media sites have, on any given day – any given minute, in fact – millions of voices holding court on every subject under the sun and the moon. Their diverse personalities and dynamic conversations are what make them so fascinating and addictive.

When Wingnut switched on, there was only one topic of conversation. One word trending. One series of photos, one video capturing the imagination of the viewing planet.

Miracle!

Images of the events at Holy Trinity Hospital, captured by smartphone cameras at the scene, invaded every inch of the web. They fought toe to toe for top spot with video footage from every angle of a glowing Junior and the miraculous return of the hospital power.

Twitter exploded in a frenzy of chatter that threatened to shut the system down. Around 700 million registered users before Junior's hospital visit grew into the billions after it. Whatever was trending before the hospital event disappeared under the unprecedented weight of one word: Miracle.

The Twitter page with the name @juniortherealdeal immediately became the most tweeted name in history.

A Facebook page for Junior appeared, equally mysteriously, and almost within the hour had just over 6 billion friends.

Facebook posts went not just through the roof but through the atmosphere, and image-hosting sites such as Instagram, Tumblr and Flickr had minute-by-minute photo updates of anything connected to the event at the hospital.

By 7pm that evening, YouTube's broadcast of the 'miracle' had clocked up over one billion hits in less than 12 hours, and the world's population was looking forward to tuning in to watch The Larry Black Show. They included believers and non-believers. Roman Catholics and Buddhists. Vatican staff and Pentagon hierarchy. The poor and disenfranchised, and the rich and famous.

Then, an hour before the show was due to be broadcast live, somebody somewhere leaked news about Homer to all the major news networks.

In 30 minutes there was so much traffic on the Internet about the miracle and the impending collision of the asteroid that the system crashed.

With the Internet down, the lure of the TV set on the wall was too great to resist.

Wingnut grabbed the remote control from his desk, punched a button and the screen came to life.

Larry Black was sitting behind a desk and the filmed backdrop was showing familiar scenes from the Holy Trinity Hospital.

Sadie, the large female hospital receptionist was saying: "It's a miracle, that's what it is." Then Larry Black asked viewers to tune into his show at 9pm to see his special guest.

The scene changed to an advert from a company with the answer to all your debt problems. It lasted about three seconds before Wingnut switched the power off and the screen went blank. "So – what you want to do until the show?"

Twenty Four

Some believed the story of Homer instantly and put their faith in their leaders to find a way out of the mess. Some thought about packing and heading for the high ground in the belief that, up there, they would miss the massive tidal waves that would surely come and destroy everything in their paths. Many completely refused to believe that anything like Homer existed and put it down to a massive hoax put about by people who had nothing better to do than scare the shit out of innocent civilians.

Others greeted the news with a sort of weird calmness mixed with awe and a feeling of inevitability. Almost as if they were saying, "Well, we had a fair crack at the whip, but we really buggered things up. So bring it on and let's get well and truly pissed and laid, before the damned thing hits us!"

Then the praying began.

All over the world, people who were either religious or had been at some time in the past, found themselves thinking of their Creator and mouthing the words that made them feel connected to Him, or Her. The consensus of opinion seemed to fall on the side of a 'Him'. They thought about the power and majesty of their true God and they wondered why such a God would send destruction on His world.

Then it was 9pm Pacific Daylight Time in Los Angeles – and whatever time it was in the rest of the world, everyone with a television set tuned in to watch The Larry Black Show. The show was even being broadcast live on radio frequencies planet wide.

At precisely one second after 9, the Internet went back up. Everywhere. Emails. Facebook, Twitter, every social networking site in existence sprang back into life and billions of voices all over the world wanted back in on the act.

At exactly one minute after 9, web technicians all over the world wondered how the Hell the Internet could be back up with no involvement on their part.

From where they were in the hospitality room inside the massive Studio City building in downtown Los Angeles, Larry, Junior, Cooper and Azriel could hear the chants of the studio audience, as they anticipated the start of the show. "*Lareee – Lareee – Lareee!*"

The room had three large leather sofas, a long table on which were various alcoholic and soft drinks, and trays of sandwiches and snacks. On one of the walls were large monitors linked to the studio cameras, showing the images being sent to every TV set in the world with the ability to receive them and, curiously, even sets without the ability.

Cooper was looking nervous.

Larry was smiling. "What's the matter, Father? You never worked an audience before? Never had a church full of halleluiah folk in the palms of your hands from up there on the pulpit?"

"Nope. Never had a parish. Went straight to the Vatican."

"You don't know what you've missed."

Azriel smiled and gulped a large G&T. "Some folks are crowd people and some folks just aren't."

Larry turned to Junior. "You ready?"

"Not without a group hug he's not!" said a disembodied voice that suddenly became very bodied in the shape Gabriel, accompanied by Bob and MoMo.

"Hey kid," said the little angel, bounding over to Junior. "Didn't think you'd get away without a pat on the back, well maybe the leg, did ya?" he said.

"What the – who the –?" said Larry, as the newcomers appeared out of thin air.

"We thought you might need a little moral support," said Gabriel. "I brought some friends. Larry – meet Bob, he's an angel, sort of. And MoMo. Well – they don't make them like him any more. He's an Oracle, but don't ask him anything. His mojo isn't operating at full power. But he can still guess pretty good."

"I got a feeling –" said MoMo, ignoring the introductions. He was standing with his giant bulk propped against one of the walls, with his head about six inches from the ceiling, holding his head in his hands, with two of his eyes, the normal two, tightly closed. The other eye, however, was doing something very different.

"Bugger," said Bob, looking at his large friend. "It's opening!"

The others looked at MoMo's forehead and they could see a slit appear in a large bump on the middle of his forehead.

"What the blue blazes is *THAT*?" blurted Larry.

"It's his third eye, kiddo," said Gabriel, excitedly pointing to MoMo's head. "He's got it up and running again."

"Oh boy – I got a feeling," said MoMo again, with a surprised look on his face.

"Yeah, we heard you the first time," said Azriel. "Now how about telling us what the feeling is!"

"It's kinda tingly."

The dark angel flapped his hands in an attempt to get MoMo to elaborate, which was completely useless since the large oracle couldn't see anything. "Tingly like what? Like a tickle? An electric shock? Is it a good tingle or a bad one?"

Cooper went over to MoMo and gently touched his arm. "Maybe if you opened your eye thing a bit more it might help."

MoMo squeezed his head harder, let out a painful grunt and the middle eye popped wide open.

"Quick," yelled Ralph, "ask him a question!"

"Will we succeed?" blurted out Cooper, before anyone else could think of anything either relevant or even irrelevant to say.

"Yes!" said MoMo emphatically. "And no–"

"What kind of an answer is THAT?"

Ralph leapt to MoMo's defence, standing in front of him and facing the others like a brave but very nervous rabbit staring down the throat of a pack of hungry hounds.

"Wait a minute – wait a minute," he said, holding his hands up, defensively.

"That's how he works. No definitive answers. Just possible options and everything's open to interpretation and discussion."

"Some kinda Oracle *he* is!" said Larry. "Either he can tell us what's gonna happen, or he can't. I mean, my aunt Alice could give you a whole bucketload of possibilities but that doesn't make her a damned Oracle."

"Hey," yelled Gabriel, "he's a very talented individual. I'll have you know MoMo has certificates of authenticity from very important sources!" He turned to MoMo and gently said, "Could you, emm – elaborate?"

MoMo's middle eye blinked. "Yes we'll succeed, but no we won't get rid of the rock," he said, then he let out another groan and the eye popped shut.

"Pardon my grasp of logic and clarity," said Larry. "But how can we get rid of the rock and still have it hanging around?"

The Oracle sighed. "Of course, it could be the other way around. Sometimes these predictions can be very sneaky."

"You mean that we won't succeed and we *will* get rid of the rock?" asked a confused Cooper, who was reaching for a bottle of very strong German lager.

At that point, Junior stood up and said, "Right, that's enough. Let's get this show on the road. Larry, do your thing and I'll do mine and with a bit of luck you'll all be happy people instead of squished bits of meat lying around on a dead planet, okay?"

"You guys can watch from in here," Larry said, pointing to a large screen on the wall as he walked to the door. He opened it and just before he went out of the room, he stopped, turned and looked at them all. "Nice knowing you. Now, let's go save the world!"

"Amen to that!" said Cooper, who took a large swig from his lager and realised that he hadn't had a drink of alcohol of any kind in years. He sat down heavily on the nearest sofa and wondered why his legs felt kinda funny.

"Before you go on," said Gabriel to Larry, "I think you should know that about fifteen minutes ago somebody leaked the news about Homer to the world's press, so things might get a little hairy out there. They don't know the full details, but they probably know enough to be scared as Hell. So who do you think they're going to turn to in their hour of need to save them again?"

Larry smiled. "Now that's what I call timing!" he said. "I wonder if we could get anyone from the military or the Pentagon on the line during the interview. Ooooh – I can feel my juices starting to flow."

"Well be careful it's just not you peeing your pants," said Azriel. "This is where we separate the men from the boys, and those with very good intentions from those with very bad breath."

Larry walked out of the room feeling the rush of excitement that normally preceded a show, only this time it was infinitely stronger.

As he walked along the corridor leading to the set and the chanting audience, the hairs on the back of his neck stood up and saluted and he could feel something approaching bliss, only without the sweaty fumblings.

The closer he got, the louder the audience was. He was completely focused on the entrance to the set – the doorway into the lion's den – and he walked onset, smiling, with his hands held high in salute, to the rapturous roar of "Lareee – Lareee – Lareee!"

The chants continued for another minute or so while the 'Applause' sign was lit up. Then the 'No Applause' sign blinked into life and the audience gradually quietened down.

Larry was wearing his sincere smile, only unlike most or even all other talk show hosts, it actually was sincere. This was his world and he loved every second of it.

As he walked across the stage to his seat he spoke to the audience. He was smiling and rubbing his hands together. "Thank you – thank you ladies and gentlemen. Boy, have we got a show for you tonight. I can't tell you how excited I am. So, let's have a big welcome to the rest of the world who, we hope, is watching this, the most unique and life-changing Larry Black show ever!"

The cameras turned on the audience who, as one voice, shouted "Welcome!" to the viewing audience. There were whoops and cheers and a few high-pitched screams here and there. By then Larry had reached his seat, which was one of two identical comfy leather armchairs with a small coffee table between them containing a large pitcher of water, two glasses and a microphone.

"Okay now," he said, sitting down, rubbing his hands together and scanning the audience. "How many of you believe in miracles? Put your hands up." Nearly all of the audience put their hands up.

"Now lets be absolutely clear. We're not talking about magic tricks or special effects. We're talking about things that can't be explained by some scientist in a lab coat. This isn't Hollywood. This is miracle time, pure and simple. So – how many of you are believers?"

He looked at the sea of hands held high and nodded his head in approval. "Pretty impressive. Okay. So, how many of you have seen living proof of a miracle? Undisputed, no doubt about it!"

Nearly all the hands went down.

"I see we still have one or two hands up," he said, grabbing the hand microphone from the table and walking towards the upraised hands.

He stopped at a large black woman with flat, twisted hair, wearing a multicoloured kaftan.

Larry turned to the audience. "Ladies and gentlemen, I'd like to introduce you to a very remarkable woman." He turned back to the woman, "Tell everyone your name, ma'am."

In a nervous, soft voice that belied her size, the woman said, "My name is Sadie Main and I'm the Head Receptionist at the Holy Trinity Hospital's Intensive Baby Care Unit."

On hearing this, the audience broke into spontaneous applause.

"I'm sure you and all the other dedicated staff at Holy Trinity do a fabulous job, Sadie. But something very special happened today, didn't it?" Sadie was nodding her head and smiling. Larry continued, " –something, if I may use the word, miraculous. You want to tell us about it?"

Sadie grabbed the mike. "Yes, Larry, I do," she said, enthusiastically. "I want to tell the whole world about it!"

Larry smiled at her. "Well, we got the whole world ready with their ears pinned back just for you. So – what's the story?"

"Well, Larry, at the unit we have 25 very sick newborn babies in incubators. These babies need all the love and care we can give them."

The audience was hushed.

Larry interrupted. "I'm sure you guys do a fantastic job, Sadie. So, tell us what happened this afternoon."

"Yes sir. Well, The power went down all over the hospital. Maternity unit, operating theatres, intensive care, everywhere!"

The audience gasped.

"Okay now, let's get this straight. You're saying that every piece of equipment that was helping those babies stay alive suddenly stopped working?"

"Yes sir!"

There was another gasp from the audience as Sadie told the story of Junior's visit and how the power was miraculously turned back on again, saving the babies.

"And this was the man?" asked Larry turning and indicating a large screen dropping from the ceiling at the back of the stage. On the screen were images of Junior, glowing, at the hospital.

Sadie looked at the screen and screamed. "That's him. That's my miracle man!"

The audience gasped again – some even screamed – and the flickering of hundred of flashes filled the studio, as did the musical bleeps of tweets arriving at, and being sent from cell phones. Half the audience immediately began punching phone keys. The other half was still mesmerized by the image on the screen.

"See that?" yelled Sadie. "That was the glow of Heaven, that's what it was! And he told me my babies would be okay and then the power came back on to the unit."

"So the electricians got the back-up generator working again?" asked Larry.

"No sir – oh no! I called them to thank them for getting the power back on again and they said 'what are you talking about, the power's still off'. They didn't get it working again for another five minutes! That man did it, Larry. I don't know how but it was a miracle. He said God heard my prayers. He saved my babies."

Sadie began to cry and as the camera panned round the audience there were tears flowing there too. Then somebody started applauding and more people joined in until the whole audience was on their feet cheering and yelling, "Sadieee – Sadieee – Sadieee!"

Larry walked back to his seat and sat down and waited for the noise to die down. "Now," he said, "my special guest tonight is without doubt the most charismatic individual who ever walked the face of the earth. He's the man who walked into Holy Trinity Hospital earlier today and did something no other person alive could do. He's the man that millions of people all over the world have waited a long time to welcome back. The first time round, they called him the Son of God. Tonight I'd like you to welcome him by the name given to him by his dear old dad – Junior."

Right on cue, with the show band playing 'Stairway to Heaven' Junior walked on stage, smiling. Gone were the jeans and t-shirt. Gone were the sports trainers. Gone was the casual air. This was Junior with his mojo turned on and turned up. This was Junior in a black suit, black shoes, black shirt open at the neck. This was showtime.

Soft as a whisper that grows in intensity, the audience started chanting, "Joooonior – Joooonior – Joooonior" over and over again, louder and louder, until you could hardly hear yourself think over the deafening roar.

Some people left their seats and tried to approach the stage, only to be turned back by large 'security' men with shaved heads and impressive muscles. Some decided that this was as good a time as any to fall into a religious fit, which brought on-site medical attendants running to help, although what modern medicine could do to stave off the effects of holy ecstasy God only knew.

Most, though, simply sat in their seats and fondled the small wooden gift crosses each had been given as they came into the studio.

Junior, who had until then been standing and acknowledging the applause, shook hands with Larry and sat down opposite him. As he did so, Larry softly whispered, "Mojo working?"

"No problemo," said Junior.

Larry turned to the audience and exclaimed loudly, "Wow – how about that for a welcome!"

"Better than the last time," said Junior. That brought a few nervous laughs from the audience.

"So, Junior," said Larry, "you say you're the Son of God."

"Oh no," said Junior. "I'm not falling for that again. Talk about being set up!"

"You mean you're *not* the Son of God?" said Larry, looking confused. "But –"

"Look Larry, I'm just an ordinary guy. Except I was in the right place at the right time – a long time ago. Of course you could say I was in the wrong place at the wrong time, but that's all history now.

"Everybody else calls me the Son of God, but He always calls me Junior, it's a kinda family thing. I don't exactly call Him 'dad' or 'pop' or 'father' or any of that. There are some things you just don't do if you want to carry on with all your organs in the right place. It's like respect, know what I mean?"

"Absolutely," said Larry, reaching for a glass of water to pour down his rapidly drying throat. He began to feel the change in Junior's voice and tried not to look into his eyes, but it was no use. He felt the power of the Holy Mojo creep over him as it was beginning to creep over the audience.

It started with a warm kind of comforting feeling and Larry felt himself relax in his chair. It was a bit like taking happy pills – through the ear.

Larry was about to speak when someone shouted from the audience.

"Fraud!"

"Pardon?" said Larry, flustered.

"Pimple-headed simpleton!" the voice shouted again.

The audience gasped and as one turned to where the voice was coming from. There, sitting in the back row, was an ancient looking, shrivelled up man dressed entirely in black, with long white hair.

"You're not the only Son of God – in fact you're not even the firstborn!" he yelled.

"And why would that be?" said Larry, thinking fast and deciding that a 'doubting Thomas' in the audience might be a great idea.

"Because I AM!" yelled the man even louder.

Backstage, Gabriel and Azriel were looking at each other after seeing the old man on the monitor.

"How the hell did he get here?" said Gabriel.

"Don't ask me. Last time I checked he was in a monastery in Tibet. This is all very awkward."

"Well, who is he?" asked a confused Cooper.

"A very large spanner in the works," said Gabriel.

"He's Arthur," said Azriel. "Junior's older brother. You could say he's the black sheep of the family."

Back in the audience, Larry was looking at Junior who had the beginnings of a frown on his face. Things were not going according to plan.

"Oh yeah," said the old man, sarcastically. "He's got you all cheerin' and gaspin'."

There was a growing mumbling in the audience as the stranger stood up with the aid of a large wooden staff and forced his way past a dozen or so sets of legs to the end of the back row and stood at the top of the aisle looking down at Junior with anger and triumph in his eyes. "Well," he said, "don't you have anything to say to your big brother?"

There were more gasps from the audience and a few very sensitive souls fainted.

"Hiya bro!" said Junior. "Long time no see." He turned to Larry. "Got another chair for my prodigal brother?"

In Larry's earpiece, the show director was screaming in Larry's earpiece. "This is bloody fantastic. I thought we had the biggest coup since – well ever! Now we got *two* coups. Get the old bugger down, this is brilliant, this is career making. There are billions of people watching all over the world. There might even be an Emmy in it, if we live that long!"

As another chair was brought onto the set, Arthur, God's eldest son, hobbled down the steps. The audience, who had been shocked at this new development, suddenly became very vocal and soon Arthur's name was being chanted as loudly as Junior's was shortly before. On hearing this, Arthur's anger evaporated and he was smiling as he reached the stage.

Larry shook Arthur's hand and the old man sat down next to Junior.

The TV show host looked shell shocked. It was almost as if he didn't know what to say or do next. As if getting the Son of God onto his show wasn't enough, he now had TWO sons and a million questions to ask. However, he also had to remember why Junior was here in the first place, so he decided to start there.

He called for calm and gradually the audience fell silent. "Guys – guys," he said, shaking his head, "I have a million questions to ask just one Son of God, never mind two!" That brought laughter from the audience. Larry immediately held up his hands and the audience gradually fell silent.

"But before we get to that I have an announcement to make. Now, it's a very serious announcement, so I want you all to listen closely. Normally, we ask our audiences to switch their cell phones off as soon as they come into the studio. We didn't do that tonight because this show is so special we wanted you to take as many photos as you want. But this also means that any minute now some of you will be learning, on your cell phones, about a very serious threat to our world. A threat that, well, I'm sorry to say, is very real and could mean the end of all life on earth. Not in centuries, or decades or even years – but in 15 days."

Larry paused to let the news sink in. God I love my job, he thought.

There were gasps and murmurs, with a few frightened screams sprinkled here and there. Nobody moved.

All eyes were on Larry.

Then, the sounds of beeps, purrs and assorted musical ringtones filled the studio and hundreds of cell phones announced Homer's imminent arrival.

Nothing is as motivating to a captive audience as a nice, juicy story about a large asteroid colliding with Earth, destroying everything and everyone in its path.

Nothing is as scary to an innocent exit door as a rabid mob looking for a way out.

There are two times in their otherwise bored lives when exit doors are popular. The first is when crowds of people head directly for them, in an orderly fashion, after enjoying themselves at a movie, or play, or musical event. Exit doors love well-behaved crowds.

The second is when similar crowds of people are told that the world is about to end and they have to get the Hell out of wherever they are as quickly as possible, with no thought of who they might have to stomp on to leave the premises. Exit doors hate bad news, ill-behaved crowds and the sounds of people screaming in pain as they're being trampled on by inconsiderate feet.

In the Larry Black studio, a crowd of the former persuasion suddenly became a crowd of the latter. All Hell thought very seriously about breaking loose as news of Homer triggered the primitive, automatic 'fight or flight' response in most of the audience. They chose flight.

Then, as the doors braced themselves for the inevitable violence of pushing and shoving, squashing and squeezing, something unexpected happened.

Junior switched on his mojo and spoke four words.

"Hang on a minute," he said, softly.

"It wasn't the kind of 'hang on a minute' that tries to persuade you to slow down and think twice about what you're about to do. It wasn't the kind that you completely ignore because it hasn't given you a good enough reason to stop and listen.

It was the kind of 'hang on a minute' that didn't need to shout to make itself heard above the loudest sound in the universe. The kind that doesn't need to go in through the ears to make every molecule in the body put on all kinds of brakes and burn rubber in the process.

Everyone hung on a minute like their lives depended on it.

They would have hung on for the rest of their lives if the voice they heard had asked them to.

Junior spoke again. "Now don't panic. There's nothing to be scared of. In fact the best thing you can do at the moment is go back to your seats, sit down, make yourself nice and comfy, and hear how the world's going to be saved."

That's exactly what they did. Without a word. All in a nice, orderly fashion.

Curiously enough, that's exactly what the rest of the viewing world did, too. All over the planet, people who were beginning to work themselves up to Armageddon fever pitch, thinking of preparing their own versions of the last supper, calmed down immediately and came back to their armchairs in front of the TV. Some with a nice coffee. Some with a very large whisky.

Others with the longest spliff they could possibly roll and smoke, without worrying about falling over.

Junior looked at Larry and nodded.

Backstage, Gabriel grinned. "That's my boy," he murmured.

Onstage, Larry looked to the cameras and switched on his show face. "Okay, keep watching, because now we're gonna find out exactly who's gonna save the world – and how."

The fact that he had no answer to either question didn't matter.

"In the red corner," he said, gesturing to his two guests, "we have the joint Sons of God, Junior and Arthur. And in the blue corner," this time he gestured to a large screen behind him, "we have the Chairman of the Joint Chiefs of Staff, General Ellis P. Crumb, on a live link from the Pentagon."

The screen blinked to life and Crumb was sitting behind a desk facing the camera and wearing a uniform weighed down with ribbons and medals. Behind him, on the wall, were photographs taken with various presidents and on the desk in front of him was a model of a lunar landing module.

"Good evening, General," said Larry, "thanks for joining us tonight, I know you must be pretty busy right now."

General Crumb looked decidedly uncomfortable. "Thank you for having me on the show–"

Larry interrupted. "So, can you give us the latest news on what measures you're taking to stop the rock, which I gather is called Homer?"

"We're doing everything we can. At this moment satellite stations all over the world are monitoring Homer's progress every step of the way. We know how big he is, how fast he's travelling and where exactly he's heading for."

Larry looked impressed and the audience voiced their approval and seemed to relax, safe in the knowledge that they were in good hands.

"So," Larry continued, "tell us how big this sucker is."

"Well, he's around 15 miles in diameter."

"Wow! Fifteen miles – that's a helluva damned big rock, sir, if you don't mind me saying so."

"It's – not small," said Crumb, in some discomfort.

In the hospitality suite, Azriel was smiling. "Larry my boy, you are a sneaky sonofabitch. I like you more and more."

Back on set, Larry continued, "And we're gonna blast that rock right out of the sky, is that right General?"

Now discomfort was turning to dribbly little sweat rivers on the side of Crumb's face. "Well – unfortunately we can't do that," he said.

There were shocked gasps from the audience.

"We can't?" said Larry, putting on a shocked face. "Why not?"

Crumb was under orders not to disclose the technology failure, although he guessed that it wouldn't be long before the word got out.

"It's too close," he said, knowing that at least that wasn't a complete lie.

"It's a fortnight away, General," countered Larry, who shrugged and turned to the audience as if to say, "What's the problem?"

"How much time would you need?"

"Well a year would be good," said Crumb, who had now taken a handkerchief from his pocket and was dabbing the sides of his face.

"A year?" exclaimed Larry. "What the Hell do you want to do, write a book about it before it hit us?"

"Well, it takes that long for the plans we have to be put into operation. But maybe we could do it in, say, nine months," said Crumb, looking and sounding a little pathetic and helpless.

"So," said Larry, "what you're saying is you can't stop good old Homer from smacking into the planet at God knows how many miles an hour in a fortnight's time. That what you're saying?"

"There's no point not being honest about this," said Crumb. "We can't stop the rock and we can't deflect it from where it's headed."

"Which is?"

"At its present trajectory, final destination should be England in the UK."

"Sounds like we all better head for high ground when Homer hits," said Larry.

"I'm afraid that won't do any good," said Crumb, sadly. "This rock is bigger than the one that destroyed the dinosaurs."

"*Wowowowow – hang on there General.* Are you saying that we might as well kiss our asses goodbye when this thing hits?"

"I'm sorry, son," said Crumb. "But right now, all the technology we have means jack shit. What we need is a goddam miracle. And they don't grow on trees."

There were shocked gasps from the audience.

"Unless," exclaimed Larry in triumph and gesturing to Junior and Arthur, "you happen to have not one but TWO Sons of God on your side!"

Crumb sounded tired. "Son – I don't mean to pop your balloon, but have you any idea how many Sons of God there probably are in funny farms throughout America, let alone the rest of the world?"

"Six thousand three hundred and forty seven," said Arthur in a matter-of-fact way.

"How the –?" said Larry, genuinely impressed.

"So I keep count!" said Arthur, shrugging. "It's not a crime. When you got that many folk all claiming to be your brother it's hard work keeping touch with them all, especially when it comes to remembering birthdays."

"What about Daughters of God?" asked Larry, who knew always knew how to throw a controversial spanner or two into the works.

"What about them?"

"Sorry, I don't have any sisters," said Junior.

"Oh yeah? Who says so?"

175

The thought of Junior having sisters brought even more gasps from the audience. Even a ripple of applause.

"Guys, guys," said Larry. "I think we need to focus on the problem. We're in deep trouble here and it seems to me there's only one way out."

He turned to the camera. "Ladies and gentlemen, I was at Holy Trinity Hospital this afternoon and I saw with my own eyes exactly what happened. Now, I'm not a churchgoer, haven't been for many, many years.

"I suppose you could say I've become a bit of a cynic when it comes to believing the unbelievable. But sometimes, science just isn't enough for an event that's so fantastic that it defies all logical explanation." Larry pointed at Junior and turned back to face the cameras.

"This afternoon, ladies and gentlemen, I witnessed what I could only call a miracle. I don't think there's any other word for it. When this man did something that nobody else in the world could have done, I found myself believing in the power of God once again."

Larry wasn't just talking to the studio audience, he was talking to the global one, and he had them in the palm of his hand. The show was his pulpit and the sermon was an object lesson in faith and belief, and they lapped it up.

As he looked at the monitors backstage, Cooper smiled and said, "Larry my friend, you should have been a priest," and realised that, after his third bottle of strong lager, he could now no longer feel any part of his body below his waist.

"Oh, it can always be arranged," said Gabriel. "A little adjustment here, a nip and tuck there. I could take that raw material and make a very nice priest out of him."

Back onstage, Larry turned to Junior and said, "Okay, you have no problem with me. I'm the guy who believes. I'm the guy who saw you do the impossible. So here's the thing. Here we are – teeny tiny planet in the middle of all this vast space. Very insignificant."

He paused. "But we're about to get wiped off the face of the Earth. Our species and every other species on this planet will become extinct – thanks to this space rock. We can't use any of our weapons to knock it out of the sky.

"And it's not about to turn around and go back to where it came from. So I guess you could say we need a miracle and we need one pretty damned quick. Now I know you can do this. I believe in you. So whaddya say?"

There was silence. Larry was looking at Junior, as was the studio audience and the rest of the world.

"Nope," said Junior, shaking his head. "I can't do this."

Now Larry was genuinely confused and shocked. "What?" he blurted out, as the audience gasped and screamed and said the things that people usually say when they see their last hope disappearing down the plughole.

"That's not how it works," he said.

"Well how *does* it work, then?" asked Larry, wondering what was coming next since Junior's refusal had thrown everything up in the air.

Then Junior switched on his holy mojo again.

"It works because you, and you, and you, and all of you want it to work," he said pointing to various people in the audience, ending up pointing at the camera to the watching world.

"The power to perform miracles doesn't lie with me. It lies with all the people who believe in God and pray to him.

"The more people who believe in Him, the stronger He is and the more miracles that can be performed with His power, in His name. The trouble is, these days there are fewer and fewer people believing in Him. Instead, you're putting your faith in the things you make. All the technology you've developed to make your life easier and safer.

"But technology doesn't do miracles. It just does stuff and makes life easier. And when it lets you down, when the technology doesn't work, there's nothing left for you to believe in, because you've forgotten to believe in the one thing that's bigger and more powerful than all the technology you'll ever create.

"You've forgotten your own Creator. Your own God."

You could have heard a pin drop in the studio. The power in Junior's voice and in his eyes was irresistible. Everyone who heard and saw him automatically and completely believed in him and in everything he said.

It wasn't as if he was preaching dissent or moral righteousness or telling them to turn the other cheek or love thy neighbour.

It was simply that, listening to him, it was as if following his words was the most natural and obvious thing to do.

Junior reached out to them. "Without each other, what do you have? Empty lives. And right now, you need each other more than ever before. This rock, this asteroid that threatens your very existence, also threatens His."

The audience gasped again and some of them started crying. There was even the odd moan of despair.

"You mean Homer is more powerful than God?" asked Larry, as he heard his director's voice in his ear saying, "Bloody hell...we just went live in every country in the world....every damned country!"

"No of course he isn't!" said Arthur. "But if His power comes from man and man isn't believing then you got a big problem, sonny."

"So what do we do?" asked Larry.

From the large screen, General Crumb said, "Well Hell son, I don't know about you, but I'm gonna go home, grab my wife and children, get down to our local church as fast as I can and start prayin'." And with that, he got up from his seat and went off-camera.

"I couldn't have put it better myself," said Junior. "Look at the math. The more people get down on their knees and pray, the stronger God gets, the more power he has. Next thing you know, we got a miracle. Homer gets blasted out of the sky, care of the combined prayers of the human race! Job done and we can all go home!"

"Except he can't get blasted anywhere," said Arthur.

"What?" asked Junior, whose turn it was now to be confused.

"That's what I'm here to tell you. That's why I made the damned journey all the way from Tibet, you wally. You can't hurt Homer."

"He's a damned rock," said Larry. "You telling us now he has feelings?"

"Absolutely," said Arthur. "He's sentient!"

Larry's eyes grew wide in surprise. "Homer's a lifeform?"

"A very large one," said Arthur, smiling. "So you see – unless you want to have on your conscience the fact that you killed the largest lifeform ever discovered, you better switch to Plan B. That is, if you have a Plan B."

That shut the audience up.

Backstage, Gabriel looked at Azriel. "I think I can feel an 'oops' coming on," he said.

"Oops!" said MoMo turning round and striking the wall behind him, leaving a large, fist-sized hole in the plaster. "I knew there was something I had to tell you. I tried to squeeze it out, but it just disappeared from inside my head before the words came out my mouth." He looked wretched. "Sorry."

"Well, big guy, small brain – just can't get the staff anymore!" said Azriel, who had taken to flicking a coin in the air and seeing whether it landed heads or tails on his hand.

"Meanwhile, back at the ranch," he added, looking at Gabriel, "how did a tiny fact like a sentient asteroid slip past the guards, eh?"

Gabriel looked back at him with a mixture of confusion and worry in his eyes.

Back onstage, Larry was glaring at Arthur, "Sentient or not, isn't it a case of either we kill it or it kills us? I mean pardon me for being a measly little planetary inhabitant who desperately wants to live, but isn't this a bit clear cut?"

Arthur pounded the floor with his staff. "No! No! No!" he shouted, angry white spittle forming at either side of his mouth. "Hasn't Star Trek taught you lot anything? You don't kill a sentient lifeform under any circumstance."

"Bugger that for a game of billiards!" said Larry, equally as forceful. "Lifeform or not, I don't care if it can compose a symphony, write a best seller or bring knowledge from the other side of the galaxy. It's either it – or us. And personally, I prefer us!"

"Murderer!" yelled Arthur.

"Dickwad!" yelled back Larry. "Anyway, how do you know it's sentient, eh?"

"I know he's alive because I spoke to him," said Arthur, softly.

Larry turned to Junior. "He can do that?"

"Oh, yeah," said Junior, nodding his head. "He might be a bit short on the old miracle talent, but he's a dab hand at lots of other spooky stuff. Like knowing what you're thinking before you even decided to think it might be a good idea to think it.

"And staring into space for years without moving a muscle or blinking. Except for eating, drinking, going to the loo and sleeping, that is. Then there's all that 'seeing ghosts' and other weird shit. So if he says he spoke to Homer, he spoke to Homer!"

"Okay," said Larry, "so what did the big rock say?"

Arthur looked kinda strangely at Larry. Like he was looking at a child who was misbehaving but didn't know any different, because he was, after all, just a child.

"Homer doesn't talk the way you or I talk. It's like he puts a feeling inside your head and you just know what he means."

"And the feeling was?" said Larry.

"Coming home," said Arthur.

"Coming home?" said Larry. "And he just said this to you right out of the blue, while you were out there in Tibet contemplating the stars or your navel or whatever?"

"Oh no," said Arthur. "Jacob Crow introduced us. Homer said it to him first and then he said it to me. And then I woke up."

Larry half-laughed. "You mean, you mean this all happened in a dream?"

"All my visions happen in dreams. How on earth do you expect me to talk to a sentient rock that's millions of miles away? By phone?"

That brought laughter from the audience.

"And who is this Jacob fella?"

"Crow. His name is Jacob Crow," said Arthur.

"Right. So who is Jacob Crow?"

"Haven't a damned clue," said Arthur.

Twenty Five

Just then, there was a commotion at the entrance to the studio. A security guard was shouting, "Sorry, sir, but you can't come in here – and you sure as Hell can't bring that in!"

The shouting was followed by the deep, sonorous moan of a didgeridoo, an Australian aborigine wind instrument. The sound lasted about ten seconds and then, through the entrance and into the studio came a small, slightly disheveled and very old aborigine male, dressed in a pair of old jeans and a checked shirt, open at the neck showing a mat of grey chest hair.

The hair on his head was long and wild and frizzy and grey, and his face was mostly covered in a white, slightly matted beard. There were two younger and taller aborigine males following him, one carrying a large sack over his shoulder and the other carrying a long, carved didgeridoo, no doubt the one heard moments before.

With his escort in tow, the old man walked up to the stage, completely oblivious to the audience who were showing a mixture of gobsmackedness and curiosity.

"Well bugger me," said Arthur, "It's Jacob!"

As he reached the stage, the old man looked at Arthur and said, "G'day, mate. I come to your country now. I'm Jacob. We spoke before, in the dreaming time about the sky rock. I think all you fellas want to know what the rock's up to. So I've come. Now you can hear my words. Hear what Jacob says is true. Not bollocks."

Jacob looked at Junior. "G'day, mate. Your spirit is strong from the father. But your God is sick, mate. You're gonna need all the fellas in every land to give him power again. The sky rock has the power, mate, so you gotta keep it safe."

He turned to the young aborigine with the sack and nodded. The young man stepped forward, put the sack carefully on the stage and undid the rope keeping it shut. He grabbed the bottom, upended it and a large snake slithered out.

"This is my totem," said Jacob, as Larry yelled and jumped out of his seat. Arthur and Junior stayed where they were, neither showing the slightest fear.

There were one or two screams from the audience.

Jacob continued, "This is my tribe's symbol of Almudj the Great Rainbow Snake. Her birthplace is Uluru. The sky rock is one of her children come home after his long journey to see the stars. His name is secret because he was her firstborn. This is his story," and he sat down on the stage cross-legged and began the tale.

"There are many stories of Uluru and how she was born. There is the story of how two boys playing with mud made her. That story is a good story, but that story is not the true story. Listen to the true story of the beginning of everything.

"In the time of Alcheringa, what you whitefellas call the Dreaming, the world was flat and empty. The Great Snake was asleep under the ground with all the animals in the world in her belly waiting to be born. When it was her time, she pushed up to get out of the ground.

"But on top of her were two great rocks, blocking her way. The Great Snake had power then. Big power. So she pushed and the great rocks came up from the ground with her.

But she pushed so hard that the bigger of the two rocks, which was her firstborn, flew off the land and into the sky. He was a boy and strong. He was sad to go but it was his job to tell the stars about the Great Snake.

"The smaller rock, the second born, was a beautiful girl. It was her job to stay and be the home of the Great Snake's spirit. This was Uluru what you whitefellas call Ayres Rock.

"Now it's time for Uluru's brother to come home. But Great Snake's power is small now. That's why you, big fella," he said, looking to Junior, "you talk the talk that helps all you fellas bring Uluru's brother home safe. These are the words of Jacob Crow. I say this truth as my ancestors before me said this truth." He spat on the stage. "Shit, mate, anybody got a beer? My throat's as parched as a sun-dried wallaby's arse!"

First one member of the audience, then another, then all the audience started chanting: "Jaaaaaacob – Jaaaaacob – Jaaaaaacob!"

Backstage, Azriel was smiling. "That Jacob is my kinda guy. Speaks to the stars, does what he wants, doesn't take any crap from anyone, looks all old and weedy but completely scary as Hell!"

"Fabulous!" said Larry.

"What the Hell are we supposed to do now? Float Homer to Earth on a cradle of hot air balloons? Eh? Or maybe even nip up there with the biggest ever bloody parachute ever made, harness him up, sing hymns as he floats to ground?"

Ignoring him, Junior handed a bottle of beer to Jacob Crow.

"Where did he get that from?" asked Cooper.

"He doesn't need a where – he's got a mojo," said MoMo.

Back on stage, the old Aborigine nodded his thanks and downed the contents of the bottle in seconds.

"Right, mate," he said, standing up, "I better get back and get ready. Up to you now, big fella. You gotta sort things out. Open folks' eyes. Show them the way." He was about to leave when Larry grabbed him by the arm and dragged him over to where Junior and Arthur were sitting. "Before you go, could you guys honour me with a group photo?" he asked, producing a cell phone and taking the most famous 'selfie' in history. Shortly after being sent to his Twitter page, the photo of Junior, Arthur, Jacob and Larry, was retweeted 15 million times over the next hour.

"Right," said Jacob, "thanks for the beer fellas. G'day." And with that, he nodded to his young companion who picked the giant python up and slid it back into the sack – and the three of them left with the cheers of the audience ringing in their ears.

"Wooohooo – follow that!" yelled Cooper backstage.

Junior did more than follow it. He flew past it on the outside lane and left it with dust in its eyes, the roar of a V16 in its ears and the smell of jet fuel in its nostrils!

He was looking directly into the television camera in front of him and he waited until the audience noise died down. Then he started to speak, with his Holy Mojo turned up to full volume.

"Once there were two children –"

"Oh bugger," said Azriel. "A bloody parable."

"Shhhhhh!" hissed Cooper, who was beginning to get some sensation back in his lower body.

" – who were playing by a river. Their parents were of different religions. So different, in fact, that they didn't even associate with each other, even though they knew each other well. They were very religious and took their faiths seriously.

"'Why is it that we can play and talk to each other and our parents can't?' said the boy to the girl one day as they were splashing about in the river. 'Because our parents caught religion,' said the girl.

"The boy thought about this for a minute, then said, 'Then religion must be a bad thing if it stops people from talking to each other and being friends. Where did they catch it?'"

"'They caught it in a church,' said the boy as he scooped up a handful of river water and threw it at the girl, who squealed in delight as the wetness seeped through her dress.

"'You mean it's like a sickness?'" whispered the girl, with fear suddenly in her eyes.

"The boy was cruel," said Junior. "He told the girl that it was, indeed, a sickness and that if she went to her church she would catch it and she would feel a pain in her belly and boils would break out all over her face and she would be ugly forever until she died.

"The girl recoiled in horror at this thought. 'Then I'm never going to church, ever,' she said and the boy said that neither was he.

"That," said Junior, "is why children wriggle and fidget and complain when they have to go to church. Because they don't want to catch religion and stop being friends with their neighbours. They need to be shown that religion is only a sickness if you make it one."

"All over the world, billions of people worship their own kind of religion. Many of these religions are tolerant of other faiths. They live and let live.

"If we want to save this world, save our people, we have to be like the two children and live, side by side. We have to push our differences aside and act as one people.

"And it doesn't matter whether we believe in one God or a hundred. Whether my God is the same as your God. We all need each other to survive. We can't do it with the technology of weapons. We have to do it with the power inside each of us.

"And if we can't destroy this rock from space that threatens our existence, then together we'll find another way."

"Yeah!" said someone from the audience. Then someone else joined in. Soon they were all yelling and whistling and applauding."

Junior stood up from his seat and every single eye in the audience was on him. Every eye watching every television set in the world was on him. Listening to his words and looking into his eyes.

"If we can't bring together all the power of our prayers to smash this rock, then we can use it to save it. To welcome it safely to Earth like the long lost brother we now know it is. But we need to pray, every one of us, all over the world.

"This is our world and this is our rock. Now it's our time to save them both. Go and pray. Pray with your friends and neighbours. Pray with family and strangers." He pointed to the exit door. "Go!" he yelled, and the audience, with smiling faces and the love of Junior in their eyes and hearts, got up from their seats and went, cheering and applauding.

As the last one passed through the door, Junior sat down exhausted, sweat pouring down his face.

Backstage, Azriel's smile had widened and Gabriel was punching MoMo in a friendly manner on the leg. He couldn't reach the shoulder.

"Oh boy," said the oracle, gently rubbing his forehead, "I got another feeling."

"A good one?" asked the little angel.

"I don't think so…"

Twenty Six

Religion is a funny thing. It brings people together and it keeps them apart. It gives them large helpings of hope and a fair sized dollop of fear. It requires belief in the, as yet, unprovable and throws logic out the window.

Since the dawn of time, mankind has huddled together in groups in draughty places and mumbled praises and pleas to various Gods.

Sometimes their prayers were answered – and other they got frogs dropping from the skies and plagues of small, hungry flying things and crop failures, the latter of the two generally coming together.

But for all that, there were times when folk realised that it was better to believe in something than not to believe at all. And it was better to believe in something you couldn't prove but felt in your heart and soul – than to believe in something that could be disproved and make you feel like crap.

The imminent arrival of Homer brought about a revival in belief of the unprovable kind all over the world.

With less than a fortnight to Homer's earth-shattering arrival, there was very little time for a gradual growth in man's ability to take up the faith. So things happened pretty damned quickly.

When non-Christians realised that the rock wasn't simply going to take out the Christians and leave the others in peace and quiet, they put their best praying clothes on and enthusiastically 'got with the programme'. The same was true of the Christians.

It quickly became apparent that whatever your religion was – Homer had you in his sights.

It also quickly became apparent that all those beautiful places of worship, so lovingly built and decorated by all those honest and well-meaning religions, were simply not going to be big enough for the numbers of people now wishing to visit them.

Teeny weeny little country chapels became so packed full of worshippers that they drafted in more priests and vicars and performed ceremonies in shifts 24 hours a day.

Massive cathedrals installed powerful speaker systems outside their doors to cater for the many thousands of visitors surrounding the ancient buildings, bringing traffic to a halt.

Places of worship all over the world had the same problem. Not enough seats. Not that they were complaining. They hadn't been so full since – well, they'd never been so full. Except for one or two extremely minority religions who hardly noticed a difference. Under other circumstances, this might have worried them. However their various leaders were wise enough to realise that religion had a vital role to play in the effort to save Homer and the world. So they got with the programme.

The day after Junior's broadcast, Cooper was on a flight back from Los Angeles International Airport to Rome, via Heathrow UK, for a meeting with Bonetti.

He, Azriel, Gabriel, Junior and MoMo had all said their goodbyes at the studio to Larry, who was not just upset at their departure but downright tearful. His biggest hug was reserved for Junior. "I don't know whether to wish you good luck or just sit back and wait for you to pull off the biggest miracle since the last one you pulled off," he said, hankie in hand, dabbing his leaking eyes. Then he stepped forward and hugged the surprised youngest Son of God a little too tightly for comfort.

"Okay – okay – okay! Let go. Emm – really. Let go!" insisted Junior, prising himself free of the hug with the aid of a small amount of Mojo juice.

Larry let go as if Junior was a hot coal, the power of the Mojo sending him reeling backwards into the waiting arms of Cooper, who caught him before he fell over backwards.

Apologising profusely, the TV show host smiled and disappeared out of a door, leaving the others to disappear from the studio as unobtrusively as possible.

"See you on the flip side," said Azriel who, without any warning, disappeared, along with the others, leaving Cooper alone in the studio green room, wondering how he was going to get back to the hotel to collect his overnight bag. Seconds later, there was a large 'thud' behind him and when he turned around, he saw the bag on the floor, zipped tightly shut. The sound of a departing laugh faded in the air, accompanied by Azriel's voice. "Taxi for the airport is waiting outside," he said.

Roughly 15 hours later, the 'no-smoking' lights went on and a message piped through from the pilot informed them that they would be landing shortly at Rome's Leonardo da Vinci Airport. Also known by its shorter, and less artistic title, Fiumicino.

About 18 miles and a couple of hours later, give or take an annoying 40 minutes at the baggage checkout, Cooper was in a black limousine complete with dark windows, being driven inside the gates of the Vatican. Half an hour after that, he was sitting inside Bonetti's private office, relaxing on a leather armchair, twiddling his thumbs. Bonetti, who had promised to meet him personally, was nowhere in sight.

There was a soft knock on the office door and, without being bidden, a small rotund priest nervously entered. He looked around the room, saw a face he knew in Cooper, smiled gratefully and waddled up to him.

"Father Cooper," he said. "You may remember me. I am Father Joseph Angelini. We met last year in New York. I accompanied The Holy Father when he met the President of the United States."

Cooper's mind worked overtime and suddenly a memory surfaced of the small priest standing beside The Pope, almost propping him up, as he stood for a photograph with the President.

Cooper smiled at him and held out his hand. Father Angelini shook it enthusiastically with both his hands and Cooper couldn't help but feel a slight clamminess to the smaller priest's palms.

"I hardly know where to begin," said Angelini.

"How about at the beginning, little round man" said Azriel who appeared beside the priest.

"Don't mind him," said Cooper, trying to remove his hand from the priest, who was steadfastly refusing to release it. "He's only a dark and mysterious angel with a very warped sense of humour."

Angelini's eyes nearly popped out of his head and he gripped Cooper's hand even tighter, causing the tips of his fingers to turn white.

"He's – he's what?"

"And that one over there," he said, pointing to Junior who was sitting on the floor in front of a large carved fireplace with his legs crossed, "is the Son of God. Well, one of them!"

That did the trick. With an almost Herculean effort, Angelini disengaged his hand and immediately crossed himself, muttering a prayer in Latin under his breath. Then he rushed over and knelt down in front of Junior and attempted to find his feet to kiss them.

Junior pushed him off, stood up, grabbed the small groveling priest by the scruff of his neck with one hand and pulled him upright. "Enough of that, Joseph," he said to the priest who was clearly awestruck. Angelini looked into his eyes and immediately calmed down.

"Now, why don't you tell Father Cooper why you're here." The small priest nodded dumbly, then turned around and walked over to Cooper.

"Hello again," said Cooper, to the priest who was standing in front of him with a smile on his face and a strange look in his eyes. The priest ignored him. "Hello!" said Cooper again, this time a little louder and at the same time waiving a hand in front of Angelini's eyes. Same result. No sign of intelligent life.

"Aw bollocks," said Cooper and gently smacked Angelini across the face.

Like a spell whose power had just been broken, Angelini came back from whatever planet he was on and raised his hand to his smacked cheek.

"Spill the beans," said Azriel, looking menacing. "And you are going to spill the beans, aren't you, my roly poly friend."

Angelini rubbed his cheek and nodded his head. "Cardinal Bellini sends his apologies for his absence. He said he would explain everything when he got here which will be in about ten minutes."

"How is the Holy Father," asked Cooper. "Is he – worse?"

"No – no!" said Angelini. "He's not worse, he's better! That's what I've come to tell you. The Holy Father is improving. This morning he regained his hearing – and this afternoon, his bowels began working properly."

"Please don't go there!" said Azriel. One look at the angel's expression and extremely bad tempered wild horses wouldn't have dragged Angelini anywhere near there. "Now scat. Unless, of course, you have something to eat and drink for my large friend here."

At precisely that moment a tall, bulky shape with a rumbling stomach decided to join the party.

"Ooooh – did I hear someone mention food?" asked MoMo.

At precisely the moment after that moment, the small, rotund priest was overcome with a sudden and inescapable desire to lose consciousness. Azriel caught him an inch or two before his body met the wooden floor.

"Correct me if I'm wrong," grunted the dark angel, manhandling Angelini into an upright position with one hand and slapping his cheeks repeatedly with the other, "but don't you think that people who worship God for a living might possibly be used to the concept of angels appearing out of thin air every now and then? Eh?"

Angelini awoke from the swoon with a startled yelp. "Eeeaauugh! Wha –" He rubbed both his cheeks and tried to stand upright unaided when Azriel let him go.

"There. Feel better now?" asked the angel, mock concern on his face.

"I – I – th–think so." Angelini's skin tone was fighting a personal battle between embarrassed red and shocked white. He was coming out a sort of light pink.

"Sandwiches would be good. Preferably lots of them," said MoMo.

"Just how much exactly can you eat and drink?" asked Cooper.

"Don't know. Never felt full and never felt quenched. I have this little empty corner inside that I can't fill up, no matter how hard I try. And believe you me, I've tried."

He turned to Junior. "Remember that wedding we got invited to, y'know – eat all you want drink all you want. Where was it again?"

"Cana," said Junior, without missing a beat.

"You were at Cana?" asked Cooper, wide eyed.

"Why so surprised? I been around, you know. Birth at Bethlehem, Wedding at Cana, Marriage of Figaro, Death on the Nile – even got a t-shirt somewhere."

"I can get you some cheese sandwiches," said Angelini. "And maybe some root beer."

"That'll do for starters."

The little priest waddled out of the door in search of refreshments. Five minutes later Cardinal Bonetti opened the door and hurried in. He was smiling.

"We heard," said Cooper. "Thank the Lord he's getting better."

"Amen to that," said Bonetti, crossing himself. He turned to Junior. "We saw the broadcast. I was sitting with the Holy Father and, even though at that point he was deaf, dumb and blind, he still seemed to know what was going on."

"He's the Holy Father. He has a direct line to the Heavenly switchboard," said Cooper.

"Very poetic," said Azriel. "This means it's started."

"What?"

"There's been a shift in the Force."

Junior butted in. "All those folk praying all over the world are beginning to affect the power levels in Heaven and Hell." He smiled and looked at everyone in the room. "I love it when a plan comes together. Especially when there's no pain or sharp implements involved."

"Well, we're not out of the woods yet, my friend," said Bonetti. "We have a very large gathering in the square outside, all calling to see the Holy Father. Quite frankly, I don't think they'll take 'Sorry, he's busy. Come back tomorrow' as an answer."

Bonetti looked at Cooper and shrugged. "I think we need your remarkable talents, father."

Cooper looked uncomfortable. "Well I – "

"You can do this?" asked Azriel quietly.

"Oh, I can do it alright. I just never thought I'd have to."

"All the other religions have their leaders, well the live ones anyway, smiling, waving and looking very confident. It wouldn't really go down well if we were the odd one out," said Bonetti. "So you see, there really is no alternative."

"How many are out there?" asked the priest.

"You know that time when the Holy Father was elected to the throne of St. Peter and the square outside was jam packed with worshippers and tourists all praying and cheering when he came out on the balcony?"

"That many?"

"Oh no," said Bonetti, shaking his head slowly. "Much more than that many."

Cooper could envisage the seething mass of ecstatic people in St. Peter's Square, all looking up at the central balcony of St. Peter's Basilica.

Packed so tightly together they could hardly move. Waiting for a sign, hanging on every single word said by the spiritual leader of around a billion Catholics in this a time of destruction or salvation for the whole world.

Of course not all of them regularly went to mass and prayed. Like a lot of things in life, saying you were a Catholic was a far cry from actually acting like one.

"Okay," said Cooper, looking Bonetti square in the eyes. "But this is a once-only deal, right? No quick Papal visits slipped in at the last minute whenever the Holy Father's indisposed."

"Absolutely," said Bonetti. "Just this once." As he spoke, he held his hands behind his body so that the priest couldn't see his crossed fingers.

Azriel leant forwards and whispered in Bonetti's ear. "He might not be able to see those lying little digits of yours, but I can. Remember that. I'll be keeping an eye on you."

The Cardinal felt a slight chill work its way down his spine and automatically uncrossed his fingers, bringing his hands to the front of his body. "It's time," he said and led the way out of his office, heading for the balcony overlooking St. Peter's Square.

Somewhere on the way from Bonetti's office to the Central Balcony, Cooper changed from a late-thirties, serious-looking priest into an exact double of the 87 year old Pope Julius IV. Except for the infirmities, of course. In fact the old Pope had never seemed so spry and healthy.

Exactly when the change occurred nobody in the small group could have said. Even Azriel, who was watching closely to witness the event first hand, was completely baffled.

It just happened in mid-stride. He simply put one foot down as Cooper, and the following one as the head of the Roman Catholic Church.

"How do you DO that!" said the dark angel, exasperated at his failure to spot the changeover.

"Aaah," said Pope Julius, with a small, mysterious smile, "there are some things which even an angel cannot be told. Papal security clearance, I'm afraid." Azriel wondered if there was such a thing as Papal security clearance – or whether it was just Cooper's way of limiting knowledge of his unique ability.

As he was wondering, they entered the anteroom to the Balcony. For the first time, the noise of the waiting crowd could be heard, filtering up from the square below.

Halfway across the room, about 20 feet from the balcony, Cooper stopped in Pope Julius' tracks. "I don't have a clue what I'm supposed to say," he said.

Bonetti, by his side, handed him four sheets of paper. "Don't worry," he said gently.

"Here's something we prepared earlier. You just read it, make a few waves, smile and put your faith in God."

"Cooper," said Junior behind him. It had an instant effect. The priest felt a warm wave of Holy Mojo spread over him, calming him and filling him with confidence.

"Go on," he said softly. "You'll be fine." And he was.

Not even the deafening roar from the crowd as he stepped out onto the balcony could remove the sense of wellbeing that Junior had given him.

That afternoon, a healthy-looking Pope Julius IV gave perhaps his most memorable speech to the waiting masses below and, through television and radio, Twitter and Facebook, photo-messaging and cell phone, to the rest of the world.

The whole thing, speech and waves, lasted almost half an hour. But in that time, the power banks of Heaven and Hell went up by leaps and bounds.

Twenty Seven

Once upon a time, a modest English farmer's son called Isaac Newton, Izzy to his mates, postulated the theory that, for every action there is an equal and opposite reaction. He called it his Third Law of Motion.

This, unfortunately, proved the long-held belief that mankind was, essentially, stuffed. It meant that whenever we were at war, peace was waiting just around the corner. And whenever we were at peace, war just couldn't wait to get its grubby big fat fingers around our throats.

It also meant, in some circles, that when one part of the world, which was due for a right royal squishing, was denied it, some other unfortunate piece of land of equal measure and on the opposite side of the planet, had to be squished instead.

This, with large apologies to the knighted Mister Newton, was the thinking behind Daisy Roper's Theory of Directional Shift Due To Unforseen Circumstances.

Her theory, really a sort of unofficial addendum to the Newton one, was first postulated when Daisy looked at the monitor on her desk about the same time Cooper and the others arrived back at Cardinal Bonetti's office after the 'Papal blessing' from the Central Balcony.

It didn't take her long to notice two things. The first thing was that every method of electronic communication that she had at her fingertips which had inexplicably ceased to work one minute, was back up and running again very quickly the next. She found herself caught in the middle of an emotional cocktail of terror and relief. The second thing was that, in the space between power, no power, then power again – something very odd had happened to Homer.

"What the bloody hell are you playing at, Homer?" she mumbled, and typed furiously on her keyboard. On the monitor in front of her, mini-screens came and went and rows of constantly changing numbers worked their way tirelessly through the calculations she was asking them to perform.

Finally, Homer's speed, size, trajectory, collision site and time of collision all blinked into view and sat there on the monitor like obedient pets waiting for Daisy's approval. She approved and screamed in delight. Wingnut, her co-watcher who was sitting about four feet away from her did a fair impression of someone coughing and choking on the mouthfull of coffee he was trying to drink.

"He's bloody done it again!" she squealed. "Don't ask me how it happened, but he's gone and done it again!"

Wingnut, whose choking fit had subsided, managed to say something that could have been translated as, "Eh?" He was trying to look at Daisy whilst mopping up the mouthful of coffee from his t-shirt front and his keyboard.

"Homer's changed direction. I don't know any law of physics that can explain what he just did – but he just did it!"

"And you're happy because?" said Wingnut, getting up from his chair and moving towards Daisy.

"Because we're not gonna get squished!" she exclaimed. "Look at the figures."

Wingnut obligingly looked. "How did he do that?" he asked.

"God knows," said Daisy. "But he just turned ever so slightly to the right. I swear if I didn't know better I'd say he did it all by himself."

Wingnut's enthusiasm wasn't quite as visible as Daisy's. "Doesn't that mean if it's not gonna land on Yorkshire, then some other poor buggers are gonna get squished?"

"No, you dingbat!" she said, pointing at the screen. "Look at the new co-ordinates. Homer's coming down smack dab in the middle of Australia. That's pretty much in the middle of nowhere, right?"

"Well, apart from maybe a few unfortunate Aborigines who will end up a whole lot flatter."

"Not if we can get them out in time. I mean, how hard can it be to round up a few Aborigines and airlift them to safety. And who knows – if Australia cops the brunt of the collision, maybe it might just soak it up enough to give the rest of us a chance."

Her enthusiasm drained away as Wingnut reminded her that it didn't really matter where Homer came down, land or sea. They were all screwed anyway. "Sorry for popping yer balloon, Oh Hopeful and Optimistic One," he said, apologetically.

Daisy sighed. "I think he was maybe just trying to make sure we didn't get squished first. Maybe somewhere in that rocky mind of his, he knew that his Daisy was down here waiting to get landed on from a great height. Then he did the honourable, gentlemanly thing and buggered off somewhere else."

Wingnut thought about this for a moment. "Naaaah," he said. "There's got to be a scientific explanation."

"What," said Daisy, laughing, "like a new law of physics - just discovered by Daisy and Wingnut."

"Oh no," said Wingnut, holding up his hands and smiling. "You can have all the honours for this one. Not that they'll do you any good. We'll say it's Daisy Roper's Theory of somethingorother."

They both thought for a minute. "How about Daisy Roper's Theory of Directional Shift," she said, grabbing a pen and writing it down.

Wingnut nodded and started chewing on the end of a pencil. He had gone back to his chair and now had his legs up and crossed at the ankles on the edge of his desk.

"Nice," he said, "but it needs something else. That extra ingredient that gives it an air of mystery or something."

"Well how about Daisy Roper's Theory of Directional Shift – Due to Unforeseen Circumstances!" she announced, grandly.

"Oooooh," said Wingnut, clearly impressed. "Now that has a nice ring to it. That way we don't even have to explain how it happened in the first place."

"Because basically we don't have a clue," added Daisy, smiling. "You think there might be a paper in it?" Then her smile faded, "Oh yeah, no world, no people, no paper. Never mind, it was a nice thought while it lasted. And maybe if we do get out of this alive I might have a think about it, with your help, that is."

"Naturally!"

Now, Daisy Roper, Person-in-charge-in-absentia, took over and she realised that she'd have to call General Parker.

The General picked up on the second ring. His gruff voice only served to set Daisy on edge.

"Hello?" he said.

"General Parker, this is Daisy Roper."

"Hello Daisy," he said, in a way too friendly tone. "What's the latest on our big boy?"

Daisy took a deep breath. "Well sir, Homer's decided he doesn't want to land on Yorkshire any more. About half an hour ago he changed direction."

"He what?" yelled Parker. Bang went the friendliness. He yelled so loud that Daisy automatically yanked the earpiece about a foot away from her head, then gingerly brought it back to her ear again.

"He changed direction, sir," she continued, trying to keep her voice calm and steady.

"And sir – his speed increased."

"It increased?" yelled Parker again. Daisy wondered whether half this man's life was spent either yelling or repeating anything said to him. She also wondered whether she would be the unwitting cause of the general suffering either a heart attack or a stroke.

"Sir, please don't shout," she said.

There was a short pause before he spoke again. "Daisy, I apologise."

"Accepted," she said, after a matching short pause. "Now, as I said, Homer's changed direction and increased speed. If everything stays the same and he doesn't throw us any more surprises, he should be docking with terra firma in about seven days time. In Australia."

"Seven days in Australia? You sure?"

"Positive – for the moment."

"Where abouts in Australia?"

"Near Ayres Rock."

"I was there once," said Parker. "The folk there were very skittish about anyone climbing it. They call it Uluru. You ever been looked at funny by an Aborigine, Daisy?"

"Emm –"

"Well you just pray you never do. You know when you get the feeling that something really bad's going to happen? I just felt this old guy knew a bit more about what happens up there than he was letting on.

"I took his picture and he went apeshit. Said I was stealing his soul. I got in the car and drove like crazy. Never went back there. And you know the spooky thing? I got the pictures developed and every one turned out except the one of him. Not a damned thing on it. Not a damned thing!"

"That's very spooky, sir," said Daisy, frantically trying to figure out how she could get the conversation back on track without offending the General. She decided that attack was the best form of defence. "But getting back to Homer. What happens now?"

"Now I talk to my superior and pass on the bad news. You did a good job there Daisy. Damned good job. You keep your eyes on our rocky friend up there and call me the second anything else changes."

Parker hung up and Daisy put the phone back on its cradle and let out a long sigh of relief. As she did so, the General was calling the man he considered his superior.

"Hello?" answered Bonetti.

"This is Parker, sir, there's been a development. Well – two actually."

"Two?" blurted Bonetti, with genuine surprise in his voice. This confused Parker, because he expected his superior to know about the development already, just as he did the last time he phoned. The fact that he was giving them new information gave Parker a vastly increased sense of his own worth. Not that it was going to last, he thought, given the circumstances.

"The rock has changed direction and shifted up a gear," said the General. "He's headed for central Australia, round about Ayres Rock. He hits in 7 days!"

"Well, well," said Bonetti, almost to himself. "The old bugger was right after all."

"What old –?"

"Never mind. Listen. We need somebody in Australia. At the scene. I think this Miss Daisy Roper of yours is perfect for the job. Call her back and get her on the next available flight over there."

Parker did something he'd never done before in all his military career, such as it was.

He questioned what he believed to be a direct order.

"But that means – I mean, that's a death warrant, sir. I mean we're all going to die when the rock hits. But what can we possibly gain by putting one of our own people at the crash site?" Parker felt his temper rising. "Pardon me for saying so, sir, but I think –"

"You think too much, General," said Bonetti. "Listen, I'll let you into a little secret. You can tell Miss Roper but nobody else, okay?"

"Okay," said Parker slowly. Dammit, he thought. His 'bringer of new information' status rapidly crashed and burned.

"Homer's not going to collide. He's not going to crash into the planet and wipe out the human race."

"He's not?" asked the General, wondering how on Earth the rock could be diverted.

"No. That big boulder of yours is going to slam on the brakes as he pushes through the atmosphere."

Parker's mind raced. "But, Homer doesn't have any –"

"Listen!" yelled Bonetti. "He's going to slam on the brakes and come to a gentle rest on the ground. That's what he's going to do. That's what you call faith, General. And that's what you call a miracle."

Parker, who believed in neither God nor miracles, began to wonder about the sanity of his superior. "Sir, I think I should point out that –"

"You don't watch television, General, do you?" asked Bonetti, almost as if he was saying to him 'you don't believe the world is round'.

"What?"

"Television. Do you watch the Larry Black Show?"

"I don't have a television, sir," said Parker. "Never had time for it."

So Bonetti then proceeded to tell Parker about the interview with Junior and about Arthur, Junior's brother, and about the funny looking old Aborigine.

"This old fella," said Parker. "He didn't by any chance have long white hair and carry a large staff and have two young fellas with him, one with a didgeridoo thing?"

"Well, as a matter of fact yes," said Bonetti.

"The bastard! That's the old sod who chased me away from Ayres Rock when I wanted to climb it."

"You seem to be missing the bigger picture here, General. That old sod, as you so unkindly put it, knew before we did where Homer was going to land. He knew it all along, but we were too thick to see it. General, that rock's coming down just like I say it will and nothing on Earth can stop it. All we can do is slow it down. And if you take the trouble to get yourself a TV, then you might be able to see how we're doing it.

"Now, get Daisy Roper on a flight pronto. And tell her to take a cell phone and a laptop, I want her to stay linked to the Foundation's systems. And tell her to look for Father John Wayne Cooper when she gets there!" he said and hung up.

Parker pressed an intercom button on his desk and a woman's voice answered.

"Yes, sir?"

"Maisie, get me a TV," he barked. "And today's papers." Ten minutes later he was back on the phone to Daisy Roper.

"You want me to go where?" she almost shouted at Parker.

"Australia," said Parker, almost apologetically.

Daisy's panic levels hit warp factor nine. "Nonononono – that's not an option. That's not in my contract and I have no intentions of bringing on a premature state of death-by-large-rock, just because you want Miss Gullible of the Century right at the centre of things when the world ends. Not me. Not Daisy Roper!"

She could almost hear Parker smile condescendingly. "Daisy, don't you have a TV, or listen to the radio, or even read newspapers," he said, in his new state of media-friendliness. "Were you the only person on the planet that didn't catch the Larry Black Show?"

"Oh, we caught it all right," she replied. "But, I mean, it's all bullshit, isn't it? We turned the telly off after he left. Why?"

So Parker told Daisy everything that Bonetti had told him, word for word in some cases. Including looking out for Father Cooper.

"And you believe it?" she asked, genuinely surprised. "General, I'm surprised at you. It's probably just some PR stunt to make everyone think that the world's gonna be saved, so they won't panic, and then whaam! End of story before they even know what hit them."

"Daisy, do me a favour. Just switch on the TV and read a paper. They're running re-runs of the Jack Black show continuously. Watch it again – and this time watch ALL of it. Log on to your Facebook and Twtter accounts. I presume you have accounts? Then book a flight down under. Call me when you've got your travel details."

Parker hung up leaving Daisy sitting open mouthed and brain spinning, looking at a recent shot of Homer on her monitor.

Until now, God was somebody she left behind long ago and a million miles away. He was somebody who didn't care when her mother and father died in their blazing car and left her, six years old and alone, in the care of an aunt who never wanted children but made it her duty to bring up Daisy in as near a state of misery as she possibly could.

She turned to Wingnut, who, all during the call, had been trying to guess the content of the conversation like the cute but nosy sod he was.

"Switch on the TV," she said, nodding to the monitor sitting high up on the wall. Wingnut dutifully grabbed the remote from his desk, pushed a button and the screen came to life. The first image they saw was of Junior speaking on the Jack Black show.

They both sat and listened to the interview all the way through. As they heard Junior's voice and looked into his eyes, the Holy Mojo did it's work on them and, without realising how and when it happened, they both felt a sense of calm and hope washing over them. When the interview finished, she turned to her laptop and logged onto Facebook.

Daisy had 1,539 'friends'. Every one of them was either posting about the miracle at the hospital or the impending arrival of Homer. There was no other topic of conversation on the site. The same with Twitter. She didn't have to wonder what was trending. Junior and Homer were the biggest double act in the history of mass communication.

"I'm off to Oz," she said.

"What, to meet the wizard?"

"You never know," said Daisy, fingerstabbing her keyboard and looking up details on flights to Australia. She reached down for her bag, fumbled around for her purse and took out a credit card. Ten minutes later she had booked herself on a flight to Melbourne, with a connection to Alice Springs. From there it was only about 300 miles drive to Uluru.

"I see, so you get to go walkabout and I get to stay at home and look after the baby?" asked Wingnut, in a tone that was only half mock hurt.

"You have now been promoted to Chief Cook and Bottle Washer," said Daisy.

Wingnut smiled, grabbed his empty coffee mug and reached for hers. "In that case," he said, "I do believe we need a celebratory mug of the old Colombian dark stuff, maybe even laced with a little of Wingnut's Special Celtic Reserve," and he reached down, opened his lower desk drawer and withdrew a half-empty bottle of smooth, malty, triple distilled Tullamore Dew Irish Whiskey.

"Tell you what," said Daisy, "let's forget the damned coffee."

Twenty Eight

Homer's little deviation from his predicted course hadn't exactly gone unnoticed by those who liked to think of themselves as the top bananas in everything that happened above the Earth's atmosphere.

The boffins at NASA and all those hard working, spectacle-wearing people with large telescopes all over the world were as alarmed and surprised as Daisy was, when they looked for Homer and discovered he wasn't where he was supposed to be. Of course it didn't take them long to find out where he was, or where he was heading.

But the alarm they felt was purely emotional and short-lived, because nearly all of them had seen the Larry Black Show and so, despite the fact that Homer was still heading for Earth like a rock on a mission, they soon became calm again. Somehow they felt praying would make the world a better place.

They were also pragmatic enough to realise that their better world would probably not exist for very much longer. However, when you're tied to the tracks and the train's coming at you full speed, there comes a time when giving in to the inevitable is the only option. After that, a curious calm sets in. Que sera sera.

NASA Administrator George McHale had been called to the office of Ellis P. Crumb. As he walked into Crumb's office, he noticed that a map of Australia was pinned up on one of the walls.

"Hiya George," said Crumb, who was standing looking at the map with a mug of steaming black coffee in one hand, and the other stuffed deep into a trouser pocket.

"Ellis," said McHale.

The JCOS Chairman turned with a smile on his face. "You ever cooked shrimps on a barbie, George?"

The image of setting light to a child's doll bullied its way into McHale's mind. Then the BBQ penny dropped.

"Not shrimps, no. Burned a few good steaks though," said McHale smiling. " Why?"

Crumb took a long drink from his mug, then turned and laid it on a coaster on his desk. He went over to the map and jabbed a finger at Australia's centre, practically covering the name 'Alice Springs'.

"That there," he said, "is where Homer's coming down. 'Bout 300 miles south west of Alice Springs, slap bang right next to that damned big rock they got called Uluru. Remember that Aborigine fella on the Larry Black Show?" McHale nodded. "Well, that grizzly old son of a bitch knew the damned landing spot before Homer even changed direction. Now how d'you figure that?" He scratched his head.

McHale shook his head and smiled. "You're asking the wrong guy," he said. "You should be asking that Junior fella. He seems to have all the answers. Or maybe even the other one...scary guy with the black clothes and long white hair. Looks like a refugee from a Harry Potter convention."

Crumb looked directly into his eyes. "You believe in God, George?"

"Absolutely."

"Friendly piece of advice. If I were you I wouldn't go around talkin' about His kinfolk like that, if you get my meaning. By the way, I hear through the grapevine that my niece Daisy is headin' down under for the big occasion. That interest you at all, George?"

McHale noticed that Crumb was looking at him very, very closely. Suddenly, a highly uncomfortable thought wriggled inside his head like a worm making its way to the surface after a hard rain. Did the General know about him and Daisy? Was he fishing or had he known all along? And what the Hell did it have to do with shrimps?

"Well – if Daisy's heading for Australia she must be figuring to be there when the rock comes down. Which means –"

"Which means *we* gotta be there too, or rather *you* do."

George McHale's heart skipped a beat. "I do?"

"Damned right," said Crumb. "You think I'd let her wander around on one of those walkabouts without the care and protection of her uncle Ellis?"

"You mean you want to know what she knows," said McHale, wryly thinking that the General probably didn't give two hoots about Daisy's wellbeing. All he was interested in, all he ever seemed interested in, was the bigger picture.

"Well Hell, if there's anything about Homer that she knows and we don't, we better get our asses in gear and find out pretty soon, right?"

McHale submitted gracefully to defeat. There was no way he was getting out of this one even if he wanted which, truth be told, he didn't. So he smiled and said, "I'll be on the next available flight over there."

"Oh no," said Crumb. "You ain't flyin' on some damned commercial airline. Hell son, that's what we got government jets for. Now you go and throw a few things in a bag. You fly out in two hours."

Crumb patted McHale on the shoulder as he walked him to the door. "I got a briefing with the President in a few minutes. I'll bring him up to speed. You call me when you get there, okay?"

McHale nodded and headed straight for his car, wondering where he could buy clothes for an Australian walkabout in Washington in a hurry.

Meanwhile, 4,500 miles away and 6 hours time difference in Rome, Bonetti, Cooper, Junior, Azriel and Arthur were all in the bedroom of Pope Julius IV, who seemed to be rapidly improving.

"It's weird," whispered Cooper to Bonetti, "I know for a fact that the Holy Father hates chicken soup, yet there he is on his second bowl of the stuff."

"You have some friends with you, Alfredo," said the Pope. "I can't see them but I know they are there. Three among you are blessed by the hand of God. Step forward, please." Holding his empty soup bowl out for an attendant who took it from him, he looked with unseeing eyes at Azriel, Junior and Arthur.

"Two Sons of God?" he whispered. "Holy Mother there are two! Please, both of you, give me a hand." Junior and Arthur gently grasped an outstretched hand each and the Pope immediately pulled them closer with surprising strength and placed their hands over his eyes. "This is the will of God," he said and as he pulled the hands away, his eyes cleared and he could see again. Bonetti and Cooper gasped.

"Hello Junior, hello Arthur," said the Pope, smiling and mysteriously knowing them immediately. "I see you've brought along an angel of the Lord. You are Azriel, I believe."

Azriel smiled. "We met once," he said. "You were a young priest then. You were about to get yourself shot for helping a Jewish family escape from the Nazis. Not a very healthy thing to do at the time."

"No," said the Pope, smiling ruefully. "I don't suppose it was. But I remember you. I remember a voice telling me to close my eyes as I was facing the firing squad. When I opened them, the soldiers were gone and only you were standing there, just like you are now. As I remember, you told me to get the Hell out of there. That's when I knew what and who you were. But for many years I wondered why you had saved me."

"And then you found out," said the dark angel.

The Pope turned to Bonetti. "Now, tell me everything. But before you start, get me some more pillows and a glass of iced water," he ordered in a tone of voice that sounded like a request but was received as a Papal edict.

The pillows and water were duly brought and Bonetti, with interjections from everyone else, brought the Pope up to date on all the events, Heavenly, Hellish and Earthly, that had taken place since the 'Papal afflictions' began. All the way through, the Pope nodded and occasionally closed his eyes.

When they were finished, the Catholic leader looked again at Junior and Arthur. "I can feel the power of God spreading over the world," he said, crossing himself and kissing the small wooden crucifix hanging on a chain around his neck.

Just then, there was a knock on the door and Father Angelini entered, carrying a tray with a steaming face cloth, a bowl of hot water and shaving equipment. He nearly dropped the tray when he saw the 'holy' gathering around the Pope. But instead, he recovered his composure, went into protective mode and barged through the gathering with one, loud "Excuse me, please".

The tray-dropping bit came when he realised that the Pope could see again. Luckily, Azriel caught it before it decided to succumb to the laws of gravity. He handed it back to a shaking Angelini with a smile.

"Don't worry my roly-poly little friend," he said. " We'll be gone in a minute and then you can play barber."

Before they left, Julius called Bonetti over and whispered something in his ear. The Cardinal nodded occasionally, then kissed the ring on the Pope's finger and ushered them all from the room.

When they were back in the Cardinal's office, Cooper said, "So, what did he say to you?"

Bonetti sat down in the chair behind his desk. "Anyone want a drink?"

"That's what he said? Anyone want a drink?"

"No," said Bonetti. "That's just me being hospitable. The Holy Father said that he wanted you," and he nodded at Cooper, "in Australia when the rock comes down. He wants you to bless it in his name."

Cooper looked confused and slightly embarrassed. What he felt was surprised and slightly alarmed. "Wouldn't you be a better choice for that, Your Eminence?"

"This is a very important task Father, perhaps the most important of your life in the service of the Holy Church. So please listen carefully.

"You have to go to the site where the rock will land. Father, you will take a bottle of holy water drawn from the pulpit here in St. Peter's and you will perform a Blessing of Thanksgiving. Is that clear?"

The priest nodded. His fate, or fortune, sealed in that single nod.

"I'll have all your travel documents ready in a couple of hours. Meanwhile, I suggest that you go pack for warm weather."

Azriel smiled, "Sounds like fun. Mind if we join in?"

"Don't you have things to do, like keep an eye on all those folk praying all over the world?"

"Oh, no," said Junior. "That's on autopilot now. Just rolls along and gets bigger and bigger. We call it the Heavenly Snowball Effect. I've never seen so many people get so holy so quickly! Just goes to show. Give them a common cause and they don't give a damn what faith they were born into. They just slap their palms together and pray like their lives depend on it...which curiously enough they do!"

"But we won't be joining you on the journey," said Arthur, who, since his initial grumpiness on the Larry Black Show, had mellowed. "I get kinda cranky on long haul flights. So we'll just, emm, make our own way there, okay?"

"Fine by me," said Cooper. "What about Bob and *The Eye of God?*"

"Don't worry about Bob," said the dark angel, "he's got his wings and his memory back and last I heard he was off to have a friendly word in the ear of my cousin Zaphir. You know, the one who, well, I won't go into detail. But let's just say that Zaphir better sleep with one eye open from now on."

"And as for *The Eye*," said Bonetti, "well that's back where it belongs downstairs, in its case, with a nice new pair of young guardians."

"Right," said Cooper, " who knows the words to Waltzing Matilda?"

Twenty Nine

About 100 to 200 million years ago, Australia decided to go walkabout – or driftabout, to be more precise.

Instead of staying joined to the large landmass called Gowanda, which sounds like an African Safari Movie, it shoved off and moved 3200 miles south to its present location. It liked what it saw when it got there, so it threw out the anchors and stayed put.

For about 80 million years, give or take a long weekend, most of it was buried under a glacier. Then about 50,000 years ago the first inhabitants, the Aborigines, discovered it, liked what they saw – and they stayed put, too.

However, according to a little known Aborigine legend, a chunk of the continent didn't stay anywhere. Instead, it was hurled into space, a victim of a spectacular explosion, and decided to go walkabout amongst the stars. This was what the whitefellas called Homer. And now, it was coming home.

In the dusty, hot heart of Australia, preparations were being made. It was now 5 days before impact and the word had got out about Homer's change of plans. About 30 miles North of Uluru, the complete Aborigine population of the continent (about 300,000), plus a few thousand slightly tanned non-native Australians, were all gathering together to welcome it back, singing songs, telling jokes – and, naturally, have a few beers.

Creed and colour notwithstanding, it's fair to say that a very small area in the middle of Australia became a very large temporary camp, with tribal music, rock bands, chemical toilets, hot dog stands, even t-shirts with artistic impressions of Homer and the words 'Homer Rocks!' hastily printed on the front.

Of course Homer didn't know this. All he knew was that something was very wrong. Instead of racing like billyo to get closer to the object of his affections, he felt himself gradually slowing down. And the closer he got to the giant blue and white rock up ahead, the stronger the feeling got.

For the first time since he started his long journey, he felt not the thrill of adventure but the fear of failure.

If he carried on slowing down at this rate, he'd come to a full stop before he even reached his destination.

Then, somewhere inside his rocky mass, inside the atoms and molecules that went together to form him into the handsome brute that he was, a feeling of calm and wellbeing grew and grew until he felt it was everywhere around and inside him.

It was as if he was being guided home.

Down on the planet's surface ahead of him, about 300 miles north east of Uluru Kata Tjuta National Park, the nice people of Alice Springs were getting nicely richer than they'd ever been.

Every room that could be let was taken. Every eating establishment was cram packed full. Every resident with even the slightest artistic talent was whipping up Homer collectibles. In fact every bit of freestanding rock in the area was hunted down and turned into a Homer lookalike. The fact that few residents had the slightest idea what Homer really *did* look like, didn't seem to matter.

About 80 miles north of Uluru, the Community Elders of the Anangu clan of Aborigines, ancestral custodians of the rock and surrounding lands, were having a meeting.

Jacob Crow was there, with his two young assistants in tow. Also there was Charlie Carpenter, a barrel-chested ancient who walked with a limp, Jim Kelly, who spoke too much but was the oldest of them all so deserved respect, Robert Kee, who had the knack of joining Aboriginal and Christian beliefs together and still finding reason to smile, and a dozen or so more. All with words to say and a right to be heard.

"I never heard of this 'two rocks' story," said Jim Kelly to Crow. "I think it's bollocks and you made the whole bloody thing up."

They were sitting round a fire in scrubland just north of Uluru. It was late afternoon and the sun was going down. Behind them, the last rays of the dying fireball were setting on the rock, reflecting off its geological contents and turning it from crimson, through pink and into a deep mauve.

Jacob Crow looked at Jim and there were mutterings and murmurings through the gathering. "Yeah," said Crow, "and I made the bloody thing up about the rock coming down from the sky right here before the whitefellas knew. And they got all their technology."

Jim Kelly and Jacob Crow had known each other since they were kids. In fact all of the elders had grown up together.

But over time, Crow had come to be regarded as the one whose advice everybody sought. It was never official, but it pissed Kelly off, who secretly wished to Hell that he was the one people came to.

"Jim," said Charlie Carpenter, "Jacob's been to see that America place and stopped them buggers from harming the rock, and that's good enough for me."

There were lots of assenting noises from the gathering.

"Way I figure," continued Jacob, " we're gonna have our hands full when he comes down, what with folk tryin' to tramp all over him and take pictures. So, first off, we gotta have a policy. The land's ours so if the rock lands on it then he's ours to take care of."

"What's his name?" said one of the others.

Everybody looked at Jacob, who picked up his staff and wrote 'Kutju' in the dirt.

"That's not a name," said Kelly.

"He was the first to come out of the ground when the Great Snake pushed him out," said Crow. "He spoke to me and told me his true name was Kutju."

"How come he speaks to you and never spoke to any of us?" asked Kelly. "And how come we're sat here instead of in the community building, I thought that's what we built it for?"

Jacob Crow took a deep breath. Kelly was a good man but, in Crow's opinion, a bit on the small size inside. "You see right here where we're sat?" he said, making a wide circle in the air with his hand, "this is where Kutju will park his arse."

"Bollocks mate, you mean he's coming down right here?" said Kelly, looking nervously above him and half getting up from where he was sat.

Crow laughed. A soft, friendly laugh and the others joined in. Kelly sat down.

"So, you brought us out here to get a feel for him, right?" said Charlie Carpenter.

Crow nodded. "Yep. And they've got all them whitefellas praying to their God to bring him down safe. It's our job to see he get's a right good welcome home, then look after him when he gets here."

For the first time since the meeting began, Jim Kelly said something that made the others nod in agreement. "So how come their God's helpin' us?"

Jacob looked at Uluru, a bump on the landscape in the distance. He thought of Junior and Arthur speaking on the Larry Black Show. He thought of the surprise in their faces when they learned that Kutju was a thinking rock and shouldn't be destroyed. And he looked at the faces of all those in his company here and now.

"You forget, Jim, we know their God and he's not a bad bloke. Best I can figure it we're all helpin' each other, 'cos Kutju's comin' down a bit on the quick side and if he doesn't slow down then we're all in the shit. They're slowin' him so he can sit down gentle after his journey. That's the way of it, mate."

"And their God's doin' that?" asked Charlie Carpenter, clearly impressed.

Robert Kee, the half-and-half Christian spoke for the first time, "Oh, that fella's got a fair bit of power, mates. And he's a big bugger, too. Hell, you should see the size of his son. Small as a whitefella one minute, and big as a mountain the next. Saw a picture of him once in that place called – emm Rio somethin'. His dad must be a helluva size!"

Jacob was about to tell them all about Junior and Arthur, but thought better of it, given the nods of appreciation the famous statue seemed to be getting. Instead, he said, "Well, Kutju's a helluva size, too. For a start, he's bigger than that," and he pointed to Uluru.

"Bugger me," said Kelly. "You know this from down here?"

Charlie Carpenter laughed. "If I buggered you, mate, you wouldn't walk for a week!"

When everyone had stopped laughing, including Jim Kelly, Crow took his staff and drew a large, rough circle in the dirt. "He's about 15 miles around."

Now it was Charlie's turn to be impressed. "How come you know this, Jacob?"

"I saw it in my dream," said Crow.

"And how long ago you have this dream?"

Crow was silent for a minute, then he looked at all of them. "I had the dream when I was a boy. When the old man came and put his hand on my head and told me I had the seeing."

The others nodded. They knew the old man that Crow referred to. He was long dead, so his name wouldn't be spoken, but they knew his reputation and knew that he spoke the truth. There was no need for any more questions.

"I reckon," said Crow, "if we take where we are as his centre and move 50 miles back towards town and keep everyone about there, then with a bitaluck he'll settle down easy like. He'll sink in a bit, but then you sink in a bit Charlie every time you park your arse." Again, everyone laughed.

"Nipper," said Jacob, and one of his two assistants got up and went to an old, beaten up Toyota Landcruiser parked about 20 yards away. As he watched him go, Crow looked up at the darkening sky then over to Uluru. "Well, girl," he said to the rock softly, "your big brother's coming home. Then you can play together like you shoulda done before he went on his journey."

The sound of the Landcruiser's diesel engine rattled him out of his thoughts.

"We're gonna have one helluva time keepin' everyone back, Jacob," said Jim Kelly, who had stood up and was scratching the forest of grey hairs on his chest.

"Naah worries, mate," said Crow. "We got the army fellas ready to run shotgun all along the line we set. We might even have fellas from that NASA place."

Kelly's eyes widened. "Fellas from the NASA place eh?" and he looked impressed. Then he thought for a moment. "Emm, what NASA place would that be then, Jacob?"

Charlie Carpenter, who was walking Kelly back to the Landcruiser that they shared on the way out, said, "That would be the NASA place in the States, mate."

"I thought so," said Kelly, nodding his head knowledgeably and not thinking so in the slightest. "Emm, which States would –"

"Jim," said Charlie Carpenter, shaking his head, "you never cared much for that learnin' stuff, mate, didya?"

Before Jim could think of a reply they had reached the 4X4's and were on their way back to the 50 mile limit. The drive took them about an hour, during which time the sun had set and they had to travel the last 20 or so miles with headlights and the full moon as the only means of illumination.

Eventually, the lead vehicle carrying Jacob Crow slowed and pulled up near a large upright rock shaped like the head of a kangaroo sticking up out of the ground.

They all knew this rock was Billy Cobb who stole a dead kangaroo from two boys who were hunting nearby and when one of the boys challenged him he killed the lad with a rock.

He would have killed the other boy but, before he could, Almudj the Great Snake turned Cobb into a rock the shape of a kangaroo's head, to remind folk forever of the crime he committed.

Crow got out of the Landcruiser and drew a line in the dirt. "There," he said, "that's where everyone stops. Until Kutju's settled we don't go any nearer."

One of the young men who accompanied him, Nipper, the one who carried the didgeridoo when they went to the States, stood near and said, "What if we got the distance wrong and he comes down a bit off target, Jacob, like here, maybe?"

Jacob Crow looked at Nipper and dug his right hand into his trouser pocket. He came out with a small stone about the size of his thumbnail. He handed it to Nipper. "Would Almudj let her firstborn land on Uluru, her second born?"

Nipper's eyes widened as he realised that he was holding a tiny piece of the sacred monolith.

"Course not," said Crow, smiling. "Now you keep that safe and give it back to me when Kutju sits down." The young man nodded and put the stone in his pocket.

"Right, mate," said Crow. "Let's get the coffee on."

As the elders settled down for a hot drink and more talk, Cooper was driving into Alice Springs about 160 miles north of them.

Before him lay the sprawling tented mass of people who had come to witness Homer's landing. The town's ordinary night lights had been augmented by so many camp fires and tent lamps that the whole area looked like a reflection of the stars in the sky above.

"I think the cat's out of the bag and this is Homer's welcoming committee," said Cooper out loud. He almost expected Azriel or Gabriel to appear in the seat next to him. The seat remained empty, but with angels you never knew. Since stepping off the plane at the small Alice Springs airport, he had been fighting hard to ignore the physical effects of being in the middle of Australia in the middle of summer.

He expected, wrongly, that he would get to the hotel quickly, shower and change into something a little more suitable.

Instead, what he found was a sea of people along the road, heading for Alice Springs and the event that was due to happen in five days.

Eventually, he reached the town and found the hotel where Bonetti had promised he had a room booked. Only then did he realise that even the long arm of the Roman Catholic Church had its limitations.

"Pardon?" he exclaimed to a hotel receptionist, who, although clearly impressed by his priestly garb, wasn't impressed enough to be the bearer of good news.

"We don't have your reservation," admitted the embarrassed woman after searching around for half an hour. "Frankly even if we did," she added, " you'd probably find yourself sharing with half a dozen other folk in the same boat, or room, rather.

"Look – Father, I'm really sorry, but I don't know what to suggest. Unless –" her voice trailed off as she looked him up and down. "Naaah," she said and shook her head, dismissing the thought.

"Naaah what?" said Cooper.

The woman leaned closer and, in a highly conspiratorial fashion, whispered, "Well, my uncle, who owns the outback equipment shop about a block down on the right is still open and I think he has a few tents left. Not many, mind you. He's been as busy as a cat buryin' shit, pardon my French, with all this and they're going like bloody hot cakes. But if you don't mind roughing it –" The rest of the sentence remained unspoken and she shrugged her shoulders. "Best I can do."

Cooper thought for about two seconds, then nodded at the woman, whose face broke out into a beaming smile.

"Hang on," she said and picked up the phone. "Stan? It's Donna," she said. "You got any tents left, I got a very special guest here in a bit of a tight spot." She nodded a few times and the smile departed. Turning back to Cooper she said, "He's got one left. It's big enough for two. You interested?"

"Definitely," said Cooper. Donna's smile reappeared. "Ace!" she exclaimed. She told her uncle to hold it until the priest fella got there.

He found the shop easily enough. A sign above the entrance said 'Stan's Store' and a very large, heavyset man was standing outside by the door, smoking a cigarette and drinking a steaming mug of coffee.

215

He looked about the right age for a Donna uncle.

When Cooper stopped outside the shop, the man smiled and the priest recognised the same family smile that Donna wore on her face a few minutes earlier.

"G'day Father," said the man, nodding at him. "You would be the priest fella wantin' the tent, then."

"That would be me," said Cooper. "And you would be Stan?"

The stranger smiled again. "Naah," said the man showing a large gap where two front teeth used to be. "I'm Dan. Stan's me brother. C'mon inside and we'll sort ya out." He flicked the nearly spent cigarette onto the road, turned and went into the shop.

Cooper followed the giant Dan inside and was surprised how light and modern the place looked. From a casual glance it seemed like the kind of place where you could get everything you could possibly need to go walkabout.

It was a camper's and hiker's and survivalist's Aladdin's cave of everything vital that was man-made, to help you stay alive and comfortable in the bush. All except for one thing – it was nearly sold out.

The shelves were mostly empty. Even the displays had been destroyed to feed the buying frenzy of visitors desperate to stock up on much needed camping equipment. A good dozen or so hopeful buyers were still searching the shop in the vain hope of coming across anything that might have been missed.

Behind the single counter stood Dan's identical twin brother Stan. Alike in every respect except for the missing teeth. They were both shaven headed and both wore faded jeans and red and white check shirts.

Stan smiled and held out a massive hand to shake. "G'day! You must be the one our Donna sent."

Cooper stuck his hand out and grasped a five-digit lump of flesh about twice the size of his. He felt like a child again. "I threw the tent in the back room, just in case it got sold by mistake before you got here. I shoved in the gear you might need. It's all we got before the next delivery in a week – but I reckon you'll be right."

He looked the priest up and down and added, "You're not gonna wear that lot out there are ya?"

"No, I was thinking maybe I could strip off and get a good tan."

Stan looked at him for a pause so pregnant it could have given birth – then he started laughing. He laughed so loud and so forcefully that tears streamed out his eyes and his large belly shook. Dan, his brother joined in, only his laugh was as different to Stan's as chalk is to cheese. Where Stan's was deep and earthy, Dan's was high and feminine. The sound just didn't match the framework.

Eventually Stan wiped his face, looked at Cooper and said, "Well I'll be stuffed! That's the best laugh I've had in a month. Mate, yer all right! I've got some spare strides and stuff that'll fit ya."

Even though he had warm weather clothes in his bag, the priest didn't refuse the offer. You could never be too well prepared. "Thanks for all your help," he said. "Listen, you know an old Aborigine called Jacob Crow?"

"Sure," said Stan. "But you won't catch him tonight. I saw him drive out this afternoon with about a dozen other fellas headin' for Uluru. Best thing you can do is find somewhere nearby, bed down for the night, and look him up in the morning."

Dan helped carry all the gear to the Landcruiser parked outside the hotel and, with the promise of dropping by in a day or two, Cooper drove south out of town and into the sea of tents, looking for a likely spot to camp.

About 15 minutes driving later, he parked on the outer edge of the temporary tent city. The sweltering heat of the day had dissipated, to be replaced by a chill of approaching evening that made him shiver as he stepped down from the driving seat.

He soon had the tent up and was shifting his gear inside from the vehicle. It felt good to be 'getting back to nature' once again, although with the number of tents and humans alongside and in front of him, nature seemed to be taking a back seat.

Ever since he was a boy, Cooper had always known when he was not alone. The feeling of someone else being physically very close by and watching him always put his 'spidey' sense on full alert. It was tingling now. Still, he was surprised when he turned round and Gabriel was standing behind him.

"Hiya Coop. Thought I'd pop over and see how you were settling in," said the little angel.

He was barefoot and dressed in khaki shorts and a black t-shirt with "My other body's a giant" in white letters on the front.

Cooper read it and laughed out loud. "It suits you."

Gabriel shrugged. "I do what I can to further the cause for the vertically challenged," he said. "We large personalities have to stick together."

"Yaay – go team!" said the priest unenthusiastically, indicating one of the chairs set outside the tent. "Park yourself. I'll be back out in a minute. I think it's time I changed into something more comfortable." When he came out he was wearing black shorts and a plain white t-shirt. Casual, but still priestly.

Gabriel did a double take. "Still can't get away from the old black and white, eh?"

"It's a habit."

"Nuns wear habits, and you're no sister."

Cooper sat down and looked thoughtfully at the tent city in front of him. The campfires were like stars in the growing gloom. "Sometimes difficult to figure out who – or what– I am," he said, looking into the eyes of the little angel.

There was silence between them as they listened to the sounds of various music styles – some recorded, some live and not always in tune – coming from the encampment. There was no guessing how many thousands of people were there. Every one waiting for Homer. Every one brought there by some collective urge to greet the new arrival like a long lost relative. Finally Gabriel spoke.

"What's your earliest memory," he asked.

Cooper thought for a long moment.

"I'm sitting on a blanket on the grass in front of our prefabricated house. I'm playing my toy guitar and singing for the factory workers as they pass by. They throw pennies that land on the blanket. It's tartan. Old and thin. I think I'm about four or five."

Gabriel reached over and touched the back of his hand gently with the tip of one finger. "Now, think again."

At first there was nothing. Then, suddenly, a feeling of wind and a sound of rushing air so strong it jolted him out of his memory. He looked at Gabriel, confusion in his eyes and a warm, tingling feeling all over his body. "Now that's something new." He looked at his hands. They were shaking.

"Close your eyes and tell me what you see?"

Cooper did as he was told. "Darkness. I see darkness."

Gabriel tutted with annoyance. "No. That's your human brain telling you that you can't see anything because your eyes are shut. Use your other brain. The one that comes to life when you change."

Cooper opened his eyes momentarily and the tingling receded. "I thought that was the same brain, just acting differently."

"Nope. This one's more like your spirit brain. A bit more flexible and a lot less physical. Take a deep breath and try again."

Cooper closed his eyes again, opened his lungs and inhaled deeply. Then he exhaled slowly, allowed his shoulders to drop and his muscles to relax. The tingling feeling returned and he shivered slightly.

"Better," said the little angel. "Now again – what do you see?"

Cooper tried to see anything except the insides of his eyelids, but without success. Then, ever so slowly, shapes began to appear. Indistinct, almost as if he were viewing them through a fog. And sounds. Like trying to hear someone speaking to you when your ears are stuffed with cotton wool.

He tried to bring clarity to the sights and sounds, but all he felt was a sharp pain in his head, in the area above his right ear around his temporal lobe. He had been familiar with that area, that name and that pain all his life. That's where the scar was. The one that caused his epilepsy. They said the scar happened at birth.

He had the first on his 7th birthday, the last on his 14th birthday, and five or six a year in between. Then nada. No goodbye nice knowing you. Nothing.

But he never forgot the feeling and there it was back again. So he pulled back. Stopped looking and opened his eyes. He was drenched in sweat and his heart was pounding.

It was dark. Gabriel was standing in front of him, concern in his eyes. "Maybe now isn't the time," he said.

"For what exactly?" asked Cooper, taking a deep breath and feeling his heart slow.

"Finding out who you are."

"I know who I am Gabriel. I'm Father John Wayne Cooper. I'm a catholic priest attached to the Vatican. And I'm a bit on the weird side. Okay – a lot on the weird side."

"The seizures won't come back, you know. They're gone for good."

The pain in Cooper's head had gone as quickly as it had come. The fear lingered on. "If it's alright with you, I think we'll do this another time. I need some sleep. Big couple of days coming up."

The angel nodded. "Nighty night then. Wake up nice and early and I'll show you where Jacob Crow is." With that, he disappeared into the darkness.

Cooper crawled into his tent, zipped up tight and climbed into his sleeping bag. As he did every night as a last action before he went to sleep, he reached for his Bible and let it open on whichever page it wanted to. It was an old routine of his and he never tired of it. The book always surprised him.

He read for five minutes then curled up, dreaming of things that no other priest would dare to dream of in a million years.

He woke with a start. There was a hand on his shoulder, shaking it gently and someone was whispering "wakey wakey" in his ear. As his eyes grew accustomed to the half-light of early morning, he could make out the small figure of Gabriel next to him. The aroma of cooked bacon was greeting his nostrils and his saliva glands were already starting to show their appreciation.

"No time for hanging around in bed," said the angel. " Landing an asteroid, saving the world, eating a bacon sandwich –"

Cooper struggled out of his sleeping bag, rummaged through the clothes he'd bought from Stan's Store and found another pair of shorts and a t-shirt, both of them khaki. He'd just slipped them on and crawled outside the tent when he saw Azriel, sitting on one of the chairs, biting off a mouthful of bacon sandwich, brown sauce dripping out the edges.

"Deelarrfymmmmous!" he said.

"Pardon?"

"He means 'delicious'" said Gabriel, throwing some bacon between two slices of bread with a blob of sauce and handing it to Cooper. "Enjoy," he said.

"I thought you lot didn't eat," asked the priest, who then attacked his sandwich with as much enthusiasm as the angel did his.

Gabriel and Azriel looked at each other, smiling. "Just because we don't have to doesn't mean we don't want to," said the little angel.

"Right," said Azriel, who had finished his breakfast and was licking his sauce-covered fingers. "Pack your things up, jump in that monstrosity you call a vehicle and I'll take you to Jacob Crow."

An hour later, with Cooper in the front passenger seat and Gabriel in the back, Azriel drew up alongside three Landcruisers and a pickup truck surrounded by about two or three hundred Aborigines. They'd passed thousands of them during the drive, all headed towards Jacob Crow.

Cooper climbed out of the vehicle and worked his way through to the front of the crowd, where Jacob was sitting on the ground with a group of old men. He was about to call out to the old man when someone tapped him lightly on the shoulder. He turned and it was Nipper, the young Aborigine who carried the didgeridoo onto the Larry Black Show.

"G'day mate," whispered Nipper. "Wouldn't be polite if you interrupted him when he's doin' some important talkin'. Best wait a minute."

Cooper noticed that, even though Crow seemed to be speaking to the old men around him, everyone present was listening intently to every word he said.

"I can't understand what he's saying," whispered Cooper to Nipper.

The young Aborigine smiled. "That's 'cos he's speaking Pitjantjatjara, mate. I got some coffee if you fancy a slurp."

Nipper looked down at Cooper's shoulder bag. The zip was open and his Bible was clearly visible.

Enlightenment threw a smile on the young Aborigine's face. "Aaaah – you're the blessin' bloke!" he said. "Jacob said you'd be comin'."

"He did?" asked Cooper, wondering how the man knew.

"Yeah," said Nipper. "He had a dream, said you'd be along and you'd be sayin' some nice words when Kutju came home."

"Who's Kutju?"

Nipper shook his head sadly. "Kutju was the Great Snake's firstborn. Then came Uluru."

The young man saw the confusion in the priest's face, so he pointed upwards. "He's Kutju. The one who's comin' back home."

Suddenly, everything went very quiet. Cooper turned to the group of old men and saw Jacob Crow about three feet away, standing looking at him. In fact everyone was looking at him.

"G'day mate," said Crow. He could feel the old man sizing him up. Looking into his eyes was a bit like looking into Junior's eyes, only without the Holy Mojo.

Crow surprised him by stepping closer and holding out his hand and saying, "How's that God fella of yours. He feelin' any better yet?"

Cooper shook Crow's hand. The grip was strong and warm. "Yeah," he said, smiling. "He's getting better by the day. When did you have your dream about us?"

"When I was young," said Crow. "Then the Great Snake sent it to me again a month ago."

Cooper had always believed that there was more to existence than humans could ever comprehend. Being a shapeshifter helped. He knew that life itself was only part of the journey and not even necessarily the beginning of it. That was one of the reasons he became a priest. And that was why he didn't even begin to question Crow's dream. A dream that happened before he was born. Some things were best simply accepted. This was one of them.

"So," he said, looking out into the flat empty plain ahead, "did your dream tell you where Kutju was coming down?"

"About 50 miles that way," said Crow, pointing towards Uluru. "This is where we stop till he gets here. Nobody goes out there."

"But, how are you going to stop people? I mean, they'll want to see it as it happens?"

"Don't need to stop my people. They already know. It's you whitefellas we need to stop. And the buggers with the cameras. So we went to the government and they gave us a few of their blokes. Here they come now," he said and pointed to the sky.

Above them, a flock of army helicopters came racing through the sky from the direction of Alice Springs. Below them, in a cloud of dust, came the trucks carrying men and supplies.

"They been trained t'sneak up on people, y'know," said Crow, smiling.

"Oh I'd never have known they were there," said Cooper. "Took me completely by surprise."

Crow tilted his head to one side. "That God fella of yours gave you a sense of humour," he said.

"Naaah," said Cooper. "He was gonna give me one, but they'd run out by the time He got round to me. I got a sense of the ridiculous instead."

Crow grunted and the ghost of a smile passed over his face.

The helicopters banked off on either side of the crowd and landed side by side, making a noisy, metal perimeter. By the time their rotor blades had stopped spinning, the lead vehicle in the army convoy, a jeep, had come to a halt behind the crowd.

There were two soldiers in it. A driver and an officer, both dressed in desert camos. The officer stepped out of the jeep and walked through the gathering to the front, where Cooper and Crow were standing. He was tall and well built with a rugged kind of handsomeness and he smiled when he saw the old man.

"G'day Jacob," he said, with a tone of familiarity which surprised and pleased Cooper. "I've brought along a few boys to help you keep order. You tell us what you want and leave it to us."

"G'day Gordon," said Crow, who turned to Cooper. "This is the man called Brigadier Gordon McNeil. He's gonna help keep folk away from the area. He was born local and he's a good bloke."

McNeil stuck out his hand to Cooper, who shook it. "Father John Cooper," said the priest. He decided to leave the 'Wayne' out for the time being. Putting it in would only begin a conversation that inevitably led to western movies. Best left for another time. "How many men have you brought, Brigadier?"

"How many do you need?" asked McNeil. The priest decided on the spot that he liked him.

"Let's talk about your boys," said Crow and the two strolled off through the crowd towards the convoy.

Cooper decided it was time he checked in with Bonetti and fumbled around in the shoulder bag for his cell phone. It rang before he could pick it up.

"Hello?"

"Hello Father," said the Cardinal, "How's Australia?"

"Very big and very hot, Your Eminence. I was just about to call you. Everything here's okay. How about your end?"

"Good," said Bonetti. "The Holy Father's just back from a walk."

"He's up and walking?"

"Better than that, he can see, hear, feel and even pee without his catheter, thanks be to God."

"Amen to that," said Cooper, quickly banishing the image in his head.

"Listen, has anyone called Daisy Roper contacted you yet?"

"Daisy Roper? Nope. Never heard of her. Why?"

"She's an astrophysicist and she's out there to keep an eye on Homer. She's the one who discovered him, so she's good to have on the team. Anything goes wrong, she'll be able to let you know about it first. Give her all the help you can."

Cooper wondered what connection this Daisy Roper had with the Vatican, but decided that, with all the fingers in all the pies that the Roman Catholic Church had, it wasn't surprising to find one firmly stuck in something floating around in space.

"Anything I need to know?" asked Bonetti.

"Not a thing. I'll be in touch soon," said Cooper and ended the call.

The phone immediately started ringing again.

"Hello?" said a young woman's voice, "is that Father Cooper?"

"Oh, yes, Cooper here. And you, I take it, are Miss Roper?"

"Well yes – but how did you know?" asked Daisy, clearly taken aback.

"Oh, don't worry," said Cooper, "it's a religious thing. Goes with the poltergeists and the exorcisms."

Cooper could hear laughter at the other end of the line.

"Well I must say," said Daisy, her laughter still apparent in her voice, "you don't look much like a priest."

Cooper's 'spidey' sense kicked in. He turned round and there, in borrowed army desert camos and filling them very nicely, was a young woman with a cell phone in one hand, a laptop case in the other, and a fat travel bag slung over her right shoulder.

"Don't mind the uniform," she said. "I was heading for the front line looking for you and when this lot came through Alice Springs I kinda hitched a ride. Pleased to meet you." She put the phone in a breast pocket and stuck out a hand. Cooper shook it. Possibly a little too enthusiastically.

"Well, Miss Roper –"

"Call me Daisy, please."

"Well, Daisy please," said Cooper, "I've just got off the phone from my boss at the Vatican and he says to give you all the help we can."

"The Vatican? Bloody Hell!"

"Probably nearer Heaven than Hell, last time I looked. Listen – my Landcruiser's nearby. Come with me and you can dump your gear. Here, let me help," said the priest.

He slipped the strap from Daisy's shoulder and onto his own in one fluid movement."

They began walking. "Well, a lot of things are nearer than we thought," said Daisy, with a sad look on her face. "And last time I looked, Homer was one of them!"

"How much nearer?" said Cooper slowly.

"He should get here about 11 o'clock tomorrow morning," said Daisy. "Trouble is, according to the latest figures, he won't be doing any slowing down before he gets here. So I guess all that noise about Homer coming in to land that we heard on the Larry Black show was just that. Noise."

"Wait – you mean he's not slowing down?" yelped Cooper.

"Nope. His brakes don't seem to be working."

"You're very calm for someone who basically thinks the world is about to end."

She sighed. "Well – we all have to die sometime. Might as well all go together."

Cooper looked at the sky then back at Daisy. "But he's meant to be landing gently on the ground! That's the plan. That's what the whole world's praying for and that's what should be happening!"

"Not quite the whole world," said Gabriel. They had reached the vehicle and the little angel was standing outside it frowning.

"Great. Who's throwing a spanner in the works?" asked Cooper.

"Who are you talking to?" asked Daisy.

"It's the atheists," said Gabriel. "They say how can they pray to God to stop the end of the world when they don't believe in God in the first place! So we can all go and get stuffed."

"But don't they realise that they'll get stuffed, too, if we don't stop Homer?" yelled an exasperated Cooper.

"Emm – they don't believe in Homer either. They say it's all a con to get more people into churches and believing in someone who doesn't exist."

Daisy flung up her hands in confusion and looked around. "Who are you talking to?"

"Oh right – forgot. Sorry. Stealth mode off," said Gabriel, who appeared leaning on the driver's door, smiling."

Daisy's brain couldn't quite figure out how anyone, especially someone so small, could pop up out of nowhere.

So it did the next best thing and instructed Daisy to faint, which she obligingly did.

Cooper caught her on the way down, lifted her to the Landcruiser and propped her sitting against a wheel.

He turned to the little angel. "How many atheists are there?"

"Oh – a fair few. Azriel went to count."

"So that's why Homer's closer than expected," said Cooper.

Gabriel nodded. "It's all a matter of percentages. The higher the percentage of people in the world who pray, the stronger the Force is. The stronger the Force is, the more brake power Homer has, etcetera etcetera!"

Just then, Azriel returned and he wasn't happy. "I got bad news and worse news. Which do you want first? Ooooh – I see the inimitable Miss Daisy Roper has arrived," he said, looking down at the unconscious 'Homer expert' still propped against the tyre.

"Does it really matter which comes first at this stage? It's all bad! Just spill the beans," said Cooper.

"You won't believe how many of these atheists there are."

"Oh I promise you, I will. How many?"

"Just over twenty six and a half million, give or take!"

"What?" Cooper gasped, not quite expecting that many.

"Just over tw –"

"Yes, yes – I heard." The priest's brain shifted into overdrive. There was plenty wrong with this planet, he thought. But dammit, he wasn't going to let anyone destroy it without a fight.

Suddenly he began to tingle. It started with the big toes of each foot and then worked its way up his legs to the rest of his body. It was the same feeling that he had when Gabriel had touched his hand the night before. The same feeling he saw and heard the shapes and sounds in the fog when his eyes were closed. Only now he remembered where he'd felt it before. When *The Eye of God* had spoken to him!

"Hang on, I can feel the beginnings of an idea," he said.

"Aaaah, you're back then," said Azriel.

"Back?"

"You've been standing there talking to yourself for the last 20 minutes. We tried nudging you and Gabriel even kicked you in the shins twice and you didn't flinch a muscle.

"It was as if your body was here but your mind was in a galaxy far, far away!"

Cooper was suddenly aware of a sharp pain just above his right ankle.

"Sorry," said Gabriel, touching the priest lightly on the leg with one finger. The pain disappeared.

"About this idea," asked Azriel.

"Oh yes. What if we removed all the atheists from the equation?"

"You mean get rid of them all?" asked Gabriel, alarmed. "Oh no, we couldn't possibly do that. They're basically very nice people and they've got a right to their beliefs, or non-beliefs, just the same as everyone else."

"No, I don't mean get rid of them. Put them somewhere else temporarily. It's just a numbers thing, right? What if they were somewhere else, say, not on earth?"

"But we don't have the power to do that without losing our grip on Homer and sending him crashing into the ground even sooner."

Cooper's brain was working overtime. "No – what if you did it really quickly. Then the negative force of them refusing to pray would be counteracted by the immediate positive upswing in power if they weren't in the equation any more. Sort of."

Azriel grunted. "And where, pray tell, would we put them?"

"How about Purgatory? I mean, when we went to collect Bob he was the last one there. The place was completely empty. They'd only be there for a few hours – a day at the most. Then, once Homer's down safely, you'll have all the power you need to whisk them back again. Then they can go on believing that there's no God, and no Purgatory, and they won't have a clue where they were because they don't believe in the place anyway!" Cooper stopped speaking and looked at both of them. "So?"

They both looked at Cooper. Then at each other. "Back in a tick," said Azriel and disappeared.

A tick later he returned with a large smile. "Well, we've done the math and all the figures add up. It might take a little time, but it can be done. We'll even throw in a slightly improved climate change for them, just to make things a bit more comfortable."

"Great," said Cooper. "Exactly how much time are we talking about?"

"Oh, about five minutes, give or take."

"All of them in five minutes?"

"What – not fast enough? Maybe I could manage four and a half."

"Oh no – five is fine. Perfect, in fact."

"Outstanding. Right – better get a move on, then." With that, the tall angel disappeared, which coincided with Daisy groaning and waking up.

"What the–?" she said groggily.

Thinking fast, Cooper bent down and helped her to her feet. "It must have been the heat," he said. "You started talking then keeled over. I caught you just in time before you hit the deck." He handed Daisy a small bottle of water from a cool box inside the Landcruiser. The astrophysicist opened her gullet and drank the lot in a few seconds, wiping her mouth afterwards with the back of her hand.

"Thanks," she said. Then she noticed Gabriel. Smiling, she reached down, grabbed a hand and shook it vigorously. "Daisy Roper, pleased to meet you. And you are?"

Cooper thought fast. "Sorry Daisy, how rude of me. This is Gabriel, a very good friend of mind. He likes asteroids."

"Large asteroids," said the little angel.

Daisy's smile grew wider. " Gabriel. Nice name. I like your t-shirt," she said.

"I like your space rock. When was the last time you checked in on him."

Daisy looked at her watch. "About four hours ago," she said, looking at the angel curiously. "You called Homer a 'him'," she said. "Not many people do that."

"Maybe it's time you took another look."

Daisy nodded and reached for her laptop. It only took her a couple of minutes to get it booted up and networked through to the servers at Falling Sky. "Holy shit!"

"Would that be good Holy Shit, or bad Holy Shit?" asked Cooper, hiding his hands behind his back and his fingers tightly crossed.

"Oh good – unbelievably good!" said Daisy. "I don't understand why, but Homer's slowed down. I mean really slowed down. In fact he's kinda coasting in with his brakes full on!"

Cooper unclenched his fingers and immediately they began tingling. For a second he thought that *The Eye of God* was trying to speak to him again.

Then he realized the feeling was brought on because the feeling was returning to his digits. "So – what's his ETL?"

"ET what?

Cooper looked at her and smiled. "Estimated Time of Landing," he said.

Daisy did a penny-drop face and punched her laptop keys some more. "About 3 o'clock tomorrow afternoon, provided everything goes according to plan."

"Why shouldn't it?" asked Gabriel.

Thirty

By late that afternoon, the crowds along the makeshift perimeter had grown and now numbered in the many thousands. Most were Aborigines who had either driven there in vehicles of every description, or had simply appeared on foot from the bush.

There was no attempt to cross the line that was now being patrolled by army units on foot, in trucks and in the air. It seemed to Cooper as if, were the army not in presence, there would still be no attempt by the crowd to encroach on the forbidden area.

The elders amongst the Aborigines simply sat and chatted patiently. The younger ones, those more touched by so-called civilisation and modernisation, bided their time by playing loud music and mainly having a good time.

Towards evening, they were joined by hundreds, then thousands, of white folk. Australians who, despite their race and colour, felt a sense of belonging and an unbreakable link to the events that were taking place.

Naturally, with them came the media, who wanted to be at the front so their cameras could get a good view to beam around the world. Thankfully, Brigadier Gordon McNeil wasn't the kind of person to let a press badge stand in the way of his healthy disregard for any kind of media, filmed or printed.

So he held a meeting with them and politely but firmly informed them that all reporting would be done behind the lines until Homer had landed – and even then they could only come within a mile of the rock and no closer. Any closer, he said, and they would be escorted out of the area and their equipment confiscated. And that was that. Freedom of the press went out the window and respect for something awe-inspiring was the order of the day.

As the chill of evening drew in and campfires illuminated the area for miles around, the first shouts went up from sky-watching folk, who pointed excitedly to a bright moving light in the darkness above.

Still small, Homer was making his visible presence felt, as he drifted towards his homeworld.

The world, in response, watched and prayed even harder. All except the atheists, that is, who one minute were doing whatever any good atheist does, and the next were wandering around a strange place in their millions. Totally bewildered, thinking they were the victims of mass hallucination, then deciding they might as well enjoy the tropical sunshine and fabulous beaches of said hallucination, before the effects wore off.

Then the welcome corroboree dance began. This particular dance was owned by Jacob Crow and was passed to him by his father Titus. Playing singing sticks and didgeridoos and wearing elaborate headgear, the ochre-painted dancers led by Crow sang and danced to celebrate the homecoming of a loved one.

Cooper and Daisy, welcomed into this strange, powerful world, were willing participants in the celebrations, particularly the alcohol drinking bits of it. Cooper conveniently forgot how new he was to the whole getting drunk thing.

Men, women and children joined in and the booming sounds and sight of the dance lasted until the dancers fell exhausted and sleep came by the warmth of large, roaring fires.

As light peeped over the horizon and fires were brought back to life, Cooper and Daisy awoke next to each other in the tent bought from Stan's Store.

"Aaaaaargh," yelled Cooper as he saw Daisy's ochre-painted face. Then the events of the night before came crashing in on him like the after-effects of a successful dam-busters raid.

"Mmmmmm," said Daisy, looking at him through sleepy eyes. "I love the smell of sweaty flesh, first thing in the morning!"

"Heaven help us – don't say that, I'm a priest!" said Cooper, as he realised that no sleeping bag coverings were in evidence. His panic subsided when he saw that they were fully dressed.

"Don't worry Father. Your secret's safe with me!"

"Emm, did I miss something?" asked a man from the unzipped tent entrance.

Daisy squinted to see the figure obscured by the light outside the tent. "George? What the Hell are you doing here?"

"Well you sure know how to give a guy a welcome. How about 'hello', or even maybe 'nice to see you'. Either would be good. Tell you what, let's start with the introductions."

He hunched and stepped into the tent holding his hand out to Cooper. "Hiya, I'm George McHale, pleased to meet you." He shook Cooper's hand and, the priest noticed, squeezed just a little too strongly.

Daisy, with something approaching a sinking feeling in her stomach, said, "Father, George here is an Assistant Administrator. He's from NASA. George, this is Father John Cooper. He's from God via The Vatican."

She turned, stern-faced, to McHale. "Okay, how did you find me?"

Cooper, sensing a personal conversation coming on, said, "I think this calls for breakfast," and made a hasty exit past the newcomer and out the tent door.

McHale held his hands up in mock surrender. "I'm not here to step on anybody's toes, honey. Especially yours. The boys back home just thought you might need some support. So here I am. Mister Backup Person at your service. I realise this is all a bit 'last minute' but I didn't want to miss the big event. And if it all goes pear-shaped and we end up getting squished, well, I can think of worse ways to go."

Daisy softened, seeing him standing there obviously aware of the awkwardness of the situation. The only reason he was there must be that he was leaned on, and that meant he felt just as uncomfortable seeing her as she did seeing him.

"That your new look?" he said, pointing to the facepaint and sitting down next to her on Cooper's sleeping bag.

"Yeah, I'm thinking of setting up my own range of tribal cosmetics, whaddya think?"

"I think you need a long, hot shower," said McHale, smiling. "It's good to see you Daisy, it really is."

"Ditto, George. But only ditto for the Homer landing bit. No dittos for the getting back into a relationship bit, okay?"

McHale nodded. "Okay. So, you wanna fill me in on Homer?"

Daisy brought him up to speed on Homer's stop-go antics and threw in the previous night's celebrations for good measure. McHale listened patiently without interruption and showed interest all the way through.

When she finished, he said, "Sounds like a pretty damned wild party, I'm sorry I missed it. That army guy called McNeil was a big help. I didn't have a clue where to start looking for you. Now, just tell me what to do and I'll do it. Gopher, tekkie-type assistant, second brain – a man of my vast experience and expertise might even be able to do a pretty mean fry-up too!"

Daisy tried very hard not to laugh but failed miserably. His weird sense of humour was what had attracted her to him in the first place. Certainly not his rugged, lived-in face, nor his lack of large muscles. He simply made her laugh. The removal of the knickers thing came shortly afterwards. But that was then, and this was now.

They were interrupted by Cooper, who shouted through the tent door, "Okay you two, put each other down and come on out with your hands up. Breakfast's ready!"

After sausages, eggs and beans, washed down with lashings of sweet coffee, Cooper boiled hot water for washing. Half hour later they were ready for what would arguably be the most important day in the history – and the geography – of the world. Maybe even the universe.

High up above them, Homer was getting pretty excited too, and he felt the warm hug of humanity reach out and cradle him gently for the last short step of his journey home. Deep inside his core, he felt a contentment he'd never felt before. So this was what it felt like to belong.

He felt warm all over. In fact he felt very, very hot. Too damned hot. Ouch-type hot. 'Help I'm melting'-type hot. And there were flames! Large flames engulfing him. He was beginning to panic when the flames disappeared, to be replaced by a refreshing cool breeze.

Down below, the day was warming up and the thousands were now hundreds of thousands, and by direct satellite link-up and the power of the Internet, thousands of millions.

Satellite tracking stations all over the earth were locked onto the falling rock and giving humanity a minute-by-minute report of its progress.

Billions of cell phone calls, emails and tweets were giving a constant second-by-second text and visual commentary of the event. Junior's Facebook and Twitter pages were celebrating by hosting the largest online parties ever witnessed.

Television stations from one end of the world to the other were shoving smiling, white-toothed experts on screen to detail every known fact about Homer's existence and every known variable about his journey home.

Every other kind of television programme was given the boot, temporarily, and replaced by worldwide Homermania.

Daisy and McHale had, by midday, taken to keeping an eye on the constantly updated information on the laptop from under a makeshift awning attached to the side of the Landcruiser.

After checking in with Bonetti who was glued to his television with the Holy Father, eating nachos and drinking cola, Cooper decided to look for Jacob Crow.

He found the old man with a crowd of children sitting in a large semi-circle in front of him. He was speaking the story of the birth of Kutju and Uluru.

When he finished, the children went off to play, some choosing to be Kutju and others Uluru. A few joined up and became the slithering Almudj, pushing her way up from the ground. Crow smiled at their play.

"Not long now, Jacob," said Cooper.

"Naah, mate. Not long now. He knows we're waitin' for him. He's very happy."

Cooper admired the strong link Crow had with the rock. It didn't depend on fear or might. Didn't have anything to do with regular visits to a place of worship or the threat of penance for sins committed. It was a natural strength that flowed from the earth and encompassed every aspect of Crow's life. He was a priest of the outback and his church was the very land he stood on.

"You got that blessin' water from your God fella?" asked Crow.

Cooper reached into his hip pocket and brought out a metal flask full of holy water from the font in St. Peter's in Rome. Crow reached out a hand and Cooper gave him the flask.

The Aborigine undid the top, sniffed it then, before Cooper could yell "*stop!*" he took a sip, savoured the taste and swallowed.

"Bloody nice, mate. Bit on the warm side, but she'll be right!" he said, screwing the top back on and returning the flask to the priest. "Now I got a bita your God fella in here," he said, pointing to his heart. "You say, 'Jacob Crow says thanks', when you see him, mate."

"I think He knows that already," said Cooper, smiling as he shoved the flask back in his pocket. "Well – it's nearly Homer time! Our big rocky friend should be landing in about an hour."

"Nope," said Crow. "He's here now," and he looked up into a bright blue sky.

Behind them, Daisy and McHale were running towards them, waving their hands and pointing to the sky. "He's early," Daisy was shouting. "Homer's bloody well premature!"

They were followed by Brigadier McNeil, winding his way through the crowd in a jeep. As the vehicle screeched to a halt next to them, kicking up a cloud of dust, McNeil jumped out.

"We just got reports from a spotter plane. The fella was babbling like an idiot. Said it was the most beautiful sight he's ever seen. Best get ready folks, looks like our boy's here."

Almost as one, the whole sea of people looked up and saw a small dot in the sky. The dot slowly got larger and larger until it's shape became apparent. A mountain-sized boulder, 15 miles in diameter, full of dents and fissures slowly falling to earth ahead in the distance.

The sight was greeted by one loud, collective gasp of awe and wonder. Then the cheering began, growing in volume and intensity until it was impossible to even hear yourself think.

Television reporters in front of their cameras were vainly trying to bring well-rehearsed words to the waiting world, only to give up and simply let the cameras roll to capture the event.

Slowly, agonisingly slowly, Homer drifted lower and lower, caught on thousands of cell phone cameras, like a breathtakingly huge alien mothership on a first-contact visit to earth.

Then, with a shuddering jolt that knocked practically every one of the hundreds of thousands who were there off their feet and sent tiny tremors for miles around like ripples on the surface of a pond, Homer touched down – part of him disappearing beneath the surface of the earth. Then, slowly, the rock's colour changed to the same red hue as Uluru, his sister.

"Now that's what I call an entrance!" said Daisy.

"Oh no," said Cooper. "That's what I call a miracle."

When the shaking had stopped McNeil nodded to Crow who got in the jeep with the Brigadier. The Aborigine turned to Cooper. "Wanna say hello to the big fella?" he said with a smile.

"Absolutely," said Cooper, turning to Daisy. "He's your baby. Want to tag along?"

Daisy grinned. "Silly question," she said, and looked to McHale.

"Go!" said the NASA man, who, without warning, reached out and hugged her. Just for a second, she hugged back, before breaking off the embrace.

Cooper and Daisy jumped in the back of the jeep and headed out towards Kutju. Behind them, the sea of watchers slowly followed, kept at a safe distance by the soldiers.

As they neared the giant rock, Cooper's mind reflected on everything that had happened to bring them here to this place with all these people. He thought back to his first meeting with Bonetti and the reservations he had taking the assignment. He thought about everyone who had joined together to save the planet and everyone in it from near oblivion.

But mostly, he thought about the fantastic journey this sentient rock in front of him had taken to find its way back home. *His* way back home!

Lost in thought, he was unaware that the jeep had stopped. Daisy was nudging him.

"Wake up," she said. "Time to go to work."

About 500 yards ahead of them, resting peacefully in the mid-afternoon sun, Kutju sat majestic and waiting.

"This is as far as you go for now," said Crow, turning and looking at Daisy. "This man and me, we gotta go talk with Kutju. Welcome him home proper."

Cooper felt in his pocket for the flask of holy water, nodded to Daisy, and stepped out of the jeep with the old aborigine. He looked back at the young astrophysicist, a look of regret on his face.

"Don't worry," said Daisy. "Homer's not going anywhere. We got plenty of time to get acquainted."

"Well mate, let's go say hello," Crow said to Cooper, smiling and scratching the grey hairs on his chest. Slowly, the two set off for the rock, which looked large and awe-inspiring in front of them.

Walking slightly behind Jacob Crow, Cooper was suddenly aware that they weren't alone. He looked to the left and there was Junior and Arthur. He glanced to the right and Gabriel, Azriel and MoMo were smiling at him.

236

Jacob stopped and turned, looking at everyone. "Well, I reckon you should all be here since you helped bring him home safe."

Cooper was stunned. "So you can see everyone?"

Jacob smiled.

"You didn't think you'd get rid of us that easy, did you?" said Azriel.

"No," said Cooper, smiling gently and glad in his heart. "I don't suppose I did. I'm just glad that we managed to discover that Junior was *The One* in time to give our large friend here a helping hand."

"Well you managed wrong, then," said Gabriel. "I have it on good authority that he's not *The One*."

MoMo yelled, "I knew there was something else I had to tell you. It was on the tip of my tongue. Then I burped and it went. It's all starting to come back to me now."

"What is?" asked Cooper.

"About Junior not being *The One.*"

They all looked at the younger Son of God.

Junior looked confused. A feeling he wasn't familiar with. "So, I'm not *The One*?" he said, disappointment heavy in his voice.

"Naaah mate," said Jacob.

"Well – who is then?"

The old aborigine looked up at the monolith in front of them and pointed. "*He* is. Kutju. That's what his name means. One.

Jeez – don't you whitefellas know anything?"

THE END

Epilogue

On a glorious white, sandy beach, sheltered by palm trees, somewhere between heaven and hell and looking remarkably like the Island of Bali, two figures were relaxing on deckchairs, sipping exotic drinks and taking in the sun. "Well," said the Devil, "that was too close for comfort."

"You need to be more trusting," said God. "I knew everything would turn out fine in the end."

"Knew my arse," said the Devil "We just got lucky, that's all. What if Junior's Holy Mojo hadn't worked? What if all those folk on Earth had told him to bugger off – that they didn't want any more sore knees from kneeling down in cold, drafty churches? What if all that technology stuff made them feel happier and safer than a lifetime of Hail Mary's or mystic chanting, eh? What then? And while you're thinking, pass me some more of that funny green drink of yours."

God reached out and poured a few fingers of Créme de Menthe from a large jug into the Devil's empty glass.

The Creator of the known Universe (and all the unknown ones, too) took a long sip of his drink and contemplated humanity's ability to put differences aside and work together to save their collective backsides.

All things considered, they weren't a bad bunch, he thought. They had distinct possibilities. Great potential. They just needed a little reminder every now and then.

"I think maybe I got it right this time," he said.

"The trouble with you is you think too much," said The Devil.

*Footnote:

The day after Kutju landed, an abandoned Landcruiser was found, doors open and petrol tank empty, a stone's throw from the asteroid's northern edge. A search of the vehicle discovered documents relating to a certain Harlan Quinn, Director of the Falling Sky Foundation in the UK.

Despite an exhaustive search of the area, there was no sign of Quinn, who was never seen or heard of again.

After a lengthy stay in Australia studying Homer and getting to know the people appointed to be his guardians, Daisy Roper was appointed the new Director of the Falling Sky Foundation. She and George McHale decided to remain firm, but distant, friends.

Printed in Great Britain
by Amazon